Introspection
From the Melvin Time Chronicles

By

Mark Wayne Allen

Other Writings by Mark Wayne Allen

AWARDS AND PUBLICATIONS

Awards
First place poem Parish Fair - Life, The Miracle
Fourth Place (Writer's Conference)

Books
Star Siege
3 Lifetimes In 1

Publications
Dementia e-zine - This Land Is Your Land
Dementia e-zine - Johnny
Dementia e-zine - Discovery

Bayou Writers Group Anthology Vol. 2
Bayou Writers Group Anthology Vol. 1
15 Articles in "The Voice of Southwest Louisiana"

Foreword

Some people say that writing a book is much like having a baby. Well, I don't necessarily subscribe to that, but the point is well taken for its intent. A lot of care and planning went into this book and over the course of time it will take on a life of its own. I'll nurture it, help it to grow, and it will be a lifelong commitment.

However, rearing a child is a much deeper level of all of the above and I have a profound respect for all parents. Have you ever thanked your parents for your upbringing? If you haven't, I suggest you should.

So, okay, some of our parents may not be the best, but we still owe them for life. Your heart is beating and your mind is thinking isn't it?

My parents have been through hell and back because my life has been far from normal. If you're curious, read the book of my life, "*3 Lifetimes In* 1."

The point I'm trying to get at is life is complex. At one time or another, I suppose that we all feel alone in the world. That's the point that the main character, Melvin Travis finds himself in, but for him it's a lifestyle.

None of us should be afraid of these low points in our lives. They make the good times be just that: good. Those moments that make life worth living are things that we should treasure. I know I do. I guess each of us remembers the good as well as the bad. As my dad always said it, "We're just making memories."

Learn to treasure each one.

This novel is one that I've wanted to write for twenty-years. I've always been fascinated by time. H.G. Wells wrote many books with time as a theme. Some say he actually traveled through time looking for the "good" future of mankind. It's easy to see why the rumor was started. His written predictions about the future are uncannily accurate. For instance, he wrote about air travel, space travel, genetic engineering, lasers, a second world war, and nuclear power.

Still, the technology of time travel eludes us. I say, thank God! Nowhere else can the human race cause such severe damage to itself. It could cause Infinite Annihilation of everything that's ever been.

My personal fascination with time travel goes beyond mere curiosity. My past has been laced with decisions that I've thought about without end and wondered how the outcome of my life would be different had I made different choices.

I suppose I look into the past and future, much like Wells, to evaluate differences as well as look toward the brightness of better days. H. G. might've been searching for the secrets of the universe.

I, on the other hand, have learned to be happy with life as it is.

I owe a lot of people through the many years of my life for the making of this book. My family and wife Kelley foremost for putting up with my eccentricities deserve the most. But, there have been scores of others. Some of the people that deserve credit I didn't even consciously meet.

To all, I say thank you and, foremost, I thank God.

To my dad whose guidance and friendship inspired me to be
more than I am

Chapter 1

Melvin did not know who was banging on the door at 4 a.m., but he knew they better have a damn good excuse, otherwise the mortician would have more business today. He forced himself out from under the six layers covering his body: hands first, then arm, then his torso. The cool air stung his flesh like he was actually in the morgue instead of wishing he could put whoever was behind that blasted door in there.

BAM BAM BAM! "Hey Mel, ... I need you man."

The voice sounded familiar, but Melvin could not place it. Anyways, at 4 a.m., they better be dying, no matter who it was. Grabbing a tattered black housecoat, Melvin headed toward the door.

He grabbed the wooden door with a furious jerk and planted his foot on the linoleum floor. Who was this presumptuous fart anyway? He cracked the door open and an enormously fat slob came busting through, letting just as much damn icy Louisiana wind into the room as friggin possible.

"I need your help, man. I don't know where to turn or even who to trust," the 450-pounder shouted through the room while gasping for air before collapsing butt first, on the couch.

Melvin threw the door just as hard as he could, trying to slam it shut with a resounding thud, but it only coasted softly,

1

leaving behind him a slightly opened door through which the January wind still blew. His lips squeezed together in rage and he could feel the warm, actively-disturbed, blood rush through every part of his now red-hot face.

Melvin closed the door with a shove of his right hand, pressed his body up against the door with fervor, and then looked at the blob sitting in 'his' chair. There this asshole sat with his cheap green jacket that had several stains, presumably from the hundred pounds of food this guy either tried to eat or just stuffed in his pockets for later. Candy bar wrappers stuck out of his pockets. He was bald with a mildly graying beard that food crumbs were in, and from the runny caramel that was oozing, it looked like the stuff was stuck for good. His pants looked like his legs were poured in and then compressed, and, the coup de gras were his wet, muddy tennis shoes from which shreds of cloth were torn.

"Hey Buddy, you better explain yourself friggin' quick or I'll throw your shameful ass back out on the damn street!"

The guy swallowed hard, tried to take a breath, and said, "Okay, Okay." Another big breath. "Just give me a second."

Melvin began tapping his foot. He wanted to get back to bed and try to warm up before he had to get to his office. Tap. Tap. Tap. The guy strained to breath. Tap. Tap. Tap.

"Okay," Huff. Huff. "Forgive me," Huff. Huff. "I ran all the way from the corner." Huff.

Melvin wanted to retain his anger, but could not help but smirk. His house, swiss cheese with a door, was only three houses from the corner.

" We were buddies back in high school." Huff.

Melvin laughed and then sneered. "Yeah, right."

"It's true. I am Tom Soren." Huff.

Melvin sneered. He had seen too much, witnessed too much, had been gullible too many times to readily believe anything. "I'm not buying it, Pal. Tom Soren was my best friend, but I have not seen or talked to him since high school."

"I know, Friend, and I'm sorry. I'm also sorry that I haven't been there for you like you were for me."

Something about that statement shook Melvin. It was true

2

that he was Tom's protector in high school... the voice matched and the face... "Tom! What in the world are you doing at MY doorstep at 4 a.m., and why now, after all these years?"

Tom managed a mild breathy laugh and then said, "I am in big trouble Mel," huff, "I figure you are my last hope."

Melvin's excitement at seeing his high school bud turned to concern about just what kind of trouble Tom had brought into his life. Not that his life was great, or even good, but none of it involved major trouble. For Tom to come to him took some courage. The two had lost contact when they had graduated. Tom was the valedictorian. He had delivered his speech, was supposed to meet him at a restaurant, then disappeared. Melvin never knew where. Some say he got into a limo, but Melvin never really knew that for certain.

Huff. "I just hope they didn't follow me here."

Oh great! ...was Melvin's only thought... "What can I help you with Tom? Explain to me what's goin' on? You hope "who" didn't follow you?"

Chapter 2

The guy that said "Friends are Forever" probably never dreamed that 20 years later a load of garbage wearing pants would break in the door needing desperate help at 4 a.m. It was definitely the last thing that Melvin expected, but there his "blast from the past" sat.

As the slob started speaking, Melvin could not help but wince about his poor sofa. It wasn't expensive mind you, but 450 pounds? It was not made for that. The odor emanating from Tom's direction was sweaty, sweet, nasty, and gut churning which made Melvin want to crawl away and hide.

"I'm in deep trouble, Buddy."

"Yeah, you said that. So how about some details? The last I saw you, ... hell, I guess I was 18-years-old," Melvin said as he raised a hand.

"Yeah, I know," the guy replied while gasping for air. He wheezed "You wrote mom and dad numerous times." Tom's hazel eyes dropped. Breathing hard, he continued, "You wrote me a lot of times after high school." Eyes lifting up, "Man, they grabbed me right after graduation."

Melvin shook his head slightly, "Who?" He paused briefly. "Who??" He patted his foot a moment, then exclaimed, "WHO?!?!?"

Tom hung his head for a moment. "I thought I could answer that for a looooong time, but today, I just don't know, man," he said as he propped his head with both hands.

"You are completely confusing me, Tom," Melvin said as raised his hand with splayed fingers. "Now," his hands found their way back to his side, "twenty-something years

4

later, you show back up into my life." His hands raised again, bouncing as he talked. "What happened to you? Where did you go? Why are you here?"

"I don't know, Guy." Tom said slowly shaking his head. "I guess I thought you could help. I am a man without any friends, except you, my high school buddy."

Melvin rubbed his stubble chin. This guy must not have any social life at all for him to not have any friends, but on the other hand, neither did he. Melvin looked over at the clock: 5 a.m. He grimaced. "Maybe I can help. Just maybe."

Tom's eye's hung low. Softly he said, "I hope you can, Friend. I know it's been a long time and I know you don't know me from a stranger on the street anymore and I know you have no reason to help me or trust me after all these years, but," he paused and stressed, "man...I need help." Tom looked up. "You, me, everybody we know, and the entire rest of the world, maybe our entire universe, and the universes beyond ours, may depend on what we do."

Melvin tried to swallow the big lump that had built up in his throat as Tom was speaking, but it did not seem to want to go down and then, with a sudden Ka-Chunk, the tension broke and the volumous mass and whatever else went down his throat all at once. HIs concerns were vast, not only because of the implications of what Tom had said, but the sheer fact that he had a friend that cared about him.

His life had been hard and, right now, at this moment in time, Tom was probably his closest friend. That's "if" he were actually here, and "if" he was the same person he knew those many years ago, He had had only had one friend in his whole miserable life and Tom had been it. The friend that Melvin knew from long ago was not prone to exaggeration. He was a dead-serious kind of guy.

Melvin took a hard look at the proverbial, blubberish slob in front of him. Was this actually the Tom he knew those many years ago? Could this guy's incredible claim be true? It seemed an awful lot to take in.

"Come on, whoever you are," Melvin said ushering Tom, or whoever this was, out of the chair and then toward the front door. Melvin tilted his head down. The odor from this guy was horrific being so close, but at this point, he didn't care. Melvin just wanted this slob out so that he could get on with his life.

Tom pushed against Melvin's arms, saying, "I am Tom Soren, truly I am."

"Okay, you're Tom Soren." Melvin said as he grabbed whoever this was by his food-encrusted jacket and pulled closer towards the front door. The whale turned his head to look at him and Melvin stared at this guy's wide-open eyeballs. "Well, Tom, this is just a little too far fetched for me to believe. Bye."

Chapter 3

"But it's ME! It's Tom! It really is!" Tom pushed back against Melvin's forcefulness. "At graduation, we sat beside each other because you had a 3.75 GPA and I had a 3.77. Remember?" Melvin stopped. Tom continued, "You told me that graduation was the best thing that had happened in your life thus far." Melvin cocked his head. "I told you that you were my best buddy all through school and that I owed you a lot."

Melvin's arms went limp and fell to his side as he backed up. His legs sprawled out like hot noodles and his feet tripped over one another and his limp body fell to the cold white tiled floor. He trembled. His insides were quaking enhanced by the cold on his derriere. "You ARE Tom! But ... but ... but ... How?!?" His voice was shaky and uncertain and the sound of it surprised even him.

As he reached his hands to the floor trying to get up, Tom said, "Believe it or not, bud, I have kept tabs on you through these many years." He paused. "The organization I have been working for confiscated the letters that you sent to mom and dad's house. They let me read them, my Friend," another pause, "and I have kept up with your activities." Tom took Melvin's hand into his and pulled him up. Tom guided Melvin back to a seated position on the sofa and then re-took his seat in the chair.

"College was a bust," Tom continued. "You majored in computers, but that degree did not help you get a decent job." Tom leaned back.

7

Melvin, startled at how much this guy knew about him, just leaned back against the cold vinyl of the sofa.

"When you couldn't get a job, your bride, Teresa, divorced you," Tom said. "Then you married Margie. Three years later you divorced her. Women..." Tom made a fist and shook it in the air. "Then you went to trade school and became a Private Investigator. A job that's apparently been keeping you afloat." Tom looked from one side to the other. "And apparently it has kept you barely afloat. This place is a mess: dirty dishes, dust everywhere, and my gosh, the neighborhood is a dump."

Melvin could feel the rush of his blood into his face. Who was Tom to criticize anybody: he was a walking dump himself. "Wait just a cotton picking minute Bud," he hurriedly stood up, "this is my house. I don't take that kind of nonsense ..."

Tom leaned forward and raised a flush hand, "Easy there, Buddy. I was just trying to get your attention. Geez, you are as hot headed as you were in school."

Melvin felt a bead of sweat roll onto his brow, wiped it away, then lowered his hand and said, "Well, I'm usually not easy to rattle, but this is," he looked over at the digital clock on the dust covered bookshelf along the wall, "5:30 in the morning." Tom chuckled. "I usually am "NOT" awake until an hour from now. Now, Tom, would you please dispense with all this doom and gloom stuff and please tell me what the hell you are doing here?"

Chapter 4

Tom hung his head and slumped. "Melvin, I was snatched by, "supposedly", our own government. Do you remember the paper that I did in high school science regarding isolated time?" He looked back up, but remained slumped.

Melvin's brown eyes widened. "That's been so long ago. I don't even remember details about my case files sometimes."

"Well, basically it was a detailed account of how to reverse time in a person, or, say, a country, or any area of space."

"Space?" Melvin asked.

"Not space, as in the stars," Tom said. "You and I both occupy area. You are, I'm guessing, 210 pounds. That requires an area of space in our universe; more appropriately called your mass, but by any definition, it is space. The area that anything in our universe occupies is referred to as an area of space."

"Okay," Melvin said as he grabbed the outside of his housecoat and pulled it in tighter to his body. "I follow you so far," he said as he silently wished Tom would hurry up and get to the damn point.

With a wave of his arms, Tom continued. "Time has always been thought to be linear. Einstein suggested that time was actually the fourth dimension. Do you follow me so far?"

"If something is linear, it is in one straight line, correct?"

"Sort of," Tom said as took a deep breath. "A better

definition, for our discussion, would be involving only one dimension and one direction. The normal dimensions that we deal with are height, width, and length. Albert Einstein said the fourth dimension was time.

He suggested that if matter, meaning the atoms that we are made up of, moved faster through space, time would begin to dilate."

"Dilate?"

Tom raised one eyebrow, "Dilate means to contract. In other words, time would move slower the faster we went...."

"Okay."

"But, Einstein," Tom said, "suggested that if matter could go faster than the speed of light, then you could go back in time, but the faster you went," pause, "the heavier matter would become."

"Okay," Melvin said. "That makes sense, I suppose."

Tom cocked his head with wide eyes as if surprised that the subject matter was actually being understood, but continued anyway. "What I suggested in my paper, was to excite particles of matter by what, in layman's terms, would be a super tazer gun. Instead of zapping the intended victim, this super gun, called Centariur, or CR, would surround the intended target, excite the atoms or, more to the point, sort of vibrate the atoms beyond the speed of light. The result would be the atoms would regress in time. They could wipe out a person from ever being born."

"Gee," Melvin moaned slowly.

"Gee, is right," Tom said. "The ramifications in doing this to a selected area, or person, could be huge; a person might, accidentally, wipe out his own existence by disturbing the influences that brought one's parents together.

"We all do billions upon billions of things that have effects on billions of other things. WE'RE TALKING ABOUT UNIVERSAL ARMAGEDDON, MAN," Tom said flailing his hands about.

Melvin could not believe what he was hearing. This all sounded too kooky to be real. His best friend from high school shows up after all these years with some end of the world, ludicrous, off the wall, story. C'mon Man!

"Tom," he said quietly trying not disturb a possible maniac, "this a wild story." His flat hands pointed toward the dingy carpeted floor in front of him, saying, I"t's not that I don't think you're a good guy and all, but before I go off and spend six months to try and save the world, I want to see some spec of evidence that indicates the truth about all of this..."

"First of all," Tom quietly said, "if I am running free, don't you think that they would be looking for me?"

"Yes."

"And don't you want to know why they haven't found me and why they haven't wiped me out of existence?"

Shaking his head, Melvin said, "Yeah, I guess those would be good questions to start with."

"They are chasing me by sight only. I've made sure of that. ... Every member of the development team had a tracking-slash-transceiver chip implanted in their arm." He pressed his left finger deep into his right arm just above the elbow.

Melvin wondered how anyone could have found anything in all that dirt and blubber and he felt like puking his guts out to even watch this guy run his fingers through all that cellulose.

"I would've never found it," Tom continued, "if I had not accidentally cut my arm at the exact spot." He removed his finger, extended his arm, then motioned with a pulling of his index finger for Melvin to go and feel.

Melvin reached over, extending as far as he possibly could to feel the arm and avoid moving from the tattered brown sofa. After a couple of pokes and prods, he felt something underneath the skin. It was very hard, but not very big, about the size of a watch-band pin, but it moved fluidly around in Tom's arm.

"I didn't say anything, other than to the medics, who totally discounted the possibility of anything foreign being in my arm," Tom said. "They told me that it could be a glob of hardened fatty tissue, but I didn't believe them. I did not say anything further because of the older people in our facility. Some of them had suspicions that they were being tracked also." He lowered his arm. "After talking to everyone that I trusted, I found that all of us had the same thing in the same spot."

"Those of us that raised questions about this to the senior staff, quickly disappeared to God knows where, probably killed. I barely managed to escape myself."

Tom raised his arms out before him and drew a box in the air. "I discovered that a key piece of their design was that they were constructing a temporal wall that they could erect and use whenever they deemed it necessary to use the CR's. They could put whoever they wanted behind the temporal wall and then the changes in the timeline from using the CR guns would not affect these few people. They want to control everything, man!"

Tom raised his hands again and Melvin gazed at their unblemished smoothness. "Imagine if you could wipe out Adolph Hitler's birth? Would that affect Einstein's development of atom fission?" He paused until Melvin tried to answer, then continued. "Of course it would have." Tom's eyes grew wider. "Anyone that had access to CR and the temporal wall would be a god of humanity with the ability to shape the world into whatever he, she, it, wanted???"

"WOW!" If all this were true, who was he to thwart the awesome powers that were behind it? He was just a lowly PI who was barely surviving from paycheck to paycheck from loathsome clients who frequently stiffed him. He didn't even consider himself very smart. It was a miracle that he and Tom ever hooked up. Tom was a brainiac. He was a nobody and liked it.

Tom was eyeing him as if he had a miracle plan, but he didn't.

Melvin's voice was unusually loud and sharp when he spoke. "Again, what proof do you have that any of this is true?"

Tom's large body rose from the sofa, "Follow me for the proof you want."' He added, "And if I'm telling the truth, can

your conscience really be clear if you don't see my
evidence?"

Chapter 5

Do you remember those days when you wish you had stayed in bed rather than face what was happening in your life? Melvin knew he didn't have a great life. He hadn't ever had any kids due to bad marital circumstances. Oh, the sex was always great at first, but somehow, he had always protected himself. If for no other reason than wanting to make sure the marriage would last.

He didn't want to be married for a year and half, only to discover that he and the woman that he was married to were at the cusp of divorcing. As luck would have it, those females he married always turned very sour. He wasn't even sure that the problem didn't lie with him. Some people are just not the marrying kind. Maybe kids would have put the cement into his marriages, but in case the coupling didn't work out so good, he had always been determined not to drag some poor kid or kids into his messes.

That just would not be fair to the kids. He had seen his few "associates," he couldn't really call them "friends," divorce. It always brought on hard times for people, but sometimes there would be as many as four kids in the mix. Those kids were like bouncing balls going from place to place to have time with each parent: even if the split was amicable.

If the split was not peaceful, "Whoa Nelly," both sides were like World War III. And where were those completely innocent and blameless kids? They were stuck right square in the middle of all the turmoil.

As Melvin was walking toward the bedroom to pack for this God-awful trip, Tom said, "I would appreciate your not bringing anything along. These people will use anything against you and, besides that, we will need to be ready to drop everything and move in a hurry."

Now Melvin was really wondering... Tom had been working at a secret lab all these years and the lab was around here... Geez! He must have been the biggest idiot of the past hundred years to go with this whalebelly. "Hey man, I am not going outside looking like this." He opened his housecoat and motioned his hands up and down his body exemplifying his candy striped PJ's and fluffy bunny house shoes complete with four ears.

He pointed to the bedroom and said, "I am going in here and change into my stealth duds. If you have a problem with that, you can leave my behind here."

Tom smiled, then motioned Melvin with his hand. Melvin turned and walked toward the bedroom. He saw the brown, partially open door and pushed on it with his hand. It sounded raspy against the brushing of his hand and it reminded him that he had recently replaced the original door with this cheap, hollow one that he had picked up at Lowe's. Hey, on his budget, the price was right.

The original door had been busted down by, none other, than himself in a rage of anger after an exceptionally bad day. He was on a missing person's case where a wife had hired him to find, and spy on, her husband, whom she suspected of sleeping around.

Sally Keller was independently wealthy and did not have the forethought to have a prenumptional agreement signed. Plum fool-hearty... If you ask him, these people that depend on love to override the greedy nature of humanity were always fools and his low opinion of human kind, especially females, proved valid every last time.

He had been as dumb as everyone else in his first marriage. In his divorce, the bitch hired a good attorney and took their car, and everything else, no matter what it was, away from him. By a miracle, he managed to keep his beloved flesh. The hussy couldn't take that away at least. In the end, she left him with the house, the clothes on his back and a hefty alimony payment.

Having to work, pay that hussy, and recoup a minimal standard of living, really taught him a valuable lesson. When he "fell in love" a second time, to Margie, he had her sign a prenumpt. She almost didn't marry him over it, but that would have just been the way it had to be. He was already indebted to one woman for the next thousand years and he was "not" going to double down.

Six months after they wed, he began coming home to an empty house every evening. Oh, she was out shopping or she was out doing this or that. Ding, Ding, Ding. The warning bells began to echo over and over in his head. He became a meal ticket and a place to sleep off whatever she was doing.

Whether she was actually fooling around on him, he didn't know or even care. He was self-sufficient anyway as well as financially capable. His fist was always available. It never talked back. It never had a headache. It was always ready and it never had to be "in the mood". So, one evening while she was off gallivanting to God knows where, he packed her a few bags, wrote her a note that said, "Goodbye. You can pick up whatever is left of your stuff here tomorrow. It was fun while it lasted," and set it atop a divorce decree.

There was no sense prolonging the inevitable.

*

With a grimace, he looked down at his frumpy clothes. They were fitting for a romp through, what he surmised to be, the back streets of Baton Rouge, Louisiana, but not much else. My gosh, he could not wait to smell the dirt, oil, and filth in the backwoods of guttersville. He grimaced. He must be crazy for even going, but, hey, a man is entitled to make a few mistakes, isn't he?

"Okay, I'm ready, Tom," he said as he came out of his bedroom.

Tom pushed with both of his whale arms and stood up. As he walked toward Melvin, his eyes wandered downward to Melvin's waist. He noticed a book of some sort fastened there. He pointed to it with his index finger and sharply said, "What the heck is that?"

Melvin's eyes drew in and he stared at Tom with unwavering eyes for a moment, then followed them to the small, black book that was fastened to his hip with a small leather strap. "Hey man, this is my book. My SANE book. Wherever I go, it goes."

Tom raised his palms and said, "Hey, Mel, I meant no offense, but I'm trying to tell ya that we are dealing with dangerous..."

"Wherever I go, this book goes! Finito'! End of story! Understand?! If you don't like it, you can leave my ass here..."

Tom took a small step back with outstretched hands pointing down. "Okay, okay. I get the point. You don't have to use long claws. I get the message. We'll do it your way."

Chapter 6

After stepping inside the green tent that was command center, Nancy walked into her boss's office and said, "Team 6 lost him again, Sir."

Petry turned from watching several video screens and pounded two fists onto a big table. His green eyes were narrowed as an angry-frown appeared on his face. For a moment, he grimaced and his head turned. "I'll have somebody's head on a platter for this. We were fifty feet from him earlier today and now this?!"

Nancy backed up slightly and she softly said, "I know, I know." She saw that the video screens behind Petry were a combination of newscasts, traffic cameras, and satellite closeups. "We'll get him, sir."

Petry's grimace softened a bit when he looked up at the thirty-five--year old woman and the small wrinkles around his eyes released some of their taughtness. What little was left of Petry's salt-and-pepper eyebrows raised as he said, "We better find him. Soon! Our bosses are not the kind of people that you want to disappoint and if we don't find the chip, the blueprints, and everything else, there will be hell to pay. Our proverbial necks are on the chopping block. Understand?"

"Yes, sir," Nancy nodded, "we'll find them. We have all 9 of our investigative teams combing the countryside. They have this entire area under close surveillance."

Petry stood up and started pacing back and forth behind the desk. "For all the good that's done us so far... the best of the best, fumbling in the dark..." He looked at the floor and started shaking his head, then jerked his head up asking, "None of them actually know what they are looking for or why, right?"

"Certainly not!" Nancy's voice trembled slightly. "We need to hold on to that ourselves. I can't imagine what would happen if ANYONE else gained access to that information."

"Well," Petry said, "Let's just hope he's still in our area." A beep interrupted the conversation and Petry reached for the view screen on his desk. He pressed one of the buttons that were underneath the screen and the image of Robert Milgrew appeared.

"This is Rob reporting in. The team has covered sections 7, 8, and 9 in grid 4," the gruff, scraggly voice was very sharp and loud. "Still no luck." He paused to take a breath. "We can't seem to pick up the trail again. Dang it!"

Petry grimaced again. "Keep at it, Rob. We can't let this guy get away. There's no telling what he'll do, free like he is. Proceed with extreme caution."

"We will. We need to get this guy behind bars."

As his right hand reached for the buttons once more Petry said, "Proceed quickly. Petry out."

Chapter 7

Robert Milgrew thought he'd always been a logical guy. He'd followed in his dad's footsteps and joined the army at a young age. His dad, Robert Sr., was a career army veteran and was retired, at the rank of colonel after suffering injuries in an Afghanistan bombing.

A year later, Robert had taken the nickname "Rob" when he joined the army. He did it to differentiate himself from his dad, but more than that, he wanted to make his own identity known to the world. Through childhood, then adolescence, he was always known as a junior. That was okay for a youngster, but a man needed his own image. He'd wanted to get away from the junior biz and be known as Rob, 'master of all in his life.'

His basic four-year enlistment had reaffirmed the major life principles that his dad had always tried to instill within him: rules, duty, honor, and courage. Those things were essential for a society to survive. If only a few people had the convictions to obey the laws, the order in the world would quickly collapse.

Rob admired his dad and wanted to follow in his footsteps. That's why he joined the army in the first place, but when his four years were over, he got an offer to help pioneer a special para-military troop. He liked the offer and was fond of the rigidness of the military, so the decision was fairly easy.

What he didn't realize is that his new job would monopolize his time. He wouldn't mind so much if the pay was a bit better. As it was, he was over a lot of armed personnel and specialized troops doing a lot of tasks that, at least on the surface, seemed unrelated. There was three times the work that he did for the army at just a fraction over his military pay.

One day he might be supervising the destruction of a truckload of narcotics, and then spend the next two weeks hunting down and killing a 'would be' assassin. It seems that at this particular time, his orders were to track down and capture a deranged madman bent on destroying Washington D.C. with a homemade nuclear device.

He didn't know the details and didn't really care to. He never did. He was just interested in carrying out his objective. The army had taught him that. "Just follow those orders son," his father had told him time and time again. He said, "There's the right way, the wrong way, and the military way. Just because you don't know the reason for everything is no excuse not to follow orders."

He loved his dad very much and had always wanted to show him that he was a success. His dad had said that he was proud of who he was, but Rob never really felt it. Nonetheless, he supposed his enlisting into the army had a lot to do with making his dad proud. Unfortunately, his dad passed away shortly before high school graduation.

So here he was, stuck in a leader position, not public or military, with little chance of being promoted.

A young man in green togs marched into his command post. It was just a green tent on the outskirts of nowhere and surrounded by foliage so as not to be seen, but, at the moment, it was home. "Sir," the youngster said as he snapped a salute.

"Go ahead, Corporal ," replied Rob as he looked up from the charts he was holding.

"We've finished looking over section 10 with no sign of the man."

Rob arched an eyebrow. "You're sure?"

The corporal responded quickly. "Yes, Sir, absolutely."

Rob looked down at the chart for a moment, then he

lifted his head again, "No chance of missing anything?"

"No, Sir."

"Corporal, how long have you been in this outfit?"

The corporal relaxed his stance. "Sir?"

Rob's stance stiffened and then he quickly and with a loud enunciated voice bellowed, "You heard me, soldier. How long have you been in this outfit?"

The lad stiffened, but with darting eyes as if looking for help. "I don't understand."

Rob's eyebrows pressed down and his eyes glared at the young man in front of him. "It's not necessary for you to understand me, Son, just follow my orders and answer my friggin' question!!!"

The young man quickly stiffened more and looked directly at Rob. "Two years, Sir."

"Two years," Rob said muttering afterwards. "You are just a green recruit. How in the world did I get stuck with you?" The corporal started to say something, but Rob cut him off. "No, for God's sake don't answer that." He grabbed the map that was on his desk. "Just show me on the aerial map what you have searched."

The corporal came forward to the desk and started pointing.

"It's always possible to miss something, Corporal," Rob said as he looked on. "Nothing is ever perfect until I say so. Do you understand?"

"Yes, Sir" There was a whoosh of air and the sound of sleeved cloth rubbing as the young man snapped a salute.

Chapter 8

As Melvin followed Tom out of his back door, which was insisted upon by Tom, he thought how improbable Tom's story was and how gullible he was for getting involved. Still, what was that pin underneath his skin? He had no clue. He guessed it could be a piece of glass, he had heard that welders sometimes get things embedded under the skin, but he really had no evidence of that. Anyone can hear nearly any kind of story. Most of the time that's all they were, stories.

As the two exited, there were numerous trees around. Melvin had selected this house because of the backyard. The area was mostly in the shade, as evidenced by the sun shining in thin streaks of daylight. "The fingers of God," he had always thought. It was very comforting for him to know that there was at least one person in this whole universe who cared about him.

The neighborhood he lived in was crappy and his first ex-wife complained about how intolerable it was to live there, but the leechy whore didn't have any indecision about taking advantage of him. He didn't care what that hussy thought anymore, he liked the yard and that's all that mattered.

The backyard made up for the neighborhood including living with the greedy thing he had once called a wife too. "Wife," that was a joke, more like, live-in harlot. It pissed him off just thinking about her.

This back yard calmed him though. It was small, measuring just 25' x 25', but had these really nice, large trees. There was a mixture of pine, hickory, and a big oak in the back corner of the lot with a few bushes mixed in, not including the pear and persimmon tree and trees which he did not know the names of. He just knew they were pretty. When the wind blew, Melvin loved to hear the rustle of the leaves. Those damn pine needles were a mess, but as a single man, he could afford the time it took to rake and bag up the needles, leaves, and such. Melvin loved spending the time to commune with nature. It was about his only reprieve from life.

Tom carefully chose a path through the yellow and green yard on the cool January day. The wind was blowing and the recently fallen leaves were slightly caressing the gray dirt with tiny movements and occasionally one would fly up through the air. The wind was not only blowing the leaves around, but it was blowing against the navy blue jackets of both men.

Melvin could see Tom in front of him, learning forward slightly as he walked. Tom's hands were in his pockets and Melvin decided to do the same as his hands were feeling the icy wind.

It was almost painful to see Tom walk. Melvin was quite certain that every four-hundred-fifty-pound-step was painful to the topsoil. The leaves and pine straw were dingy brown and they made a sharp, crinkling sound with every step.

Both of Melvin's parents had weighed over four-hundred pounds ever since he could remember. His dad had died when he was only 5 and his mom died when he was 6. Both died of heart attacks brought on by obesity complications. Obesity had ripped the two most precious people in his life from him at the age when he needed the most from them. He loved them very much as. He supposed, all kids love their parents, but for them to die with ensuing complications of something that they could prevent was insanity to him. It was just one more thing in his life that was screwed up.

In front of him, Tom, pressing a lone finger to his lips, at the back corner of the property, began stepping out from the trees. The area beyond was a crossroads of residential properties. Tom crossed the black top road carefully and, when they had both crossed, he pointed south.

In the distance was a stoplight and Tom turned and drew a circle in his palm indicating that they would go around the light.

"Why?" Melvin asked.

Tom quickly turned around then abruptly raised one hand in front of his mouth. He pushed the other hand forward a bit and then turned back around.

Melvin didn't understand the need for silence, but obeyed the leader. Tom led the way through backyards, across roads, and through bushes. This went on through the housing district and into the vacant parts of town. Tom was leading them to God knows where, but definitely heading somewhere. Through ditches and trash areas they traveled headlong south. They stopped frequently for rest breaks with Tom huffing and puffing hard enough so that Melvin could see Tom's eyes bulging with each heavy breath. Sometimes he would shake his head and raise a flush hand as if to apologize, but never said a single word, and would not allow Melvin to talk.

Their trek continued on and on through one dismal area to the other. As soon as they were close enough to get a glimpse of an intersection with a stoplight, Tom would change their path. Melvin did not realize that Tom must have walked all the way to his home on poverty lane. He wondered how Tom got in such bad physical shape. In high school Tom was not in great condition, but he was far from the worst of the kids.

Tom moved in and out of alleyways so much so that Melvin was confused as to exactly where they were. He knew that they were on the south side of town, but not exactly where.

The weaving in and out of streets, alleyways, backyards, wooded areas, and other mucky areas continued for hours. Occasionally Tom would stop and rest a few minutes, but mostly it was a steady pace now as the sun was getting lower in the sky. Melvin took the breaks, but he didn't really need them. Being a PI kept him in pretty good shape. His legs would cramp a bit every now and then, but other than that, he was okay. There was nothing like being a glorified bounty hunter to keep you in great physical shape.

A lot of his cases were just missing persons and a lot of them didn't want to be found. Other cases involved people who wanted to shoot at him. He didn't respond too well to bullets buzzing his ears. Quite frankly, it royally pissed him off. There's nothing like a near-death experience to get the blood stirring. It was that sort of thing that caused him to give his chasee's 'a friendly beating' whenever he finally did catch them. It calmed them down instantly and, frankly, it gave him great satisfaction.

They were nearing a virtually paint-stricken house. Melvin recognized the architecture as Victorian. He had always loved Victorian architecture with its romantic style. Its overly-accented awnings and the swooping nature of a roller-coaster ride were a true romantic's dream. It was not a big house, maybe two or three bedrooms, at best. It was hardly worthy of the styling. In his opinion, larger houses were much more romantic and better suited to the styling.

This house was very quaint and Melvin supposed that, at one time, this little house had been a roomy little home for whatever family dwelled there. The years had not been very kind to the old house. The roof and eaves had pronounced sags and there was even a small hole on the left side eaves. The back porch, struts include, looked in good shape, but the screening around it was rusty brown. Tiny holes were everywhere including several large rips and there was not a drop of paint on the entire gray house.

Tom appeared to be heading directly towards the back porch of the house. He pressed a perpendicular finger to his lips and whispered, "Shhhhh......... Follow quietly and step EXACTLY where I do."

Melvin was sure going to try to do exactly as directed. He didn't know much, but he had seen enough war movies to know that to fail in this game of "follow the leader" might have serious consequences.

Melvin stared with wide eyes at every imprint of Tom's two-toned brown Reeboks. He could see every wave and dimple in the grass blades that were crushed by Tom's weight and the impressions in the bare grey sand underneath what we coonass's call wood dirt. Most of the countryside in this area was gray sand or wood dirt. Well, either that or the red gumbo clay.

Mud truckers loved the red clay because it was like trying to navigate in a road of super glue. That is, until they finally stuck their truck in some. In that event, it was "hello tractor, goodbye money," because once you were stuck in the stuff, you have a hell of a problem trying to get out of it. Melvin knew how tough it was from going mudding with a friend back in high school that got his 4-wheel drive Dodge Ram stuck.

Mudding in the red clay was fun, but his granddad had always told him that anything could be grown in that red gumbo mud because it was so rich with nutrients. He didn't know. He had never tried, but he sure wanted to.

Once they had tip-toed through the assumed minefield, Tom grabbed the D-style backdoor screen handle and swung the door open about a foot. A blue jay began chirping and Tom raised up to look around with wide-eyes like a scared rabbit, then he leaned back over and inside the cracked-open screen door.

With hidden motions, Tom opened the porch door and they both stepped through. As they walked, the boards creaked, which made Melvin wonder about whether the flooring was sturdy enough to support their combined weight. Hidden motions by Tom opened the house door and Tom ushered Melvin inside. After closing the door, Tom did another hidden maneuver. Abandoned houses, secret meetings, what was next?

"Whew!" Tom wiped his brow. "I'm glad the trip is over with, for now at least."

Melvin marveled at his surroundings and noticed wood cabinetry. He instantly recognized the dark, wide, stained wood grain to be pine as similar to his own house. Pine was

27

cheap. The grain was unmistakable underneath the edges of peeling paint, a sure sign of lead based paint. Underneath the cabinets was a dusty countertop with an empty slot. Dirt was on the floor and there were some black hoses and other connections coming out of the wall. On the opposite wall, there was a gas nozzle on the floor, but no stove. The entire floor was dirty, dingy, with warped tiling and it was all stain ridden. The sand popped underneath Melvin's shoes as he turned. Thick dust was layered on the surface of everything. There was about a 3 foot by 3 foot window above where the sink would be. The basin was missing and the window had a long diagonal crack.

Beyond the kitchen to the left was an open door to an empty storeroom or it might have been used as a walk-in pantry. Melvin could see warped shelving on the left wall.

In the other direction, opposite the now closed back door, there was an entranceway to what Melvin assumed was a dining room.

"Come in," Tom said as he walked into the next room. "You better not try to open any doors or windows. I have the whole place booby-trapped."

Melvin followed Tom into what would be the dining room still wondering what he had gotten himself into.

Chapter 9

Inside the command center, the screens in the back were all tapped into assorted video cameras of the area. In front of the cameras, sitting in a tan leather office chair on wheels, was a blonde woman. Her shoulders were pulled back and, rather than slouching, her torso was rigid and away from the back of the chair. When the phone started ringing on the fold-out side table, she twisted around, reached over, and grabbed the maroon receiver. As she was about to put it to her ear, she put her feet flat against the floor and stood. "Hello."

"Nancy, please," a high-pitched female voice said.

"Phone call for you, Nancy," the woman said as she looked over at Nancy. She extended the phone towards her.

"Thank you, Tracy," Nancy said as she walked over. Tracy's hand released the phone slowly into Nancy's and then sat back down. Nancy took the receiver and put it to her ear. "Hello."

"Nancy?"

"Yes."

"Red Scramble," the female voice said.

Nancy said, "Understood," and hung the phone up.

As she turned around, her head collided into Petry's chin. He looked down at her and asked, "Who was that?"

Nancy calmly said, "Oh, that was just my husband telling me about the kids. Sorry for the bump." Petry nodded and then she circled around him. She darted out from the command tent and into her own without saying another word to anyone along the way. Once inside she pulled down the zipper opening, and then pulled the inside cover. She walked to the far side of her bed, knelt, and then pulled a leather bag out. Reaching her right hand in, she began roaming through it.

She unfastened a Velcro closure in the bottom and pulled from the bag a small device. She entered the unlock code on the top keypad and put the phone to her head.

"Status report."

Nancy said, "We have not found the device yet."

"That's not good enough," the female voice said.

"I know. I know, but we are doing everything possible, Senator."

"Damn you! Don't you dare use titles or any fucking thing else on any frequency. No one else has any friggin' idea that I'm involved. You're a dead woman if you expose me."

"Y-Ye-Yes, Ma'am." Nancy said with a trembling voice. "I'm terribly sorry."

"Don't you forget how much I can do to you and the people around you. If this thing goes right, I will greatly reward you, but you've gotta get on the friggin' ball or I will shred you and everyone around you. Your husband, your kids, your life are all in the palms of my hands and don't you dare forget it."

"I, I, won't. I will try my best, Ma'am."

"I want the missing piece... You have your orders..."

"Yes, I will accomplish the task," Nancy said.

"You better! "

As Nancy hung up the phone, she let out a whistling exhale. She then put everything away and exited her tent.

She was walking back to command center with a renewed sense of purpose when she saw a slim figure walking toward her. She squinted her eyes and saw that it was Eric Kandle. He was headed in the same direction as she was and she began walking toward him. "Eric," she hollered.

Eric stopped and looked around. After a moment, his eyes finally saw Nancy walking toward him. He raised his right hand, smiled, as he began walking toward her.

"Has your team gotten anywhere," Nancy asked as she walked. The lack of reaction on Eric's face told her that the answer was negative.

"No, Nancy," he said as he neared her. "We are finding some clues, but the trail is cold. He has really managed to keep himself well hid."

"Damn it!" Nancy lips stiffened. "Satellites, cameras, audio sensors, police, detectives...! We have everything turned on and still this guy eludes us!" She slammed her fist in midair.

"Yeah, he's good alright. I'm just here to report to Petry and then I am off to re-join my team."

"I'll come with you and then, I'd like to search with your team for a bit."

Eric's eyes widened. "Sure, you're more than welcome."

Chapter 10

Melvin gathered himself into a ball while he tried to sleep on the thin mat that Tom had handed him. The mat was not much comfort over the hardwood floors that were throughout the abandoned home. Now Melvin realized why they were called hardwood floors because his body thought he was sleeping on a damn cement slab. Every inch of his body was yelling at him. Was he an idiot for even being here? Were it anyone but Tom the answer would have been a resounding, yes.

Melvin knew that time changes people. He had known a lot of people over his many years that had changed. Jerry Horner from high school was kind hearted and honest. He was the kind of guy that gave the girls flowers or helped a wounded dog, but his first case as an investigator was from Jerry's ex-wife. Jerry owed twelve-months of back alimony and child support. What a change that was. Jerry used to be such a great guy and now look at him, a down and out deadbeat.

He learned, quite by accident, that Jerry had become a child abuser and wife beater. The clerk at the jail was friends with the, now, ex-wife, and he knew him well enough to talk about the situation without it being a breach of confidentiality.

You never know what is going to happen to people through the rip-roaring course of time. Look at him. His life had certainly changed since high school. First, both of his parents dying suddenly and nearly back to back... What a colossal shock that was. Second, his first failed marriage sent him spinning into a depression. He never expected but to marry once and live happily forever in a two-story house with a white picket fence. It was every young man's dream, his included. Then there were a number of busted jobs, deaths and other deplorable things. It made him angry. It was life.

He was lying on his back which hurt from an awful night. He turned to his left, then to his right, but nothing was making his aches and pains any less. He just wanted this night to end. Tom had wanted to postpone viewing all the evidence until they both had some sleep. Melvin was just now realizing that he would have much preferred staying up all night if need be. It felt as if the flooring had metal spikes that were poking his body in places that he didn't know were even there until now.

He still didn't really know if Tom had gone bonkers or what? His investigator alarms had been buzzing in the back of his head ever since Tom had stepped through his doorway. It was hard to believe that a lowly guy like him was somehow mixed up in an attempted global domination scheme. Ding, ding, ding. Hello? Was he crazy? Was Tom crazy? It made Melvin's brain ache just cogitating the possibilities.

He nestled as well as he could between the floor and the thin, tan cover that Tom threw his way and tried to drift off to sleep again, but the cold wasn't helping things. His house may have been cold, but not this cold. The heating unit at his house was at least set on 64 during the night. The weatherman had said that it was supposed to get down to 46 tonight. He didn't know what the temp was, all he knew is that was cold enough to make his body feel numb. Unfortunately, not enough... He still felt the cold bite on every inch of his body.

The cover might have been thin, but at least it was flannel so it was a minor barrier. The worst part of it was the high humidity caused by the mighty Mississippi River running between Port Allen and Baton Rouge.

Combine the river with all the creeks and lakes in the area and you had a perfect mess. The humidity ranged between 75 and 100 percent year round, usually staying near 90 percent. If you had lived in the area long enough, you learned to adapt, but if you were from anywhere north of the Mason-Dixon line, it was tough. He was born and raised in the area, but on several trips with school friends he got to see and feel how northeners live. It was not bad up north and he thought about moving to D.C. once.

A company up there had offered him a job doing personal investigations. Getting dirt on politicians would have been a terrible life. Besides, he hated politicians. Yuck! One of his high-school 'associates' had called him, but the job definitely was not for him.

He was warming up a teeny bit. That blanket turned out not to be too bad and it allowed Melvin to warm up just enough to drift off to sleep.

Chapter 11

The night passed long, slow, and painful, but at least it passed. Melvin was never so happy to see the sun come up as he was this morning. He could see light begin to shine through the almost sheer white cloth hung over the bay window along the bare, nearly black, wood-paneled wall. In true Victorian style, it was hung in the outside corner of the room.

The window stood there as a testament to the old days when cars were simple and being a man meant taking full responsibility of yourself and your actions. Melvin couldn't help but gaze at the beauty of the design. His past was anything but beauty and he certainly was no hero, never had been. In school, he was never a model student and his passion was the boxing team. In fact, his whole life was exactly the antithesis of Victorian design.

In his youth, boxing had taught him patience. Wait for an opening, then throw a punch, but he also had to learn that one punch was never enough. You had to throw in combinations. It was a sport of the quickest and smartest.

He couldn't help but think about his coach. Myron was dead now after having had a heart attack before Melvin had graduated, but his philosophy of never quitting even when your face was buried into the canvas had always stuck with him. "They might win the match, but you're never beaten until you're dead," Myron had always said.

As a student, he was nothing special. His grades were

mostly A's, but it wasn't rocket science. You study, you pass. And he didn't have any friends, besides Tom and he was rock solid. He kept in touch with some "associates" through the years, but he had always wondered what had happened to Tom.

Now he knew or thought he did anyway that if Tom were not telling the truth, it would be the first time that Melvin had any knowledge of that happening. He had always been honest, and at times, too honest. There were never any secrets kept with him, because, if he knew it, he would tell it. It was not a character flaw, it was just who he was.

That was the reason for pursuing this grand scale conspiracy that Tom talked about. It may have sounded like insanity to some, but Melvin knew Tom's character too well to just pish-posh it off. Something would have to radically change for him to be that different. Still, Melvin could not help wonder if his feelings of friendship were clouding his judgment.

People change. That was a fact of life. Oftentimes not for the better...

Chapter 12

By the time that Tom walked into the room, Melvin had balled up his thin, but somewhat useful, cover and was sitting on it. He had been standing for a while to try and get the achiness out of his body. He had taken out his book and had been writing into it, but supporting it in midair proved to be unsteady. His penmanship was not the best anyway. The midair antics proved to be too challenging so he had elected to sit as near to Indian style as his middle-aged body could manage.

After his second marriage had started to crumble, he started writing a daily journal to ease his mind. He had seen all of his dreams turn to dust after high school. His best and only friend had disappeared, parents were dead, couldn't get a job, marriage was in the toilet, no other relatives to speak of. Life had just shit on him and it was getting ready to flush. Keeping a journal of his thoughts and feelings about what was going on in his life was the way that he clung to sanity.

And it was a Journal, not a friggin' diary. Girls wrote diaries. Others had seen him writing in his books and called it a diary and he took pleasure in setting them straight, sometimes with his fists. Over twenty years, it amounted to lots of writing books and he treasured them all. He had a large locking fireproof cabinet in his bedroom that he kept them in. Recent events gave him lots to write about. His fingers started to cramp so he finished his last sentence and then clipped the pen into the wire binding. With limp fingers, he shook his hand.

"Good morning," Tom said as he pulled out a small, wooden, deck chair from the bedroom he had slept in. Melvin put the book and pen away. He found himself envious of the chair that Tom was sitting in. He could feel warm blood rushing to his face to show it too. A warm face was welcome in the cold house. He could have slept far better in that chair than he ever could have on that lousy mat. The chair creaked and squawled under the weight as Tom sat down. It had seen much better days. There was black bailing wire around parts of it and Melvin supposed that Tom had gotten it out of a trash pile somewhere. The bare wood looked to be dry and pitted with a dingy light-brown in multiple shades running throughout. It was a miracle that it held Tom's 400 pounds.

"Are you ready to see more evidence?"

"I would love to," Melvin exclaimed. Translation: 'Yeah, let's get this over with so I can go back to my sorry life.'

"Okay, but keep your voice down. We don't want to attract anyone. Ever since the 1970's all televisions have integrated in them a non-serviceable microchip that is for government eavesdropping. Even repairmen can't replace or even remove the chips."

"Wow!" 'Okay, everybody knows the government spies on us.'

"No one knows who makes these microchips or even where they come from." Tom paused. "Over time, they got far more sophisticated. These days, one of these microchips can piggyback audio signals from any electronic device within 100 yards. The V-chips that the government mandated be in all TV's made the problem worse. Those things monitor everything we watch and they can monitor us by video. Modern TV's can project a picture or be used as a video camera."

'This I didn't know.'

"Those types of things are why we couldn't make any sound in coming here. Every traffic light in the United States and pretty much the entire civilized world is equipped with these monitoring techniques. They have video capabilities also along with numerous other electronic devices. They can even monitor with infrared at a lot of locations." Tom paused a moment to clear his throat.

'Gee! I never knew it was this advanced.'

Continuing, he said, "The age of George Orwell's book 1982 and big brother are here, man. It just got out of control before we or even the government ever knew it. Over the years, our government has started numerous secret societies and all of them with a different objective."

Melvin slowly became aware that his eyebrows and cheeks were moving in opposing directions and making his eyes bulge. He could definitely feel the increased airflow to the edges of the sclera of his eyes.

Tom must have noticed. "This must be somewhat of a shock to you. I mean, even detectives don't have access to this kind of information."

"No. I didn't even know these things existed. I mean, I knew it was possible, but...."

Tom's eyes widened. "It is not only possible, but it is used to control the masses by learning how to sway people's opinions through their own words and actions." Pause. "Beware of all electronics that are near even minor public areas such as parks, playgrounds, etc. People that use the Internet, search engines, Facebook, etc., they don't realize how much of their life they are giving away to our government. Think about a common thief. Through the social media and the Internet they learn our mother's names, even maiden names, our relationships, our likes and dislikes. People expose their entire world and with just a little digging through public records, they can come up with our social security number and all kinds of other stuff. As a detective, you know that much."

After pausing to absorb the last statement fully, Melvin answered, "Yeah, I knew that, but I didn't know about TV's and consumer electronics."

"Okay, my friend, let's get to the stuff you came here about."

Chapter 13

In the back seat of a black four-door sedan, Eric Kandle was sitting beside Nancy on the velvety black seating. "Eric," Nancy said, "how do you feel about politics?"

Eric cocked his head. "What do you mean? Just saying "politics" covers a very broad area."

Nancy lifted her medium length dirty-blonde hair and rubbed the back of her neck. "I mean just in general."

Shaking his head, he replied, "I dunno. I guess it's okay. I mean, I don't trust any politicians, or their policies, but I guess none of us have any alternative."

"You are such a strong person and you ought to know that we always have an alternative. Everyone has an alternative to everything in our lives. We may not always like the choices, but nevertheless, we have them," she said as she finished straightening her hair.

"Well, you are right about that, but the feasibility for changing anything in the government is doubtful," Eric said as the car stopped at a red light.

Nancy turned her head in all directions. "But.... suppose you had the opportunity to change anything in our government for the better... would you take that once in a blue moon chance?"

Eric cocked his head again and laid a finger alongside his face. "I suppose I would if in doing so I did not have to break any laws. Besides, why are you asking?"

It was Nancy's turn to shake her head, "I dunno. It's just

a question. We have known each other a long time, my friend, and I just thought I'd ask. I often think about the 'what if's like this. It's sort of a pre-emptive thing that I do. I like to think about all possibilities."

"I see," he said with a slow voice. "How are Rex and the kids?"

Nancy swatted at a fly buzzing her ear. She'd rather have not changed topics, but she had planted her seed. "Oh, they're fine. Tim just turned 12 and plans on playing football next school year and Laura is involved in some cooking classes sponsored by the school."

"I'll bet all the boys are crazy about her. All boys like blondes."

Nancy took a deep breath and exhaled slowly. "Thank God, no. She's only 10, after all. It will be a few more years, I hope, before we have to worry about that. Besides, I think Rex would kill'em if they got too close to the house." She laughed. "He is totally not ready."

"How about you?"

She looked at him, stared a moment, then chuckled and said, "Not yet. In a few more years," The car stopped. As she starting looking around, she continued, "maybe I'll be ready by then."

There were a number of people standing slightly beyond Nancy's side of the car. One was holding a tablet pointing between it and, intermittently, at the wooded area beyond. The area itself was mostly pine trees, bushes, and weeds. There was tall grass in a mostly clear field to the left. The tallest of the grass had narrow burnt yellow stalks with tops that were bigger and spoked. "Barnyard grass," she mumbled.

The wind was blowing strong and the grass, trees, and bushes that were in the area were leaning over with each gust. Nancy noticed the top of a particularly tall pine tree was swaying about three feet over. The wind was coming from the west wher she saw dark clouds blowing in. Below those dark skies were blurry vertical streaks, which could only mean one thing, rain. They would all be soaking wet within minutes. "Liquid sunshine. Dang!"

She looked down and beside where the car had parked and saw that about five-feet from the car was the man holding a tablet around his neck. His body was swaying slightly and his navy jacket fluttering with each gust.

Nancy clutched the door handle and gently pushed it open, but a gust of wind tore the door out of her hand. She yelped slightly in surprise, not only of the wind, but the coolness of the air on her skin. Folding her arms together, she got up and out of the vehicle.

She felt a bump in her derrière from Eric following her and moved out of his way. She looked back at him and groaned slightly. Had he just wanted to look at her ass or what? She quickly decided that it wasn't worth questioning him about and side-stepped his exit.

When they were both out, Nancy took a moment to unfold her arms and straighten her clothes when out of the corner of her eye, she saw Eric as he went ahead. Reaching her hand around the car door, she slammed it shut with a THUD.

Eric walked up to the man seated at the tablet and asked, "Well, John, what's the news?"

John looked up from the tablet. "We know the guy is headed south. Satellite images picture a whale making his way to the south end of this berg. That's got to be our guy. I can't imagine there being too many half-ton men waddling in these streets. The strange thing about the video is that there are two people, one portly, one slim."

"Where?"

"Right about here," John said, as he pointed to a map on the tablet. "We lost them in the trees."

"At least that gives us something to go on." He looked back down at the tablet.

Nancy looked around at the agents who were searching for clues and shook her head. Softly she said, "We gotta get this guy. We gotta get him quick."

Chapter 14

Tom stretched his belly up from the chair, using his arms as leverage, and walked over to the kitchen wall. Leaning against the wall in the corner was a small metal tray that Melvin had not noticed. It was the only extra item in the room so he was not sure why it didn't stick out like a cop at a mafia convention.

The tray appeared to be an old dinner tray that someone had thrown away. The tray itself was warped with bowed legs underneath and was tediously standing upright. It had dings in a number of places all of which were stripped of paint. The thing barely stood on its own but at least it stood. There were patches of dingy orange rust covering large and small areas, particularly where the dings were. Tom grabbed the tray from the side, waddled back, then re-seated himself.

Melvin was reminded of the long, hard night by the stabbing pains in his joints as he waited for this fantastical unveiling. With bodily contortions that would make a gymnast jealous, he tried to manage a comfortable position. Not succeeding, he stretched his head up and rubbed the back of his neck. It felt good, temporarily, then he looked back down and put his hands at his sides.

Tom leaned down to his right and grabbed a black shimmering bag from the floor. Putting the bag in his lap, he pulled out several devices and laid them on the table. The table wobbled a bit. "I have removed the tracking chips from these devices, so don't worry."

Nodding, Melvin quietly said, "Okay."

Tom held up a slim circuit board by both open hands placed along the edges and rotated it to show both sides. The board was green with a lot of lines and microchips on it. Here and there were spots of rosin core solder. The length of the board was about 3 inches, width was about 4 inches, and along the bottom of the width was a black connector. "This is the key thing that makes the temporal wall work. The wall protects up to twelve people from any changes in the timeline from the use of the CR guns. There are plans in place to put the CRs into satellites, but they have not done that so far, thank God.

This board is a temporal phase discriminator. They have been working on this for forty-six years. Research began when our illustrious government found an alien probe that crashed in Colorado. Examining it, they found that it was designed to study the effects of time dilation in space."

Melvin scratched his head. "What is time dilation and what does it have do with space?"

"It doesn't really have anything to do with space, but apparently someone thought it did. Anyway, time dilation dates back to Einstein. He would test theories such as whether a lightning strike would be seen the same on a fast moving train as a person standing on solid ground. What he discovered was that the lightning bolt would seem to move slower on the train because it was moving.

The probe had scooped up some kind of particle from a black hole, star, or something totally unknown, that allows for particle excitation up to, and beyond, the speed of light. Einstein said if you moved anything faster than light, it would go back in time. Every CR gun has a spec of this element."

"If they only found one particle, how does each CR gun have it?"

Tom's thin lips pressed tightly together and the tops of his lips curled inward so that the skin poofed outward. "They were able to reproduce it in a lab. Unfortunately, I did not have access to the lab where the particles were held.

Moreover, I didn't know how many guns there were. They were not all kept in the same place. I found out about these particles by accident when I was doing some hardware design on the mainframe. I was kinda bored and began poking around. Found out about the particles and the reason that they had me on the team designing this board. I decided right then and there to look for a way to escape."

Melvin lurched forward and held a hand up. "Whoa! Were you being held prisoner or something?"

"No, but our outings were very restricted." Tom paused and lowered his head. "I should have known something was up." He looked up. "As a kid, I was just excited to be sought after, which is most likely why they get kids fresh out of high school.

Anyway, I waited until they had the prototype board completed, then erased the memory banks and all the backups, grabbed the board with my chip, the blueprints, as much stuff as I could, and then got the hell out of there. I've been on the run for about a month."

"What does the circuit board do?" Melvin asked looking at the board.

"It senses ripples in our timeline and when it's plugged into the temporal Dyson super computer, it can block a limited area from changes in our timeline."

"By changes in our timeline, I assume you mean through the use of these CR guns?"

Tom nodded, "You are exactly right. The rulers of these powers would almost be like gods, but there is no way to control which direction the changes would go. They may make things better or worse and, as with all things, better or worse depends on your point of view."

"How does the board work?"

"My friend, it is far too technical to try to go into right now, but," Tom leaned over and pulled a small box out of the bag. It was about the size of a box of kitchen matches. It was clear on all 4 sides with a small hole one of the sides. Tom leaned forward saying, "This is one of their experiments that I found and stole as I was escaping from the research center."

He pulled down on one of the short sides, then reached into his pocket and pulled out a dead roach.

Melvin couldn't help but make an unintelligible noise of revulsion and recoil a bit.

"Easy there, my friend. I found this roach in a spider's web when I came to this house. Just watch..." Tom put the dead roach inside the box and closed the side. It was upside down and Melvin wondered what in the world one simple roach could mean, especially a dead one. "This box has a protective layer so that the CR beam will be enclosed inside the box."

Tom then pulled a bronze looking object from the black bag. It sort of looked like a .32 revolver, only the barrel was extremely short. There was no cylinder or hammer, but there was a button on the side.

Tom put a finger on the button and put the barrel into the hole. "I would not do this with anything else, but I need you to believe what I'm telling you." He paused. "This is a dead roach, correct?"

"Correct."

"Keep your eye on the roach." Tom pulled the trigger on the gun. A yellow light shined into the box from the gun. A few moments passed and there was no change. Tom released the trigger and adjusted something in the rear of the gun, then pulled the trigger again. Another few moments passed without any change.

The roach's legs started moving in almost circular motions and Tom released the trigger. The yellow light vanished and Tom pulled the gun barrel from the hole.

Astonished, Melvin's lower jaw dropped open. He felt it drop, but he felt every muscle in his body go weak and numb at the same time. He didn't know how long he stood there like a stupefied statue. All he knew is that it seemed like forever.

He could not wrap his brain around what he had just witnessed. This was totally impossible. Time was the one constant in the universe. It always moved forward, never in reverse.

No, he thought, this was some kind of trick. You can't bring anything back to life. You can't alter time. You can't... you can't... you can't... This was worse than a Frankenstein horror movie. The ramifications of this kind of thing were...

"It boggles the mind, huh?"

Melvin closed his mouth and swallowed the lump in his throat. An enunciated, "Y-Y-Yes," was all Melvin could utter.

"It seems impossible, but the reality is that this actually exists and it works." Tom laid the CR gun on the table. "This small box just limits the beam from going anywhere else. Our timeline has been affected to a very small degree. The spider that was saving this roach for a snack, I'm sure, will be disappointed, but not much else will happen. I don't think. It was just a necessary demonstration to show you the reality of what I was saying."

Melvin opened his mouth again only blowing air. There was nearly an audible whistle as the air escaped. "If I wasn't totally convinced before, I am now, and I must admit that I was a bit skeptical."

"Yeah, I know you. That's why I knew that I needed a convincer. I mean, not just you, but who in the world would believe this stuff?" Tom paused and raised both hands in the air. "Even I wouldn't have believed it twenty years ago." He dropped both hands to his legs with a plop sound as they hit.

Melvin put his hand to his chest and in doing so finally realized just how much life had changed. "Buddy! We are in a bunch of trouble! Our lives aren't worth anything. They will stop at NOTHING to silence us and get this board back."

"I know. I know," Tom said slowly.

Chapter 15

Suddenly Melvin's mundane everyday life meant exactly nothing. Suddenly the world had changed into a highly dangerous, foreboding place. He felt very small, microscopic even, in a world that wanted him dead or even worse than dead, in screaming agony until they had these resources back.

They were dead men, they just weren't dead yet. Melvin looked at Tom who simply stared at him. There was the roach alive and well in the box when he should be dead. Why was it alive? Couldn't Tom have let it stay dead? But this faucet had been dripping long before Tom even got involved. Melvin wished he were still in his cold bed at home. His life was not perfect, but at least he didn't have the fate of the entire world, hold that, the entire universe, maybe even all universes, right square on his shoulders, his and Tom's. It was sheer insanity for anyone to even mess with this stuff. It was universal Armageddon. How could anyone think they could control such awesome power? If was like a sci-fi disaster movie gone wild...

They were dead men, they just weren't dead yet. Insanity, he thought, total and complete insanity. The other part of their problem is what could they do? What was the next step? Tom had convinced him with a resounding THUD. A ton of bricks... Ha! That was mere child's play. How about a quadrillion tons or even more? What would they do? What in this entire world was possible to do?

They couldn't go to the press. Ever since a few years

ago, all the news was entirely distributed through government computer networks. Ah, the perils of the information age. Everyone's gone crazy with the lightning speed of anything digital. If a news story was submitted it would be screened out and they would kill whoever the story came from including both he and Tom. Moreover, they would kill anyone that had even remote knowledge of the incident.

That's what they would call it, too, an incident. An incident, my foot! It was more like a damn catastrophe! It would naturally look like a suicide or an accident, but it would be a murder of necessity for the government. Government and their secrets, sheesh... They were so compartmentalized that offices could be side by side and neither one know what the other did or that the other one even existed.

Melvin leaned over to stare at the roach a bit closer. He was hopeful of finding out that this was some elaborate trick for a Candid Camera type of show. He picked up the box containing the squirming roach who had managed to right itself and was crawling around in the box.

This technology could have some positive aspects, too. Take someone with a failing heart for instance. The heart could be removed, reversed to a time when it was healthy, then put back in. Assuming that you could suspend all matter in all universes while you do it. It would work splendidly that way. Zero chance of rejection, too. But without suspension, the repercussions of that scenario were inconceivable.

No, this is wrong, Melvin said to himself. This shouldn't be, it damn well shouldn't be. It wasn't right. He must not allow himself to think positive. This was bad, really bad, incredibly bad, enormously bad. There was just no other way to look at it. Anyone that thinks they can use or control this power was out of their fucking mind.

Melvin hung his head and closed his eyes. As he sat motionless, all he could do was whisper, "Damn, damn, damn," then a pause and then whisper the words again. He knew that their lives were nothing. They must not let this horrendous force be used. They must destroy all materials and equipment for this technology.

What about the God factory? What about fate? What about destiny? This went against everything natural. How many people could you change until you wipe out everything that exists or will exist? This could potentially be ruination of everything. It was too dark to even contemplate.

Melvin reached up and grabbed his head on both sides and whined. This shouldn't be used. He looked at Tom and then back at the roach. Capturing Tom at such a young age stunk of government. The crooks! Damn them anyway! What they did openly was bad enough, but this is a covert disaster. Even the government should have better sense, but they employed any tool that they could to control the people and the world, including strategic assassinations. So, it was he and Tom against the whole entire government and that's assuming that other governments were not looking for this technology.

It was upon he and Tom to destroy this reprehensible technology. The biggest question was how?

Chapter 16

Melvin looked over at his pigpen friend. He was becoming thankful for the cold absorbing much of the odor. He put his hand to his head, brushed his hair back, then asked, "Okay, friend, what's the plan?"

Tom's eyes looked like twin lighthouses. Melvin saw that frightening look. The lights were on, but nobody was home. Tom wilted and hung his head, shaking it. "Mel, I just don't know."

"WHAT do you mean??? You have no idea??? I thought you had a plan, Man."

Tom quickly righted himself, frowned, and spoke, only this time the voice was sharp, forceful, and with accented volume. "Well, I do. ... I stole the board and erased the data." He leaned as far back as the dilapidated chair would allow and started separating hairs with his fat, nubby, fingers. There was a definite tone of resignation in his voice when he spoke again. "Even that won't stop them for too long though."

"What do you mean?"

Tom's fair complexion washed away, leaving only off-white. "I mean the damage that I did to the project as a whole was minor. They still have the technology and, worse yet, the will to use it. To really eradicate their ability to use this God-forsaken technology, all knowledge, materials, and mechanisms must be destroyed."

Melvin shrugged. "And just how do we do that?"

Tom put an index finger to his lips. "Very, very

carefully. The security around that place is near to impenetrable. I'm certain that my security codes, even the ones I confiscated to get into other areas, have been revoked."

"Listen bud, you and I are nothing in the grand scheme of everything. We cannot let this thing be used. The consequences could be devastating for everyone and everything that exists or, maybe, has ever existed." Melvin paused as he shook his head vigorously while making sounds of gibberish. "I'm saying this stuff and part of me still can't believe that this is actually happening."

Melvin saw Tom raise an eyebrow. "I know, Man. I was totally blown away when I learned what these folks were really up to. I'm sure to you it is even harder." He rubbed his hands together.

Melvin saw Tom's hand coming together and asked, "What are you doing?"

"I'm a diabetic. Rubbing my hands together tends to bring back some of the sensation. I've been out of my sugar meds for days now. If I lag behind at any time, leave me."

Tom sat up, thought a moment, then leaned over and grabbed the small board with his right hand and grabbed a hard casing from his bag with the left. He put the board in the case and snapped it shut. There was a crooked safety closure on the side which he fastened as well. "I don't really want to do this but hook this case around your belt loops," he stressed, "all of them, just like a belt. The twining is reinforced steel and the case is made of a tough metal. Inside the case are the board, the blueprints, and all the things you need. You are my life insurance policy." He grabbed the bag and stretched his hand toward Melvin.

"Hey, are you sure this is what you want?"

Tom shook his head up and down several times. "Yeah, my diabetes is kind of bad and I don't know when I will crash. ... You take the stuff. I trust you. I wouldn't trust anyone else in the world, but I know you. You will stick up for what's right."

Melvin took the case and began strapping it into his belt

loops with the strap. "I don't really think it's wise for me to have this thing on me in case I am caught."

Tom tilted his head. "This is true, but they don't know about you yet. Besides, if we get separated, I suggest that you hide it somewhere. Somewhere safe."

"Why don't we just destroy this stuff, then go after the rest?"

"Because this stuff will keep us alive. What do you think would happen if they knew this stuff was destroyed and either, or both of us were captured? They'd kill us in a heartbeat, old buddy. Dead, dead, dead! There wouldn't even be enough left for fish food."

Melvin's head bobbed up and down in an exaggerated fashion. "Yep! You are right about that. Forgive me. Sometimes my head is not screwed on straight. Years of women twisting my brain, I guess." He chuckled slightly. "But that still leaves us with the question of what to do now?"

Tom hung his head and shook it slightly. "I don't really know. Honestly, I don't. Just remember something. If I fall, stumble, or if I lag behind even, leave me, regardless."

"No, Man, no. I wouldn't know what to do."

"Mel, I seriously don't how much longer I have." Tom paused, but when he spoke again, there was a high-pitched urgency. "Promise me?"

Melvin looked at Tom's face and how unmoving it was. Tom's eyes were narrowed by his down pressed brows. He still paused, but finally squeezed out the words that Tom wanted, "Okay, I promise."

There was a quiet calm that had come over the room. Tom was obviously confused about how to rectify this terrible situation. Melvin knew he was in the same shape. Obviously, the security at the installation was nearly unbreakable and while Tom managed to get this stuff out, it was an inside job and those were always the easiest. With inside jobs, you know everything and nobody ever suspects a Benedict Arnold to be in their midst.

Now they would be breaking into the secure building.

Melvin was certain that security would be even tighter than before Tom escaped.

"We need someone to help us. Someone on the inside like you were." Melvin put his flat hands together and pointed them straight up. "Please tell me you still have contact with someone on the inside?"

"If I did, I'd be telling a fib. I barely escaped with my life. Keeping in contact with anyone would have been entirely too dangerous for me and whomever I would have been contacting."

Melvin hung his head for a moment while leaning forward a bit and rubbed his face with his hands. The warmth felt good, comforting somehow. He wished he was a teenager again. Times were so much simpler then. He knew what he had said was true. They needed a person inside the complex to help them. "Do you have any way possible of making contact with anyone inside the research complex?"

"No way, Mel. There are only two or three people in there that I would, sort of, trust, none that I would have one-hundred percent faith in."

Melvin put his hand on Tom's shoulder. "Then, no matter how tight the security is, you and I have to try to break in there."

After a long pause, Tom finally said, "What do you need from me?"

"Do you think you could sketch the layout of the place for me?"

"Yes, I lived there for a long time you know. I can also write down what I know about the security."

Melvin reached into his pocket and grabbed his book, turned to the back page, and set the book on the rickety table. He reached into the wire spiral and brought out the pen he had been using. As he turned the book toward Tom, he said, "Here, write everything you can think of."

Chapter 17

The sky was filled with dark clouds as Robert felt alligator size raindrops fall on his full dark hair. He crouched low enough to put his head into the open window of his black Ford Escape. He grabbed his cap and jacket from the passenger seat and put them on as weather shields. "Idiot," he said softly as he clutched the door handle, squeezed, and pulled.

A gust of wind blew the door open and almost out of his grasp. He pulled the door back to him, rolled up the window, then slammed the door closed again.

A young blonde officer with the face of an eighteen year old boy ran up to him. He snapped a salute and said, "Sir, we have a request from HQ that you call them directly." The young man was trying to take in air in big gulps as if he had run all the way. Rain pellets were hitting his cap and bouncing off.

As Rob stared at the boy, he could see that it was raining harder. Streams of water began trickling off of the boy's face. Robert stared at the rigidness of the kid a moment and admired the diligence and faithfulness of duty. Once upon a time, Rob was the same way, stiff and rigid. That kid still believed in the system. "I'll be right there, private," Rob said as he snapped a salute toward the young man. He broke into a fast-paced walk heading straight to an army green tent. The raindrops were pelting his jacket and he could feel the water rolling off of his cap onto the back of his neck. Not wanting the rain to flow beneath his jacket collar, his fast walk soon escalated into a run.

There were a group of men huddled around a tablet that one of the men was holding and Rob could hear the men talking as he approached. He walked past them and into the tent. On the center table was a black satellite phone that had began ringing. Picking it up, he said "Robert Milgrew here."

"Robert, this is Petry. Alphi-Pi 87."

Rob nodded. "Access for this contact is verified. Go ahead."

"We have reason to believe our suspect has picked up a second party of unknown origin. We believe the two of them are working together. Rob, I trust you. We have known each other for a long, long time."

"Yes sir, we have. About twenty years, I think. All the way back to the middle-east war."

"Yeah, those were the days. I am awfully glad that you came to head the security for our research project though. For some time, I didn't think you were going to sign on."

"Well, you know, sometimes you have to think things over. In the end, it made sense."

"I'm glad." Pause. "Rob, we can't let this bastard explode 'any' nuclear device on U.S. soil. He was one of our top men until he sold out to a foreign power: which one, we still don't know."

"How do you know that he is a turncoat?"

"Intercepted communications."

"Okay. Well, I love our country, sir, and totally agree with you. We cannot let a nuclear device be detonated here. My team and I will stop this guy."

"I dearly hope so. Remember, we need this guy alive so we can beat it out of him where he's hidden this bomb, if indeed he has hidden it."

"Oh, don't worry. Captures are what my team does best."

"I know, dear friend, I know. I want you to personally check out grid 11 in section 13 with a few of your best men. There is an abandoned house in the center of that area that we believe this guy may be at. We need onsite intelligence to know anything for sure. You still have your photos of this S.O.B?"

"Yes, sir."

"Well go to it."

"Roger."

After waiting for the ending click from the receiver, Rob slowly hung up the phone. His lead person, Matt, rushed up to him saying, "What are the orders, sir?"

Rob looked up and down at Matt's pseudo-military uniform, army green togs with a cloth green cap, then said, "Round up Ryan and Brent. We four have to do some advance scouting."

"Yes, sir," Matt said. He immediately ran off.

Chapter 18

Inside Petry's tent, the thunder and rain were reverberating in his ear, yet it sounded soft as his mind was focused elsewhere. Nancy had said one word on the phone and immediately exited the command tent. One word... How can one word have such great meaning? ...especially to a woman that was talking with her family...

He could not recall even what word it was yet he knew that it was a simple word. He had just entered the command tent to check on everyone's progress and it surprised him to see her pick up the phone, say 'Yes', and then one word. There was not even 'Bye' or anything like that. It caught him off his guard.

He was in his own tent, at the moment, away from the hustle and bustle of the command center and staring at the army green surroundings doing what some would call a 'spit bath'. The brown paper rag was on his hand and he had a basin of cleaning solution in front of him. It was anybody's guess what the solution was made of, but it was what all the field people used to clean themselves. He guessed that it was the same stuff he had used many times before. The one constant in the universe was that there was always wars to be involved in.

Petry was not normally in the field. His job was usually in a nice, cushy office somewhere, but this case demanded his personal attention. There could be no screw-ups this time. The higher-ups would have his head cut off if he messed this up and a thousand years from now somebody might be able to find the ashes.

He put the paper cloth over his palm and fingers, dabbed some of the cleaning solution, and put his face into it. He rubbed the cloth vigorously over his face, into and outside his ears, and in a low voice said, "Crappy wash." The coolness felt good, yet he was still sweaty and dirty.

As he moved his hand down to his armpit, he mumbled, "Better than nothing, I guess." He rubbed the moistened paper against his left armpit, then changed hands with the paper and cleaned the other side. Then proceeded to clean his groin and legs. When he reached down to his right leg, his hand knocked over the picture of he and Nancy, taken just outside the Lincoln Memorial.

He carried that photo everywhere he went. It was one of his prized possessions. He had no wife, no kids, not even a dog. His work had always been his life. When he and Nancy got back from the Middle East war, which neither thought they would survive, they were both dragged to D.C. for a CIA debriefing.

The meetings were long and laborious, but, after they were over, they had taken the photo as a celebration. Now, he was looking at it differently. He stared at it a moment, picked it up, then moved the picture into different positions while he stared, forward, back, tilted, and side to side as if he was hoping a magical answer would appear to an unknown question.

They were both about twenty-eight at the time, neither had wrinkles or gray hairs. There they were standing with shoulders wrapped in the others arms, smiles bearing teeth, and leaning on each other. It was a picture of perfection and a testament to their war bonding. "Damn," he whispered.

He set it back on the small table and folded out the kickstand that was in the back. "Damn," he whispered again. His lips tightened together as he grabbed the phone that was laying beside the photo. He pushed a few keys, then put the phone to his ear.

"HQ Team 6, Arney speaking."

"Arney, this is Petry. Is Max Thomas in there at the moment?"

"Yes, sir."

"Send him to my tent in 10 minutes please?"

"Yes, sir."

Petry took the phone away from his ear and pressed the end button then lifted the thinly blue striped shirt up from his makeshift bed. One arm went in, then the other, and then he fastened the buttons from bottom to top. His underwear and pants were laying on the bed beside where his shirt had been. He looked at them a moment, then shook his head slightly. "Damn," he whispered again this time a bit louder. He put the underwear on, then the khaki pants. He stood, snapped the pants, then pulled the zipper with his back arched.

He stood a few moments staring down at his grass and dirt flooring, then re-seated himself on the bed. He grabbed the electric razor on the bed, turned it on and rubbed the heads over his black and gray whiskers. Left cheek, right cheek, chin, underneath, lastly the lip. He was halfway across when the razor pitch changed for an instant. "Ouch!" He pulled the razor back, looked at it curiously, then rubbed his upper lip. He put the razor back next to his lip, and finished his shave. "Can't cut yourself. Ha!"

He was putting the razor away when a voice from outside said, "Knock, knock, Mr. Petry, sir, it's Max Thomas. You wanted to see me?"

Petry turned and said, "Yes, Max, please come in?" Max's twenty-eight-ish muscular body parted the seams of the outside and then pressed through the netting inside the entranceway of the tent as he entered. There was a small fold-out table just inside the entrance with a laptop on it. Around the table were two folding chairs, one in front and one behind where the laptop was facing, ready to be used: Petry motioned to the chair in front and said, "Please, have a seat."

Max seated himself with his best attention to proper stance as he could manage. Petry could see the nervousness and rigidity of the blonde-headed young man. "Relax," he said with a nonchalant wave of his hand. He pulled the remaining chair out from the table a bit, then seated himself facing Max. "First of all, Max, this meeting is to be kept top secret. No one is to know except you and I. No one can know what is discussed here. Do you understand?"

Max's eyes bulged a bit. "Yes, sir, you can count on me."

Petry nodded. "Can I also trust you to do exactly as I instruct? No variation, no nothing. I need total and complete devotion and commitment to the tasks that I give you. This is imperative, son."

"What's this all about?"

"I can't tell you that yet. I can tell you that the fate of this mission hangs in the balance."

"Yes, sir, you can count on me," the young man said.

"Put your right hand on the table." Max raised his right arm up and sat his hand down near the edge of the table. Petry leaned forward and laid his right hand over Max's and gripped it. "I am putting a great deal of trust in you, son. Probably more than I should, but I have no other choice." Getting up from his chair, Petry said, "Please, come with me."

Chapter 19

Sitting in the back corner of the virtually vacant living room was Melvin sprawled out on the grungy hardwood floor. The floor was caked with sand, dirt, and dust. Here and there were streaks of the stuff from where he had spent the restless night. In the midst of the mess was a small area that He had cleaned away, just big enough to lay his book open. He was still in shock of what Tom had demonstrated to him minutes ago. A moment like that happened once in a millennium. As he held the pen in his hand, he still could barely believe what he had witnessed. What power...

He felt a vibration coursing through his body and looked down at his hand only to discover that his written words were jagged from a shaking hand. The knowledge that he now had was affecting him much more than he even realized. Why? He paused his writing to ponder the question for a moment and thought about his life.

He had no attachments to anyone in this world. Why was he so upset? It was no sweat off his nose if someone wanted to kill the world or even the universe. His life might even become better if certain things were changed. He'd love to have had his mom and dad around longer but no one could be certain that that would happen. As he sat thinking, he finally decided that the thought of potentially changing the universe, in any way, was totally unacceptable, especially without knowing the exact consequences of any actions. One might inadvertently change the fate and shape of all universes and then some. The ramifications were just too immense.

Melvin looked up at the dark wood ceiling, and closed his eyes. He could feel his eyelids trembling as he took one deep breath after the other. Slowly, he could feel his quaking body relax. It was a good feeling after being so tense for over twenty-four hours. His aching body that had been tormenting him for the night's abuse finally was showing signs of its forgiveness. His muscles were beginning to relax.

He finally opened his eyes slowly and looked down at his hand. It had stopped shaking.

Tom had the look of suddenly being held at gunpoint when he said that he needed a few minutes of quiet to try to cope. It was no surprise to Melvin. He felt the same way. At least his body had stopped shaking. He looked down at the open book in front of him. It had kept him sane after having the emotional trials of a troubled life. The trials were many while the solutions were few, or in some cases, there were none. By writing in it when he was stressed, it calmed him. Some people meditate, some create art, and uncountable other ways to de-stress. He wrote.

The sun was midways up and shone through the limbs of the oak tree outside the window. "ten A.M.", Melvin thought as he looked up from his book.

"Hey, Mel," Tom said from just behind him. Melvin clipped his pen in the metal spiral of the book, then turned around a bit. As soon as he did, Tom said, "Hey, man, while you settle out, I'll go down the block and get some food."

"Are you sure that you want to risk that, Tom? Maybe I should go."

Tom shook his head. "Nah, man, I know how to avoid the surveillance better than you. I haven't been at this spot very long so I doubt they would know to look here. Besides, buddy, the exercise is good for my diabetes."

"Okay, as long as you're sure."

Tom nodded and put up his hand. "Yeah, I got this, but if you hear a high-pitched beeping sound, get out as fast as you can. The safest way is to go out the back. If that happens, go to Hollywood Street near Airline Highway and I'll find you.

Don't worry about the booby traps, you don't have time; just haul your ass away quick."

"What if there are people after me?"

"Don't worry about them. Just run."

"Alright."

*

Tom exited the back door and quickly off the porch. As he stepped into the backyard, he noticed a plane flying overhead. He looked up at the trees covering him and shook his head. The leaves were dripping water all over the place. One drop hit him on his left cheek. He wiped it away with one hand and dried the hand on his blue jeans.

As he stepped out from the yard, he quickly spied the convenience store just three blocks down. He kept to the tree-covered sidewalks amid the small houses that were in the neighborhood. Most of them were largely devoid of paint, had shingles missing, torn screens, or structural problems. Some of them had condemned signs or keep out. Those that didn't had junk cars and assorted trash in the yards. All had overgrown grass encroaching on them.

The store was a mom and pop operation with no major signs of commercial affiliations. It was on the corner with the rust-covered signs hanging on top of the two gas pumps that read, Regular $5.09, Supreme $5.95.

When he reached what he thought to be the hundred-foot mark, he stopped and reached into his left pocket and brought out a small remote. It was octagon shaped and had two buttons. Tom pressed the top one which had an indented label above it. The label was worn from use, but still legible: 'JAM'

Tom put the remote back into his pocket and continued walking. As he neared the store, he started walking faster. The front door and windows had all kinds of different signs. There was everything from ads for cigarettes and liquor, to snack cakes and lottery tickets. There was a newsstand out front. Tom leaned over to look at the headline, 'NATO meets with world leaders'.

He huffed and straightened himself, then pulled the handle on the door and walked in. The small bell over the door dinged. Inside the store were six aisles of dry and miscellaneous goods. There was some assorted fishing equipment to his right and a glass countertop to his left. In the back there were some various refrigerated goods. Behind the counter was an overweight man, about three hundred pounds, with a black handlebar mustache, neatly twisted at each end, and a slightly graying fringe of hair.

"Good morning," the man said huskily.

Tom lowered his head. With his left hand raised, he said, "Good morning." He quickly perused the aisles, grabbed several items, and made his way to the counter. His hands quickly laid the items on the counter while keeping his head down.

"Heck of day isn't it, pal?"

Tom muttered, "Yeah."

"You from around here?"

"Just passing through."

The clerk started pushing buttons on the register while picking up the items. "Oh yeah, where ya headed, friend?"

"South."

"You mean to New Orleans."

"Sure."

"Be sure to check out Bourbon Street while you're there."

"Sure."

"Cash or charge, buddy?"

"Cash."

The clerk pushed more keys on the register and the thing dinged. "That'll be $39.75."

Tom pulled a wallet from his back pocket, opened it, and fished out two twenties from the scads of bills. "Keep the change." He grabbed up the two plastic white bags and exited the store.

Once he was a good distance from the store, Tom pulled the remote from his left pocket, pushed the button marked 'OFF' and started on his way back to the house.

Chapter 20

The clerk twisted the ends of his mustache with his right hand. He looked up at the surveillance camera mounted in the far corner and then turned to look at the one behind him. "Peggy," he shouted as he looked toward the service area in the rear of the store.

A blonde girl walked out. She looked to be still in high school; her face was still plump with baby fat, although she looked slim overall and she bounced slightly with each step toward the register. "Yes, Mr. Roberts."

The clerk eyed her, smiled slightly for an instant, then said, "Would you come take over the register? I want to go in the back and look at something."

"Sure, Mr. Roberts," she said as she walked behind the glass cabinet. As Peggy opened the small security latch on the half-door guarding the register, she entered and the clerk exited.

"I'll be back in a minute," he said as he walked toward the back. Rounding the corner, he saw a great many boxes of stuff that were kept there for stock. He turned to the right and looked at the black digital video recorder on a small shelf attached to the wall. Four of the eight lights on the front were bright red. There was a small desk below the shelf which held a black and white monitor. The picture was segmented into four sections that showed different areas of the store.

He picked up the remote and pushed the 'rewind' button. All four of the sections on the monitor, within a few seconds, were distorted and he pressed 'play' on the remote. He could hear the conversation, but the sound was very scratchy and the picture was all distorted and jumbled. He pressed 'rewind' again and held it until the distortion went away, then pressed 'play'. Moments before that mysterious dude entered the store, the monitor flaked out.

"This is too weird," he said. Beside the monitor was a black, cordless phone and he picked up the handset. He looked up on the white wall to a printout of phone numbers. At the top of the list, was a heading, "EMERGENCY NUMBER." He scanned the list of numbers until he found, "Police," and he started dialing.

"Baton Rouge Police. This is Sergeant Ernest Powell, how may I help you," asked a male voice.

"Yes, sir, this is Paul Roberts over at Roberts Grocery at 11145-P Bluebonnet Way. A hefty gentleman was just in my store and he acted suspicious. Is there someone that I can speak with?"

"Sir, I can help you with that. Now, this guy, what made him suspicious to you?"

"Well, sir, he came in, and very quickly gathered up a bunch of stuff, barely talked, always kept his head down, and after he left, I was curious so I pulled up the video camera footage. The video was so distorted that I couldn't see much of anything."

"That does sound odd," the officer said. "Could you hear the audio, sir?"

"Yes sir, it was distorted, but you can make out what was being said."

"What did this guy look like?"

"Well, sir, I couldn't honestly say. He kept his head down, but he was a whale of a size. Something else was odd too. He was walking."

"That is odd, you would think that being overweight, he would've been driving. " Pause. "Are you going to be there all day, Sir?"

"Yes, sir."

"I will send a car out there. Officer Hicks will investigate this further."

Chapter 21

Petry was walking to his black sedan with Max at his side. Petry's office administration physique paled by comparison to Max's lean muscular body. Max looked like a professional bodybuilder with bulging muscles that were easily evident through his brown button-up shirt and khaki pants. Although the colors didn't quite match, Petry told him, "Nice clothes."

"Thanks," Max replied.

As they reached the sedan, Petry opened the driver's side door while Max circled around and did the same on the passenger side. They both stepped inside the vehicle. Petry pulled his keys from his front right pocket. After a moment, he found the ignition key among the giant wad of keys, then seated himself in the crushed velvet black seat and put the key in the ignition. Max had seated himself and pulled his door closed with a THUD while Petry leaned out, grabbed his door, and pulled hard.

"Petry! Petry!"

As the door closed with another THUD, Petry's ears registered the shouting. He looked out of the dirt speckled window to see short stuff Dan running toward him. He clicked the door open again and pushed on it.

As Dan neared the sedan he quickly said, "Petry!" Dan grabbed the outside door struts as he slid to a stop in the loose gravel and sand mixture. "Petry, we tapped in on a call to the police about a really large man that was keeping his head low and walking. The shop owner said the security footage was distorted, too."

Petry looked over at Max and said, "Max, I'll be right back. Wait here!"

As Petry raised up from his seat, Max looked over at him and said, "Alright, boss."

When Petry exited the sedan, he closed the driver door behind him. "Where did this happen?"

A bit winded from his run, Dan said, "S-S-South, just like we thought, but Southeast, not Southwest."

Petry put his chin in his hand and rubbed his fingers a moment. "You know, this may be a fluke or diversion like before. This guy is a smart S.O.B." He took his hand away. "Have Robert Milgrew and Team 6 investigate and report back. We'll be back in a few minutes. Max and I are going to investigate something."

"Will do."

Without saying another word, Petry got in the car again, cranked the engine and drove off.

#

Petry drove 10 miles down the road without saying a word. Up ahead was an open field with a dirt road running through the middle. There was a wire fence around the near side of the field and after the corner post was a small dirt road. On the other side of the road was a picnic area with a mushroom shaped, rather large, oak tree, as shade over the driveway on one side and a picnic table on the other. The table was gray with age and weather-worn cracks could be seen in the wood.

When Petry drove into the area, he parked under the tree. He exited the sedan, leaving the door open, and looked around the area closely. He leaned under the top of the car, looked at Max while putting his index finger to his lips, and then motioned Max to exit the car with his other hand and circle around.

Max did as Petry indicated, closing the door behind him, and, when he rounded the front of the sedan, opened his mouth a bit as if about to say something. Petry shook his head and took Max's hand into his, closed his door, and guided them both around to the far side of the bench about 20 yards away.

Petry looked up and saw the plethora of limbs and a mixture of colored leaves above them, then looked down at Max. His head bobbed as he said, "Sorry for all the secrecy, Max. When you've seen as much as I have, I guess it makes you very cautious."

"No problem"

"We are under the cover of trees here so satellites can't view us and we are away from the car, which could be bugged."

Max nodded.

"Max," Petry hung his head slightly, "We've known one another for a number of years, haven't we?"

"Yes, sir, I think it's been seven or maybe eight years that we've worked together.

"I think that's right. Well, you remember Nancy?"

Max nodded.

"We have been friends for about 20 years. I know her about as good as I know myself. You know what that's like?"

"Yes, sir, I do. I have a sister. A lot of times we can actually finish each other's sentences.

Petry shook his head. "Well, that's sort of the same thing, but not quite. It's close enough that you know what I mean." He paused while he cleared his throat. "It pains me to say this, but I have reason to believe that Nancy is either a traitor or a spy."

"How do you know this?"

Petry looked at the pitted surface of the picnic table and let out a heavy stream of air through his mouth. "Let's just say, I know, period." He paused. "What I need your help with is keeping a close eye on her to see just what she is hiding. Not only that, I need to know who all is involved. I am trusting you because you have always been honest with me. You have told me things out of sheer honesty that really were nothing to be concerned with. I respect that, Max, I really do." Petry raised his right arm off of the table and offered his hand.

Max took Petry's hand into his and gave a firm shake. "I appreciate that and I'll do my best to find out who or what organization she's reporting to, if any. I know she has a family, but beyond that, I don't know much."

Petry smiled and winked his right eye. "Thanks, pal. From now on, you will be my eyes and ears as far as she is concerned."

Chapter 22

At Team 6's headquarters, Tina sat in front of a table of electronics. She was watching the blips on the screen in front of her while intermittently monitoring several view screens behind her.

A man walked up behind her and with a deep voice asked, "Anything new, Private?"

Tina turned her head and saw it was duty Sergeant Wayne Peters. "No, sir, Sergeant, sir," she said calmly. "They've just about covered sections 12, 13, and 14, with no sightings or evidence to..." The phone laying on the table in front of her made its shrill sound of an incoming call. With her right hand she grabbed the phone, picked it up, and said, "Team 6, this is Tina."

"Tina, this is Dan Fielding at HQ. I have new orders from Petry for Robert."

"Rob is not in camp at the moment. He had already received orders from Petry at HQ."

"It's important that I speak with him immediately. New information has come our way. Can you get him by phone?"

"Maybe. As long as he doesn't have it turned off."

"Thanks."

*

At 3am even the big city of Baton Rouge was calm. Airline Highway had sparse traffic and side road stores were mostly dark. They had outside security lights on, but that was about it.

Airline had been a major traffic zone of the city for a long time, but with the newest beltway encircling the city, it became just another road. It is a north-south road which was mostly only two lanes. They tried to expand it a few times but it was eventually deemed unfit for the population size. It intersected with Interstate 10 and was the main road leading out of Baton Rouge on both ends of the city, but has virtually been abandoned for inner-city travel. As a result, vegetation was encroaching on it. Its surface, once bustling with traffic, had a great many cracks and pits. Here and there were jagged lines of tar where repairs had been done.

Rob, Matt, Ryan, and Brent were walking southward on the narrow shoulder of Airline. Rob had them walking because with short distances, he had learned, all too often, that you could easily miss critical details. The sound of any vehicle could also give their prey a heads up that they were coming. That's the last thing you wanted to happen. Once the element of surprise had been eliminated, on cases with learned opponents, especially, they almost never went right.

Rob was walking in front of the group when the phone clipped to his belt began vibrating. He walked from the road's shoulder into the grass, grabbed the phone, slid the panel, and put it up to his ear. "Rob here."

"Rob, this is Tina. I have an urgent call from Dan at HQ. I am patching it through."

Rob could hear the phone make a slight click.

"Rob, this is Dan. A lead just came our way and Petry thought it was important enough to call you."

"Hey, Dan. We are already following up on a lead that Petry sent us."

"I know. You will confirm the cancel code, C-107, and take these new orders."

Rob cocked his head while he thought. Righting his head, he said, "'Cancel confirmed. What's the new orders?"

"You and your men will proceed South to Roberts Grocery at 11145-P Bluebonnet Way. Paul Roberts, presumably the store owner, called the police and reported a strange man that came in, matching our guy's description, and disrupted the video and audio recording equipment. If it is our guy, there may be an abandoned home in the area that he is using. Investigate with extreme caution."

"Roger. Will do. Rob out." When Rob looked up, he gathered the men around and in a moderate voice said, "Alright guys, we have a possible location for this guy just up ahead, possibly in an old house. Our orders are to investigate and report, not to take action."

The group said a chorus of, "Alright, Okay, Let's get to it." Rob laid his hand flat in mid-air and said, "All in," with a voice trailing upwards. Hands piled on top of each other with an audible, hard slap of skin. "Go team," they all whispered in such a great, husky harmony that it would make a huddled football team boiling with jealousy.

"It's not far... Just two streets down from where we are, so we're on alert status yellow. No unnecessary talking." Each one nodded their heads. Their green togs made a whisper of noise as the stiff fabric rubbed together when they turned sharply and got into single file position. Rob, now at the rear, stepped up to walk beside his small platoon of compatriots looking at them from their heavy, black boots upwards to their faces and green caps. He saw the hardened look of military on them. None of them were technically in the military anymore, but he had recruited them all when he first leaped from army to this unit. They could have each had their own unit to command, but instead chose to remain by his side.

As they walked, Rob started rubbing his hands together. The humidity in the air combined with the cold was numbing Rob's hands. He stopped, ran in place for a moment, then continued walking. The cold was not as bad as it had been the last few days, but it was still rotten weather. Combine the temperature, which he supposed was in the teens, and the high humidity, which was probably ninety percent, and it made staying warm unlikely.

Rob sprinted forward to take the lead. When he did, the rest of his band of crusaders started following in his footsteps, literally. As Rob looked back, the corners of his mouth rose. Once you had been in the military, you never forget the training. It sticks with you, even though you might wake up at night in fits of sweaty terror at things you had done, tried to do, and on and on as the military life inspired you to do. Onward, just follow the orders, and don't forget to kill the enemy because if you don't, the enemy will kill you. Destroy or be destroyed, that was the military. Just follow those orders. Right or wrong means nothing. Just follow orders. That might work for a young kid, but not him, not anymore at least. Age teaches you better. There were a lot of gray areas in life.

The Army teaches you to kill the enemy. Well, if your enemy is lying there in a pool of his blood, broken legs, or another debilitating condition and begging for help and mercy, he is no threat. That's really why he got out of the Army. He could not force himself to blindly follow orders anymore. Common sense was beginning to take over and he knew that reeked of trouble, for himself and whoever was around him.

Rob looked at the street sign in front of him, Bluebonnet Way. He looked East down the empty street. Most of the street lights were lit and Rob could read the first two house numbers: 111095, 111097. He waved his arm at the other three, and then, with a lone extended finger, pointed down the street.

The men followed Rob downward from the mound of dirt and gravel that road crews had built up Airline Highway with. Years ago, when it was first resurfaced, back in the 1990's, they had done a fine job, but in the process, they had lowered the road so much that it flooded every time a cloud dropped a few sprinkles. They came back, some years later, and corrected the matter, at the taxpayer's expense, of course.

He could see the convenience store which Dan had spoke about. In a primarily run-down neighborhood, he was surprised to find that the lights were on, both outside and inside. He stopped and held a flush hand pointed toward the pea gravel, sandy, dirt mix that they were walking through and each man came to a halt in quick succession.

He turned and leaned into them. Whispering, he said, "I am going to go into the store to scout. You wait here. All of them nodded and Rob turned and starting walking at a normal pace toward the store. As he walked, he began contorting his neck to try and peer through the windows seeking signs of movement; he found none.

As he neared the door, he saw on it in red lettering on a white background the word, 'OPEN'. He pulled the rusted metal ring on the door and walked in. As he looked around the small shop, he saw that there wasn't a soul in the place except for the big, fat, Ron Jeremy clone, behind the counter.

Rob noticed the camera in the corner of the room, but, nevertheless, strolled up to the counter. The clerk, who had been watching a small TV in the top corner of the checkout cubicle, turned to eye the Glock pistol strapped at Rob's side.

"What can I help you with, fella?"

"I'm John Brady, a special investigator for Baton Rouge. I was told that you had an unusual customer come in."

The clerk's green eyes bulged. "Gee whiz! You guys must not have much of a life. It's friggin' Four A.M.!"

Rob opened his stance a bit and clasped his hands behind his back in true police fashion. "Well, sir, when you work in a city as big as this, you end up working all hours." He paused, looked down and stepped closer to the counter. The clerk started to say something, but Rob cut him off. "I have the details of the incident, the regular police will be following up on that. My only question for you is, did you see which way the guy left from here?"

"Not really sure, but if I had to guess, it would be down this street. There's not much on the other side of Airline."

Rob unclasped his hands and said, "Thank you, sir. This city appreciates your help." He turned and walked out of the store's front door.

Chapter 23

After Rob exited the store, he took several steps forward before doing anything else. The pebbly dirt beneath him shifted its position each time one of his feet came down with a crunching sound similar to eating cereal. Once he was at the furthermost point of the stores lighting, he then twisted his body toward the other men, and motioned to them.

Ryan, Brent, and Matt burst into a slight jog. When they neared Rob, they slowed back to their cautious pace. A slight breeze had started and a few of the men started intermittently rubbing their arms and hands. Rob put his hands together in front of him and pulled them up to his cold chapped lips. While rubbing his hands together, his lips parted and he blew warm air on them as best he could. A momentary puff of steam appeared, then he lowered his hands.

He pointed to a dilapidated old house. The roof was sagging in several areas and there was barely any white paint on the walls, the edges of which, were peeling off in thick sheets, a sure sign of lead based paint. They were at the rear of the house at the moment standing just outside of the fence line, but still on the road.

Rob huddled the men together and spoke in a low voice. "This looks like a location that our guy would use. You three circle around and try to look inside, but don't enter the yard area at all. Use your radio vibrator to indicate any progress. One buzz, you see something, two buzzes, you don't. Then wait for me, but, at all costs, nobody shoot."

The men nodded. Rob made motions with each hand in both directions around the house. He held one to his ear, pointed to the fence line on each side of the house, and then undid the strap that was safeguarding his Glock pistol. The silver, round clasp made a faint, hollow, click.

He watched his three men circle around and then cautiously studied the side of the house. The area seemed quiet enough, but most houses would at four A.M. The windows that he could see were completely dark with, what appeared to be, semi-shear tan curtains in most of the windows. The curtains were still and most of the glass in the windows was intact.

There was a shallow ditch on his side that would be very traversable while the front and back of the property seemed flatter. The yard was mostly dirt and, although Rob tried to scan it for disturbances, the darkness prevented him from seeing anything. What little light there was, was coming from the nearby streetlights. The ones on this block were out. Beyond the dirt was a big oak tree that was growing into a rusty tongue and groove fence that was being pulled downward by the plethora of vines and weeds that were growing in and out of the wires. The bark of the large tree was growing over about four inches of the fence wire. Large veiny gashes were in the wooden posts and the wood looked to be rotting with large pits that were scattered throughout the surfaces.

The radio on his belt vibrated: one-two. Another: two-two. Then: three-two. Rob put his right hand to his lips and blew. He pulled his hand back and then lowered it to his waistline to grab the radio. When his thumb was over the button on the side of the walkie, he pressed it down. Speaking softly, he said, "Hold your positions, I'm going in closer."

Rob stretched his legs wide and stepped over the ditch with his right foot leading the way. When the foot was on the other side, Rob felt something hard, yet spongy press into his foot. A thousand thoughts went through his mind all at once when he heard a metallic "CLICK."

Amidst the silence that rang out, there was the distinct sound of a loud heartbeat and a short, quiet but troubled comment, "Oh shit!"

Chapter 24

All was quiet in the dark house. Melvin was tightly
wrapped into as much of the thin tan blanket as he could
possibly gather around him. His aches and pains from the
previous night were seering every inch of his 160 pounds.
Last night was nothing. His aches and pains were being
amplified tonight and the friggin' thin pad was very little
protection.

A high pitched beeping noise started and Melvin sat up
quickly and just in time to see Tom run out of his room. His
hair fringe was all mussed up. The black and gray hairs were
going every direction, but not the right ones. Tom's face was
pale, but he managed to scream, "Mel! Out the back! Run!
Don't stop for nothing!"

Melvin gave a violent shove to his ratty cover and
quickly slipped on his white and blue-striped tennis shoes,
laces never undone, and propped his hands on the floor.
When he raised himself to full height with his legs, his lower
back sent a bolt of pain through his spine. "Ack," he muttered.
He felt like shouting, but knew that it was a bad idea. He
started to run, but thought of his book: his lifeline. The
urgency inside him was great. His insides were trembling and
his guts were tied in the biggest knot. His breathing was in
big gulps and it made him feel light-headed. In a desperate
attempt to hurry, he leaned over and grabbed the tan cover
with an out-stretched right arm and shook it. His black book
fell out. He threw the cover to the side and grabbed it from

off of the floor and straightened the pages quickly.

When he rose up, he muttered, "Damn it," because his back had jolted him again. He quickly stuck the book in his beltline near where he strapped the black box that Tom had made him take. He saw Tom exit his door and point toward the back.

"Go! Go! Go," Tom shouted.

Melvin burst into a run heading toward the back door. He sprinted through the kitchen and to the back door and then looked behind him. Tom looked to be moving slower and Melvin considered going back to help, but Tom's instruction of leave him was reverberating through his mind.

"Go! Open it, quick!"

He grabbed the door handle and turned it. To his surprise, it opened right away. He knew that he had seen Tom do something, presumably a lock, but what? He shoved the door open completely and ran through the porch hearing the boards underneath his feet crackle and groan with the abuse on its aged surface. He opened the handle at the back door and did not see anyone beyond it. The yard was totally empty. Was this a false alarm?

Suddenly, he felt both of Tom's hands push him out of the doorway. "Go, go, go!"

Melvin noticed that Tom's voice was much more subdued this time, but still had that urgent tone and quick speed. He started running through like he was running from a rifle shell. Perhaps he was, he thought. The semi-clear night sky and the clearing cloud cover which had formerly eclipsed a full moon gave him good light to see where he was stepping. Don't fall, don't fall, he kept telling himself. He looked back at Tom to see how he was doing. He could see Tom struggling to run fast and panting to breathe. Tom raised his right arm and with his hand, pushing Tom onward. Tom wasn't too far behind. He snapped his head forward again, then back at Tom who was then flat on his face this time with two men rushing toward him.

One of the men, pulled out a gun and shouted, "Stop or I'll shoot."

His head was halfway turned back forward, when he saw his black book drop away from his belt. All of the sudden, he could feel his life drain from him as it slipped. Down and down it went and with it, his mind. Please God no! Please! Please! Please! The book just kept falling. Please God, let me keep it. His life was slipping away.

His mind could see flashes of his life. ...two marriages, jobs as a detective, and his childhood.... He could feel his emotional life being ripped from him and there was not a thing he could do. His guts quivered, his heart pounded, and his mind was in catastrophic overload. At this moment, the world stopped. Time was still, but still HIS book kept falling.

Somehow, his legs kept running, arms moving back and forth. ...His body knew what to do even though his mind didn't.... He snapped his head forward and realized that if he grabbed for his book, then they would surely see it and find it. If he did nothing, maybe they would miss seeing it. He could do nothing except let it fall. He looked down at it once more. ...Down, Down, Down...

Once it fell below his knee, he managed to kick it to the side with his foot. He looked forward as he was nearing the edge of the yard. Through the opening he went and from behind him he heard another voice say, " Stop or I'll shoot." He kept running.

POW! POW!

Oh my God! Melvin knew that he was as good as dead if he was caught. Power hungry people like to keep their power and so he just kept running. His insides were quaking and quivering all once, but his legs kept moving. Keeping those legs moving was his only thought as he neared the convenience store. There was a woman pumping gas into what looked like a Ford Escort. Not the fastest car in the world, but it would have to do.

He glanced behind him and saw a man chasing him. The man was firing his gun in the air and shouting, but falling well behind. Cops, ha! They must be eating too many doughnuts.

When Melvin reached the blue car, he ran around the

back to the driver's side and shoved the woman backward. "I'm sorry lady, but I gotta." He jerked the gas nozzle from the tank, closed the lid, not even bothering with the cap, and jumped in the open door. He turned the key and almost simultaneously shifted into Drive, then drove away watching the poor lug in the rear view mirror run on foot after him.

Chapter 25

Rob saw Brent walking back to the yard. "Hey, Brent," he yelled while waving his right arm wildly from side to side. "I need help here." When Brent saw his brother in arms, he turned and started jogging toward him. Rob managed a small sigh.

He dare not move his foot. He did not have any idea what his foot had activated. It could well be a landmine; it certainly felt like one. If he moved off of it, he might lose his leg or his life. So here he was, with his legs spread about as wide as humanly possible, and, to make things worse, the backs of his thighs were starting to ache.

He could feel his body trying to waver with gravity pulling his face toward the dirty ditch in front of him, but knew that he was necessarily frozen in this awkward position.

The more seconds and minutes that he spent here, the wider his legs became. His hamstrings were starting to ache from the stretch. He was a fool for ever getting into this position. In unknown territory, you never underestimate the terrain. Well, he did, and his ripping, burning, stretching, legs were making him pay for it too.

The ditch itself was not deep, maybe a few inches, but it had water residue from the previous day's heavy rain. Not knowing how much longer he could still his movements, he called out to Brent "Hurry, hurry." The approaching body was not well lit, but instead, it was more of a silhouette against the darkness of an early morning sky.

When Brent got near him, Rob pointed at his foot and said, "Be careful. My right foot over there is on something. It may be a pressure mine."

Brent was still on the pavement of the road and looked down at the predicament Rob was in. "Kind of in a jam, huh, pal?"

Rob grimaced. "Ugh! No shit, Sherlock! You want to help me out here?"

Brent stepped over the small ditch, knelt down on one knee, and started brushing away the brown dirt. There was a small amount of gumbo red clay mixed in, but not much. When he felt the hard surface of whatever it was, he paused, and thought a moment. A few anxious minutes passed before he reached down to the ground. He removed the soil with one hand and put it in a pile to his left. With each movement of his hand, he became slower and more careful.

His slender fingers wrapped around something on the right side. It was slender and protruding outward. It's surface dimly reflected the early morning sun's rays as it was starting to peek out from between the open area behind Brent. As his now dirt layered fingers covered the length of the protrusion, he found that the further out it went, the more slender it got, with a round, flat tip at the end.

"I think that it's a proximity sensor, very old style." Brent pushed his hands over the top of the device to wipe away the sand. Looking at it while brushing more, he said, "Model: PW90821. Yep. You're good to go Rob. It's a remote sensor."

Rob slowly moved his foot back and, as he did, he heard the device release. "This guy is really pissing me off!" He shook his head from side to side furiously making quirky noises. "Did we get anybody?"

"One guy fell down back there. We got him. The other one got away. He hijacked someone's car before we could even get a good look at him or the license plate."

"Damn!" Rob shook his head as put his hand to his side. "We're gonna get nailed!"

Chapter 26

Rob sat a moment, his butt being cooled by the coarse tar in the road. "Well," he said, "you go see about the guy we did get while I phone this in." As Brent started walking toward the rear fence opening, Rob unstrapped the black phone from his belt and started pushing buttons, then raised the receiver to his ear.

A female voice answered. "Command Center."

"This is Rob Milgrew. Contact code: Beta-Pi 108."

"Code verified, Mr. Milgrew. What is your report?"

"Is this Nancy?"

"It is. What's up, Rob?"

Rob paused briefly to clear his throat. He began moving his feet and legs toward the opening to the yard. "Nancy, our suspect or suspects were definitely at the location that Petry sent us to."

"Were?" Nancy asked with a bitter undertone.

"Yes, were. We were still investigating the site when I inadvertently set off an alarm system."

"What!?!? Your orders were to investigate, NOT to move in!"

Rob moved the phone away from his ear. "We didn't move in. We were simply looking at the area."

As Rob rounded the corner of the fence, he saw Ryan and Brent kneeling over a large body on the ground. Ryan had a flush hand on the guy's chest and thrusting while Brent was apparently waiting. Matt was standing up talking on his

87

phone.

"Then how in the name of hell are they not STILL there?"

Rob burst into a run toward the others holding the phone nearby to his ear. "One is still here, but is receiving CPR at the moment."

Nancy's voice, much more subdued, said, "I'm sending our medical team right now. Investigate the scene and report to me later."

"Roger," Rob said moving his arm to his side and clipping the phone to his belt. He approached the others and asked, "What's the story, guys?"

Matt was still on his phone so Brent said, "This guy has gone into some kind of damn arrest." Ryan stopped pumping with his arms, leaned over to Tom's mouth and put his lips to his, pinched his nose, and blew air. Tom's chest rose a bit as the air filled his lungs, then receded. Ryan's loose, medium-length brown hair flopped a bit as he rose up and began the compressions again. "I don't know if this will do any good," Brent said.

Matt put down his phone. "We found him flat on his face and rolled him over. His heart was beating, but it was weak, then it stopped altogether. Ryan started CPR, but..."

"Okay, a medical team ought to be here any minute." Rob pointed at Brent and Ryan. "You two take care of him. That's tiring business. Matt, you check inside the house while I check out here and speak with the medical team when they arrive. Watch out for booby traps."

Matt looked down to carefully choose his steps as he walked towards the back porch door. Parts of the dirt and grass seemed to sparkle as the morning sun shined on the frosted ground. Rob walked toward the back porch to trace over the path that the two men had run. He stopped when he was near the almost rotten back step and pivoted on his right heel. When he did, to his left, he spotted a mound and knelt down to it.

With his right hand, he lightly felt of the ground then started brushing back the dirt until he had reached a hard surface that was underneath. As he kept sweeping with his hand, he unearthed another proximity mine. "Geez!" He walked slowly onward and unearthed several more as he neared the center of the yard. "This guy is very cautious," he muttered.

Where Melvin had ran was obvious to Rob. There were chunks of unsettled dirt and grass everywhere with indentions from the sole of the shoes in each one. Sometimes there would be an impression of his shoes, other times it would be chunks of dirt that his tennis shoes had ripped up. Rob was nearing the edge of the yard and came to a complete stop. He straightened his head, then looked up, and rubbed the back of neck with one hand with one closed eye. When he opened his eyes, he saw a brown leaf falling to the ground.

His tired mind watched the leaf float with the mild morning wind. The wind was cool, but his warm hand rub felt so good to his neck that he took a deep breath. The stress of the morning, night, and circumstances were dismissed from his mind for a moment. As he took a few relaxing breaths, he watched the leaf float in the air. As it neared the ground, its surface grazed something black and finally nestled itself on top of the surface of the object.

Rob walked toward the object, carefully, and brushed the leaf away from it. When he did, he saw that the object was a small notebook. It was about five inches wide by six inches long with the words, 'Journal 67' written on a white sticker and stuck in the top right corner. He opened the book to the last written page and read the entry:

*

"I can barely believe it. An
actual gun that reverses time.
Somewhere out there is a room
filled with exec's and rich
people that want to control the
world by reversing time to wipe
out anyone that stands in their
way. Worse yet is they have a
chamber that insulates them

89

from changes in the timeline and I have the key to it strapped to my waist."

"I can't believe I am a part of all this. Who am I to try and thwart an evil plot against the entire world, perhaps the entire universe, and the universes beyond ours. The technology must not be allowed. It cannot be used. There are too many unknown possibilities."

I wouldn't have believed any of this was possible, yet Tom had 'the convincer'. He actually brought a dead roach back to life. It's totally unbelievable! Who would have ever thought!

"Thank God I have Tom's help! "

*

Rob closed the book, then looked back at Ryan and Brent. They were still looking down at Tom's unmoving body. Rob looked down at the ground and moved the black book to his right hand, then snuggly put it along his right leg. He walked carefully to the corner opening in the fence and around the back fence line where the weeds had grown up to his waist, then dropped to one knee. Bending low to the ground, with his left hand, he lifted his jacket, and un-tucked the rear of his shirt. His right hand reached behind him and stuffed the book into his green pants. He re-tucked his shirt over the book, pulled his jacket back down, and then stood back up.

Chapter 27

When Rob walked back to the fence opening, he saw Matt stepping out of the back porch doorway and onto the rotting steps. Matt walked toward Ryan and Brent while swinging his arms slightly. His jacket was ruffling a bit as he walked toward the men and he was careful not to step on any of the booby traps that Rob had exposed. With slow and cautious steps he walked and finally reached Tom's prone body.

As Rob walked back toward the body, he unearthed several more booby traps along the way before nearing the group. "Did you find anything, Matt?"

Matt put his hands on his hips and with a whoosh of air said, "Nothing." He paused, then continued, "I found some booby traps. Nothing explosive, just things designed to give an early warning."

"Same here. I thought I might have found something over there," he pointed behind him, "but it was a black piece of trash." Hearing a noise, Rob turned around and saw that two red and white marked vans had arrived. No sirens, but there were red flashing strobes on top of the front of the vans. Each one had its headlights on, although there was plenty of daylight outside now to see by.

Two men and two women, a mixture in each van, threw open their doors. Equipment in all eight hands, they ran towards the body being tended to by Ryan and Brent. Brent was now the one leaning over Tom's still body. The only motion of Tom's body was coming from being beaten on by the pair. As they neared the body, one of the men and one of the women grabbed stethoscopes hanging from around their necks and plugged the rubber tips into their ears.

The four dropped to their knees as they neared Tom and slid on the dirt sending particles of the brown, sandy soil up into the air. Their knees came to a halt an inch away from Tom's shoulder. The two placed their stethoscopes to Tom's chest and listened as Brent and Ryan pushed themselves away with their hands and lifted themselves to their feet.

"How long has he been like this?" the second male asked.

Brent said, "We've been doing CPR for about 15 minutes. Shortly after we got here, he just collapsed and about a minute later, his heart stopped. The second woman unwound multi-colored cords from around a white box, then hooked silver looking paddles to the cords. The first male removed his stethoscope and ripped Tom's shirt open. "Charge," he said followed by a crescendo-ing high-pitched whine from the box.

"Ready."

"Clear!" He raised up and put the silver plates to Tom's chest. Tom's body bounced on the ground and trembled. The first woman felt his neck and shook her head. "Raise it 10 points." There was another crescendo and when it stopped, he said, "Clear!" When the paddles were thrust onto Tom's chest, his back heaved backward followed by his body trembling. She felt Tom's neck and shook her head again. "Maximum," he said and when the crescendo stopped, "Clear," then the paddles were again pushed to Tom's chest. She checked the neck again and shook her head.

"Okay, let's get him to the van quick and put him on full life support."

As they got Tom on a stretcher and carted him away, Rob could only seem to whisper one phrase over and over. "It doesn't fit... It doesn't fit... It doesn't fit..."

Chapter 28

Melvin had already driven to the northern end of town. He had been considering ditching his ill-gotten transportation for nearly 15 miles, but something inside him was saying, 'Press on.' The steering wheel had a leather cover on it with a nylon rope stitching material on the inside. The leather felt cold in his hands and the stitching made his mind wander to Tom's poor body lying back there.

He could see himself running away from Tom's flattened body, lying face down, on what must have been a cold ground. Tom was the only friend that he ever had in this rotten, miserable, life. If he was still alive, what would they do to him? If he was not alive, what then? If he was or wasn't alive was moot. It was almost certain that he would never see him again. A tear rolled down his left cheek.

His life was not safe. What was that street Tom mentioned? Oh yeah, Hollywood near Airline. Did he risk going there? "No," he answered himself in a breathy low tone. He could not chance that. But where could he go? Where?

Poor Tom. He was a smart guy that did not ask for anything that happened to him. Snatched right after high school, then to live in an isolated building away from everyone. That's not much of a life. Did he ever get laid? Melvin chuckled and smiled. What a silly thing to think about? After all, Tom might be dead or, worse yet, in an unscrupulous doctor's bed somewhere. Well, a piece of ass was not all that teen peer pressure would have the young male to believe.

There was a small shopping center just up ahead. The sign read, 'Twin Villages,' and Melvin got in the left hand lane, waited for a clear opening, and steered the car into the center of the almost empty lot. He threw the gearshift up into park and leaned over. His forehead hit the steering wheel with a loud THUD and there it stayed. "FFFFUUUUUUCCCCCCKKKKK," he moaned. "Dear God, what do I do?"

His insides were quivering. He closed his eyelids and rolled his forehead on the black leather. From one side to the other he rolled while moaning unintelligible sounds. "What to do, what to do... FUCK!" He began to moan the word over and over, "FUCK!"

There was no one in his life. No one that he could depend on... No one to turn to... No one. As his forehead rolled on the leather, he wondered why his life was so dismal. In this dark hour, he regretted not being more open to new things and people. Maybe he could've had at least one person that he could have turned to. If only...

'If only' was somehow descriptive of his life. 'If only' he wasn't such a loner. 'If only' his parents had lived into his adulthood. 'If only' he had not married 'the bitch.' 'If only' he had made more friends. It's always easier to look back rather than forward. 'If only...'

His closed eyelids became small slits and he looked at the dirt laden floorboard below him. In addition to everything else, he now had to deal with grand theft auto. Compared to his current problem, theft charges seemed trivial, but it was just another burden laid on his back. His brown eyes rolled downward toward his crotch. His barely open eyes stared at his navy blue jeans where white specs of aged cloth were prevalent. In recent months, the white spots had been becoming larger with wear. His eyes followed the zig-zaggy pattern to where the fold of cloth hid his zipper. "Damn it," he mumbled, then said, "What should we do, Willie?"

With a sudden jerk, Melvin leaned back. Pressing both

hands to his face with a pop, he screamed, "Margie!" He
opened the door of the car and rushed out leaving the keys in.
"Free car for somebody! Unlucky bastard!" He started
walking toward the shopping center's payphone in the corner
then paused a second, grabbed his fancy wireless phone, and
turned it off. Melvin then turned it lengthways in his hand,
thumb on the touchscreen, and threw it towards Airline
Highway as hard as he could. The phone hurled over to the
northbound lane, and shattered against the pavement.

Melvin burst into a sprint toward the payphone. It was at
the far corner and Melvin put both hands into his pockets
with sifting fingers feeling for change. When he reached the
phone, he brought up everything he could from within his
pockets. The left pocket netted him lint, while the right had
$1.25. He shifted hands with the money and reached in again.
$1.50 more... "That's enough," he said as he clinched the
coins into the palm of his fist. He raised the fist in triumph
and marched up to the phone.

The three-quarter glass panes were there with their red
and blue shades and dirt encrusted onto all three, but when
Melvin picked up the receiver and put it to his ear, there was
the familiar buzz of a working phone. He put $2.00 worth of
coins into the slot and pushed '411'.

"Information. Say a city and state. "

"Baton Rouge, Louisiana."

"What listing?"

"Margie Walker."

"The number is 225-555-9890. Please wait to be
connected."

As the phone clicked and started ringing the number,
Melvin started bouncing on his toes.

"Hello," a female voice answered.

Melvin gripped the receiver tightly and stopped
bouncing. "Margie! It's me, Melvin! For God's sake, don't
hang up."

"Melvin!"

"Yeah, it's me, but PLEASE don't hang up.," Melvin
pleaded. "I need help. Desperately!"

"Give me one good reason, just one, why I shouldn't just hang this phone up and forget that you ever had the nerve to call?"

"Because I'm trying to save you." There were a few moments of dead silence and an intense shudder of worry went through Melvin . What if she won't help? Was he a fool for ever calling her? She had to listen to him! She just had to! She was one of the strongest women he had ever known. Her compassion was one of the things that made him fall in love with her in the first place. Was he too late? Had her compassion for him gone?

"In what way," she demanded.

"I would rather not go into it over the phone. Can you come pick me up?"

"Yeah, yeah, yeah. Where at?"

"I'm at the Twin Villages shopping center off Airline."

"Alright, honey. Don't shake your tail feathers too much; it'll take me about twenty minutes to get there. This better be worth it! Bye."

Well, she didn't sound too happy about it, but at least she was coming. Melvin crouched down, propped himself on the cold concrete with his hands, and sat down on the curb. He stretched his legs out and started watching the highway.

Airline Highway was nearly always busy at the North end of Baton Rouge. Not that there were many stores on it or much of anything worth visiting here. It was just that this section of town was above the Interstate and people still used the highway to get to the Interstate.

The North end had long been the main center of all crime in the city. A few of the cops that he had worked with had warned him of a few sections in town that they wouldn't even go into if the sun had gone down. Gangs were taking over the north side altogether. What a waste. Millions of dollars in development costs just going to the dogs. No wonder this shopping center was virtually vacant.

Well, screw'em all! Maybe he should let, whoever it was, try and make a better world. From what he knew, there's wasn't too much to love about the world right now.

Everybody is trying to screw everybody else anyway. Fuck them all!

No! No! No! He pounded a fist on his leg. This could have disastrous consequences and could make things a lot worse. He reached his hand down to grab his book, but realized that he had done the worst thing imaginable. He had lost his current book. His guts became as hard as the concrete his butt was on and quivery. Moving his hand up to his waistline, he felt the all too important box fastened there. At least it had not gone away. Melvin reached both hands underneath his legs, interlaced his fingers, and put his head on his knees.

He closed his eyes. He felt tears forming in his eyes and then felt the moisture as it began to pour down his face. He didn't know why fate would put him in such a mess. Why? Why now? Why him? Why, why, why? Was Tom dead? He was the person that got him into this. It's all his fault! Now, that rat bastard left him with one hell of a mess. He wasn't really a bastard, but what... Tom may be rotting somewhere for all he knew. It wasn't a good way to think about an old friend.

An old friend.... Hell, Tom was 'the only friend,' he ever knew, trusted, dealt with, you name it. Tom was it. There had been many 'associations,' but no friends except Tom. His body jerked in convulsions of emotions as he sat there. As he wailed, he balled his right hand into a fist and knocked himself in the head with it. "Damn it! Rat bastard... Fuck everything!"

Melvin tried sucking up the mucus running through his nose with an extended sniff that sounded like a motorboat. Failing at that, he began wiping up mucus from his nose by wiping it with his fingers. He leaned backwards for a moment, rubbed his fingers on his nose again, and then looked at his hands. Seeing the wetness, he sniffed, grabbed his shirt tail, and wiped his nose. He heard a bang and raised his head. As he rubbed his eyes trying to clear his vision, he heard the sound of an engine crank.

As his vision cleared, he peered into the parking lot and

he saw his stolen car drive away. "One problem solved," he said as he continued wiping at his face.

Chapter 29

Outside Robert's Grocery, a police car rolls over the sandy-gravel driveway and parks on the far side of the twin gas pumps. The blue florescent lights on top were not lit. The driver pushed open his door with a creak and stepped out of the car. Splash! "Son of a gun," The middle-aged gentleman said as he felt his flat-bottom shoe fill with water. His black sock, halfway submerged, had that yicky feeling of being soaked. When he looked down and saw his ankle was nearly submerged, he slammed the car closed, then picked the foot up and shook it as he started towards the door.

He opened the wooden door to the store and immediately noticed that there was no one in the store except a young blonde girl behind the counter and eyed the video camera in the far corner. As he walked toward the counter, he pulled his navy blue cap off.

Light glinted off of the officer's badge and it shined on the young girl's face. She turned her head away from the TV to the direction of the door. "May I help you, officer?"

"Yes, ma'am. I am Sergeant Dwayne Hicks. I was told that a Paul Roberts had reported a strange encounter with an unknown man. I'm here to follow up."

"Sir, he went home a little while ago. He would be the one to talk to."

"I see. Does he stay far from here? I really need to speak to him."

Peggy picked the phone receiver from where it was hung

on the far side of the register and put it to her ear, saying, "His trailer is out back. Let me just call him." She pressed a button and paused while the receiver sounded the familiar pitch, then dialed. There was a low-pitched, beep beep followed by a click and then a greeting. "Mr. Roberts. A policeman is here to talk to you." Pause. "They say it's about the report you filed yesterday." Pause. "Okay." The young lady put the receiver in its cradle with one hand while looking at the policeman saying, "He said that he'll be right here."

"Thank you," the Sergeant said. He then looked up at the TV and pointed to it. "Whatcha watching?"

The young girl run her fingers through her hair and said, "It's just some kind of game show. I try to watch meaningless stuff like this in case customers come in."

Dwayne's head turned toward the back when he heard the squeak of a dry hinge squealing followed by the KABLOOMP of a door closing. After a few moments, a big, rounded figure walked through the opening to the back room.

As the figure walked into the room, he said, "Can I help you, officer?"

Dwayne looked at big man, asking, "Yes, sir. I am following up on a call you made yesterday concerning a strange man that came into the store."

The big man shook his head. "Geez Louise! How many of you people are there?"

Dwayne's eyes widened so that most of the white could be seen. At the same time, both eyebrows raised and he replied, "What in the world do you mean, fella? I am the first one to come here regarding this."

"No. No, you aren't. There was a tall man in here about 4 A.M. this morning asking about where this guy went to when he exited the store."

"Oh!" Pause. "What did the man say?"

"Just that he was from the city and was investigating the incident. He wanted to know which way this guy went."

"What did you tell him and what did this guy look like?"

The big man pointed. "I told him that the guy probably

went West. As far as looks, come on and I'll show you the video." He ushered Dwayne into the back room.

Chapter 30

Max stood outside the command center tent looking at the tablet in his hands and reading the recently submitted reports from the search teams. Eric Kandle's team was always aligned westward of where the main search was it seemed, but not significantly so. It was probably just a matter of containment. As he slid his finger on the surface to advance to the next report, he sensed motion, lifted his head, and saw Nancy coming toward him. He took a step back.

When her figure rounded the corner of the door, she and Max collided hard enough for Max to loose his grip on the tablet that he was carrying. It fell to the ground and quickly slid into a brown puddle.

"Oh! I'm sorry, Max," said Nancy as she stilled herself. She pulled at her clothes a tiny bit, then reached down for the dropped tablet. Max clutched it in both hands and was bringing it up by the time Nancy's hand arrived. She withdrew her hand and reached into both pockets of her green jacket and withdrew some pink tissues.

"Here, you can use these. I think they're clean." She put them on the brown speckled tablet and rubbed slightly.

"Good thing these are waterproof, huh?"

"Yeah."

She stopped rubbing and withdrew her hand. "I wish I could stay and help, but I am in a hurry."

"S'ok. I can manage."

"Thanks," she said and then walked off.

Max continued wiping for a moment until he saw a young technician start to enter the command center tent. He waved to her, saying, "Hey, miss."

The slim, blonde woman stopped walking and turned toward him. Her arms were cradling some yellow paper with splotches of blue ink on them. "Yes, sir?"

Max shoved the dirt soaked tablet toward her. "Take care of this."

"Sir?"

Waiting a moment for the young girl to obey, Max finally said, "Just take it!" The young woman shifted the load in her arms and reached out with her right hand to grab the device. The mud splotched surface slipped on her fingers and the tablet fell. She lifted her right knee to try to keep it from falling; to no avail, it went to the ground and back into the puddle.

As she looked around for help, Max had already disappeared.

Chapter 31

Nancy had just finished informing her taskmaster of the latest news when she pulled open the green mesh curtain of her tent with a raised right hand. As soon as she did, she noticed Max standing on the right just outside the doorway and she felt the warm blood drain from her face.

"Hey Max, what's up?"

Max reached over with his left hand and grabbed her right wrist; his index finger was touching her green shirt sleeve and the jacket covering it. His knuckles turned white and the black hairs on his arm protruded. With his right hand, he swung the open end of a quarter-inch wide steel cuff around her wrist and closed it with a loud click. "You are," he said as he closed the other cuff around his wrist with another click. With flared eye sockets, Nancy groaned while Max testing the cuffs with a jerk of his left wrist.

She pulled her arm against the cuff, wriggling her wrist. Not being able to free herself, with a sharp, high-pitched voice, she said, "My God... What's this for?"

"Being a traitor. Let's go." He leaned his body toward the command tent and started to walk, only to have his arm yanked by hers.

"Wait, wait, wait," she pleaded.

Max turned and looked at her. "Wait nothing. Come along or I'll drag you."

Nancy looked him in the eyes. His green eyes were as hard and unwavering as blocks of cement. She huffed and then moaned. "Alright, let's go settle this." She started walking beside Max toward the command tent. "This is moronic. We have a nuclear threat out there and I'm having to deal with this crap."

Max marched on silently, chained arm stretched backward.

"You could at least let me explain whatever's got you upset."

Max marched on silently. His pace quickened as people in the vicinity had started gawking.

Max stopped suddenly about fifteen feet from the command center tent. He shoved Nancy's right arm down beginning at the wrist, where she had no choice but to be jolted from the cuffs. Helplessly, she was forced to turn and face him and saw that his face was candy apple red from anger, disappointment, and resentment at having had to catch her in such a despicable and treacherous act.

With a trembling voice, he asked, "You and I both know that I have you nailed to the wall." He paused and looked down at her shoes and then slowly back upward to her face, then pulled her wrist down even more and leaned forward into her face. "There's only one thing I want to know before all hell breaks loose and that's why?"

His face was so near hers that she could feel his hot breathy words on her face. She paused a moment and then tried to look away, but her nose was bumping into his.

Max finally pushed her away with his free hand. "Ah hell, it doesn't matter anyway." He turned toward the command center, then put a flush hand on his jacket. "Damn it!"

As he started walking, Nancy took a step, then pulled at the cuffs. Max's body jerked from the shoulder and he looked over at her, still red faced. Nancy's lips parted slowly and softly she said, "You deserve an answer, it's a long story."

Chapter 32

Melvin spotted Margie's car turning into the lot. It wasn't a challenge, by any stretch. She was a sucker for old cars and forever had been. The car was a sleek design, four doors, and somewhat narrow. The wheels had rims with four rectangular holes and no caps. "Yeah, that's her 2001 Plymouth Neon for sure."

Still seated with his rear on the curb, he began shuffling his legs in preparation for getting up. "Ooh," he moaned. He reached a hand to the small of his back and started rubbing. "I need to be younger." He removed his hand and laid it flush against the edge of the cool, concrete curb and pushed with his right arm. Using his outstretched arm as leverage, he rolled his body and stretched upward. Sitting still had not been a good idea as his back muscles started screaming at him when he was at a standing position. He put his hand to his back again and rubbed. "Got to keep moving."

The maroon Plymouth rolled up next to him, the passenger door at his side. The window powered down and as he ducked to peer in, he saw Margie with her shoulder length brown hair. She bent over long enough to see his face.

"Get in."

There was a very obvious sharpness to her voice. Colonel Margie had given him an order that he better not ignore or else he would get left behind. There were definitely consequences to calling the very person that he had treated so harshly. Ah, but the kicker was, he had no choice. Being a loner has it consequences. This is why he kept to himself in the first place: people always have baggage. He did not want to wade through all the crap to find the few good qualities inside people. Too much time, too much energy... Not that he thought he was perfect, he had as much crap as everybody else, but it was his crap. The effort it took to merge his crap with everyone else's crap was just too much of his precious time and energy.

There was Margie inviting him in. "Well...."

"Fuck," Melvin moaned in a nearly silent voice as he grabbed the handle of the door and pulled. The door swung open and he stepped inside the car, crouched, then seated his butt on the crushed velvet passenger seat.

Margie glared at him. "Okay, Mel, what in the hell is going on?!?" Long pause. "I know you're in trouble, otherwise you would never have called me!"

"I'll explain everything, but first, can we please not stick around here. It's dangerous for both of us."

"I must be absolutely nuts," she said as loosened her hand from the steering wheel only to hit it with a fist and grab it again. She paused a moment. "Okay, Hero. Where to?"

"Someplace north and isolated."

Chapter 33

There were five people in the command center, three men gazing at onscreen charts, Tina was sitting at the front right desk gazing at the monitors, head in her hands, and Petry with the receiver end of a phone stuck to his right ear. When he saw Max enter the room, Petry blinked to filter the bright glint of the office light's reflection from the shiny cuffs around Max and Nancy's wrists. His eyes bulged and his normally tannish skin grew pale.

He pushed his chair backwards and stood. When he did, the steel desk inched forward a bit ripping the top layer of grass blades underneath. He looked over the room and with a shaky voice said, "Ya'll carry on. I'll be back in a bit." He turned toward the opening and glared at Nancy's downcast head for a moment, then looked straight into Max's eyes, saw the steely gaze and reddish face. He pointed the index finger of his already raised right hand. "Let's go to my tent."

The three exited the tent and, once outside, he heard Nancy clear her throat. "Save it until we get to my tent," he said trying to steady his own voice. The three walked quickly to the tent and after they had entered, Petry closed the tent, then sat in the rear chair of his small fold out table. With his elbows braced on the chair, he pointed his right finger at Max and said, "Max, you first. Tell me why we're here."

Max reached into the right-side jacket pocket and pulled out his phone. "I saw Nancy head out from the command center and go into her tent, and," he paused and swallowed.

The sound seemed to permeate the room; there was a dead quiet in the room while Petry waited on his teammate to bolster himself. "... well, sir, I recorded this." He sat the phone on the table and touched the screen.

*

"Hello, ma'am, it's Nancy. I have updated information for you."

Pause.

"We found Tom Soren."

Pause.

"No, ma'am. The chip and data were not on him and a thorough search of where he was at produced nothing. Unfortunately, Mr. Soren collapsed at the scene and so far, all attempts to revive him have been unsuccessful."

Pause.

"No ma'am, but we do have another lead to follow. There seems to have been a man with Tom, but we were unable to catch him."

Pause.

"It wasn't the men's fault! The whole area was booby trapped."

Pause.

"We strongly suspect that this mystery man has the stuff with him."

Pause.

"We'll get him."

Pause.

"I know very well what the consequences would be. My whole life and the life of everyone I know."

Pause.

"I won't. I can't. Nancy out."

After some shuffling noises. A faint, "I'm screwed."

*

Max reached a right arm to the table and tapped on the screen. "What the hell was that conversation about?"

"Save that question for a moment," Petry said. He looked at Nancy's downcast head. "Look at me," he said in a loud brutish voice. Her brown eyes looked up while she righted her head. "Explain."

Chapter 34

Nancy's downcast head looked up at Petry, then cast her eyes downward again. From outside the tent the sounds of people walking and talking could be heard. The voices were distant, muffled, and unintelligible. Inside, the room was stone quiet.

Petry picked up the tablet that was laying on his desk and started bringing up data about the investigation on the screen. When he looked back up, he turned his head and looked into Max's brown eyes. He could tell from the pinpoint pupils, the younger man was filled with questions. "Max, I am promoting you to my second in command." Max's head bobbed backward. Petry touched a few areas on the tablet, then laid it on the table. "Remove your cuffs and bind her wrists together, then read what's on the tablet."

Max did as instructed. When he finished reading, he looked up and straight at Petry with his mouth open ready to ask questions. When Petry saw Max's mouth start to open, he held up a flush hand. "We'll talk later. Right now, I want to handle this situation." Max closed his mouth and saw Petry look over at Nancy. "I am trying to think of why you would be exposing our confidential information to someone. I suspected you were, but I had hoped that I was wrong. The only answer that I keep coming up with is someone, either a person or a group, has a vested interest." He picked the tablet up once more and started fingering through the screens. "There is a hell of a lot of data here." He stretched his arm toward the table's surface and, when his four fingers slid out from underneath the tablet, there was a klunk sound that permeated the stillness of the tent. Putting his hands on his knees, he arched his back and with a stretch of the legs, stood up. The chair behind him scooted backward. When it did, he walked around the corner of the table and grabbed underneath both sides of her jaw using both hands and squeezed. Her skin became white and taught under the intense pressure. He pulled up so that her head was jutted backwards. She had no choice but to look up into his piercing eyes. "I'm only being this nice because of our long friendship, but this, my dear, is the last time I will ask. What's going on? Last fucking chance..."

There was a long pause. Nancy sat unmoving.

When Petry spoke again, he leaned his body toward Nancy's helplessly positioned body, and his voice had the loud, harsh tone of a volcano. "ALRIGHT, YOU BACKSTABBING BITCH! WE'LL PLAY IT THE HARD WAY!!! DAMN YOU ANYWAY!!!" He pinched the fingers of both hands tightly against her cheeks until his thumbs slid downward over her cheekbones and finally released. A pair of symmetrical red streaks appeared on each cheek, speckled with pools of blood. "Fuck you!" A few droplets of spit flew out of his mouth like nuclear missiles full of rage and smashed into her blood gorged, reddish cheeks. As the droplets began sliding down her face, Nancy lowered her head. "This project will continue without your sorry ass!"

When Petry turned toward Max, his eyes were streaked with jagged red lines and his cheeks, forehead, and everywhere else on his face were blood red. "Max, my car is parked in the rear. Put this treasonous whore in on the back seat, hogtie, and gag her." He backed up behind the desk.

"Hogtie?!?"

"You heard me!!! In the back seat... With my tinted windows, nobody will ever see her. Until she talks, she's not a human being, just a backstabbing pig. She needs to be treated like one." Nancy looked up and Petry closed the fingers of his right hand into a tight fist and then swung in the direction of Nancy's face. Her eyes flinched and tears formed in the inside corner of each eye. The tears slowly trickled downward in her eye sockets and began to flow down her cheeks. They gradually rolled to the top of her cheeks, around the curves, and then fell to the floor.

In a low, shaky, voice, she said. "I'm sorry."

Chapter 35

Bits of paper were swirling in the whirlwinds that had appeared on the outside of the downtown police station. Inside the flesh-toned brick building, Sergeant Dwayne Hicks was busy typing on the white keyboard at his desk. The four black filing trays on the edges were almost overflowing.

A man with thinning gray hair in a fringe walked up to the desk. The florescent track lighting glinted off of his head. Dwayne leaned sideways away from his boss, threw up a hand, and chuckled. "Get out of here; you're blinding me, Chief."

The Chief put one hand on the corner of the desk and laughed. "You mean my dazzling beauty? Yes, I know it's a burden, but, hey, if ya got it, flaunt it." He paused. "Seriously, I came to check out whether you found anything about our imposter at the convenience store?"

Dwayne's large body righted itself in the rolling office chair that he was in and the brown leather upholstery squeaked from the movement. The smile that was on his face moments before, turned to one of stone. "Nothing. I checked records and no one from any office in the city went there and the Mayor's Office didn't know about anything either."

"So we have an imposter of some sort. That represents a danger to everyone. Did you put it out on the wire?"

"Yes, sir, but according to everything that I can dig up, I can't even prove this guy exists. Facial recognition from the video turns up nothing."

As the two were talking, from the large opening in the front of the room came two men in suits, one gray, one navy. The navy-suited man was taller with black hair, parted to the left, and a slim face. His face was pitted, as if as a teenager he had had uncontrolled acne. His skin had the look of a leather saddle, dingy, grainy, and dry. The other man was older with swirly, receding, gray-white hair. He was fair skinned and pale with a solid gray tie matching his suit. Both men's faces were expressionless.

The two policemen at the desk abruptly stopped talking when the pair stopped in front of Dwayne's desk. The fair one reached into the left side of his suit and brought out a brown leather flap which he opened for the men: 'FBI', with a photo ID. Looking at Dwayne, he said, "I'm Agent Mike Curry, this is Agent Roger Christian. Is there somewhere private that we could talk?"

The Chief said, "Sure. Let's go to my office."

The foursome walked silently to an office in the back of the room. Once inside, the Chief closed the door. "What's all this about?"

Mike said, "I understand that you are investigating an unknown imposter?"

"I am."

The Chief looked at Mike and said, "I'm Chief Hunter. Can we help you, gentlemen?"

Mike looked up at the Chief with an expressionless face. His deep voice was vibratory. "Effective immediately, you will turn over all your records on this investigation."

Dwayne's eyes widened. "This is our case!"

"Not any more. This is no longer your responsibility or concern."

Roger's voice was still manly, but a significantly higher pitch. "Also, it would be in your best interest to totally forget this incident. Our national security depends on it."

Chief Hunter leaned forward a bit and said, "By law, once we open a case, we have to follow up, file reports, etc."

Mike glared at him. "Sir, are YOU aware that according to the Terrorist Act that I can have you both incarcerated in solitary confinement until you die for obstruction? No attorney, no family, nothing."

"We'll do anything you need."

"That would be in your best interest," Mike said.

The Chief pushed the intercom button on his desk. "Yes, Chief," asked a female voice through the speaker.

"Ceceila, round up all the data on the convenience store case and bring it to me. I want copies, originals, everything, and put the digital data on a flash drive.

"Yes, sir."

Chief Hunter looked at Mike and said, "It'll be a few minutes. When she gets here, I'll wipe out the data on the computers."

Roger said, "That'll be fine. The government thanks you for your cooperation."

Chapter 36

Not a word was said on the trip North. They had been in the car for about ten minutes on Airline Highway, when Margie finally asked, "How far do you want to go?"

Melvin had been trying to look forward only. Somehow, he couldn't bring himself to look at her. "We're on the outskirts of B.R. now, so pull over at the Shell station up here." The station was about a mile in front of them and Melvin knew that soon he would actually need to look at her. She was probably already mad enough to eat bullets; I mean who did he think he was anyway? Show back up in her life in a split second begging for help. YICK!

He could barely believe that he was asking another human being for help anyway. That defied every principle that he used. YICK! Now he was the one with the troubles going to another person. As a P.I., it was always him helping others and, damn it, he liked it that way.

The closer they got to the turn, the harder and faster his heart pounded. As soon as Margie turned the car into the area, the rush of blood became greater. He felt light headed and euphoric. The jolt of the large curb reminded his body of a few, not-so-good, nights of being cold and on a very hard floor. The million aches and pains overwhelmed his mind and he grabbed at the dashboard to steady himself, but his hand fell short and he brought the arm back to his side. He grunted from the pain which apparently was unnoticed or uncared about by Margie.

Thump...thump......thump...thump...... the sound of his heart became louder and he could feel the pulsations deep within his ears. The insides of his stomach were inflamed with acid caused by his jittery nerves and it was making him queasy and jittery. He lifted his right arm, studied it a moment and noticed almost imperceptible tremors. Deep breaths.... calm and cool... settle down, self.

Abruptly, the Plymouth turned again and then rolled over to a vacant area by a green dumpster bin, slowed, and stopped. It was like she slammed her foot on the brake pedal and it jolted Melvin's body, giving his aching body something else to complain about. From the corner of his eye he could see that she had twisted her body towards him, but he did not budge.

"Alright, bub, tell me what the dire emergency is?"

Oh no! Here we go. He turned his head slowly toward her. He stared at her from the visible foot, to the loosely sprawled thin legs. Her buttocks were resting below and behind as she was slightly leaning towards him. Her pants were a light shade of pink cotton without any wrinkles. She had always commented 'dress well, then you'll feel well.' Her blouse was mostly white with pink swirls in odd shapes of flowers and her perky 36C's were sticking out as prominent as ever. The blouse was V-cut so the tops of her white bosom's were visible and her face was oval shaped, not short, not fat, just right. Although she had no makeup on, it was the face he remembered -- soft.

Her green eyes were staring him down at the moment. With her eyebrows pulled down, those big eyes became smaller. "Well?"

He rearranged his position in the seat and faced her. In doing so, he put his back against the door. "I'm in big trouble, Margie."

"You said that already."

"You are going to think I'm crazy. Hell, I thought I was crazy. I still can't believe I am mixed up in all this." With a tone of indignation, he added, "Me, the turd of the century."

"Well, I won't argue that."

Melvin hung his head for a moment. "I know. I know. I'm an asshole. Go ahead and tell me."

"Okay. You're an asshole! A supreme asshole! Asshole of the century!"

"I deserve every bit of that. If not for our marriage, then for other stuff. Okay?"

"Oh, you deserve it alright and much more, for our marriage and then some."

"Can we please put our differences aside for the moment and focus?"

"I suppose I can. Can you?"

"Yes. I am in a real jam. Do you remember me talking about Tom Soren?"

"You didn't talk about a whole lot in our short time together, but, yes, I do."

Melvin looked at her and raised his hands with palms up. "Please, Margie?" He paused long enough for her to nod briefly. "Well, three mornings ago, he showed up at my door telling me this wild story. Well, I heard enough to convince me to find out more. I thought I was crazy."

"That makes two of us."

Melvin hung his head briefly, looked up, then his brown eyes latched on to hers. "He showed me a gun that this company or whoever has been developing that reverses time to whatever its fired at."

Margie's head rocked back. She put her hand to her stomach and rocked backwards with open mouth laughter. His mouth tried to say something, but all that he could utter was, "Umm... Ahhh... Ummm... W... Ummm."

She raised a loose limp arm and extended her index finger, but still cackling and rocking. "That's the best you could come up with?!?" Her voice was filled with indignation.

Melvin leaned heavily against the door and just sat there. Maybe she would be finished soon and then he could convince her. While he waited, he curled his left arm and placed his hand on the black box strapped to his side.

Margie extended her right arm to the dashboard and

pulled out a tissue from the tall black box that was sitting there, grabbed one, and put it to her watering eyes. "Mel, I never thought you were a kidder."

He stared into her eyes. "I'm not."

Chapter 37

The wind rocked the old car a bit as Margie's smiling face from moments before changed. The smile was gone. The eyebrows pulled down and in.

Melvin knew that his words and the way he had said them had caught her attention. "I'm not joking," he reiterated in an even tone. He paused. "I wish I were. Boy, do I wish I were." He pointed to the box strapped to his side. "Everything is in here. I don't even know how to work the damn thing, but my friend Tom sure did. I damn near came unhinged when he brought a dead cockroach back to life right in front of me."

"He what???" She looked down at the black box, then back up at his face.

"You heard me right. He brought a dead roach back to life by reversing it in time."

Margie's eyes were wide open and getting wider. "You can't be serious?"

Melvin looked at her and shook his head. With a lowered voice he said, "I wish I wasn't." Pause.

"Gee," she said with a long breath. Looking back toward the box strapped to his waist, she asked, "What's in the case?"

"The gun and other stuff." He took in a big gulp of air and slowly exhaled making a faint whistle.

"What are you going to do?"

"Well, I'm a dead man for sure. Tom and I were going to..." In sheer horror, he let out a bloodcurdling scream that rattled the windows with the sound of cheap tin. Margie leaned back and her eyes widened. Melvin balled up his hands and his slammed them over and over against the air. "Screw it all anyway! You hear me, Tom! Damn you anyway!" His hands cradled the front of his face and he tipped his head backwards against the glass with a klunk sound.

Margie's eyes grew soft when she leaned forward again. "What's wrong, Mel???"

Melvin slid his hands down his red face while he lowered his head to look at her. "It's my book. My SANE book." Pause. He shook his head. "It had the friggin' map and the security details. Which leaves me nowhere."

"What book? What map?"

Melvin klunked his head backwards repeatedly against the glass. "No. No. No. No. No." He sat up and stared into her eyes. "Ever since you and I parted, I have written in journals. They have kept me sane." He swallowed. "Tom wrote the layout and security measures of the building we have to penetrate on the last few pages of my sane book." He raised his arms, palms up. "I lost the book when we ran from whoever the hell the bad guys are. Tom and I had decided to break in and destroy this technology to preserve everything and everyone."

Margie tilted her head with a dull look in her eyes.

"Don't you see? If this stuff is ever used it can change the future of everything. If I reverse your body and wipe you out of existence, that would mean that everything you've ever done, and everyone's life that you've came in contact with, would be wiped out. It would change everything."

Her eyes bulged and her face became pale. She nodded.

Melvin put his hands in his lap. "Yeah, now you get it." Pause. "I had the exact same reaction: stupefied." He leaned slightly forward away from the door. "Now, I'm lost. I don't know what to do." He lowered his head, put his hands to eyes, and sighed.

Margie, unmoving, stared at him. A few moments had passed by in silence when she finally reached her right hand across and laid it atop his leg. In a low and sweet voice, she said, "I'm here for you, Bean. We'll find the answers."

She had not called him Bean since a few months after their marriage. It felt good. He didn't really know how to respond. Here he was sitting beside a person that he had kicked out of his life with an iron boot, and yet she was being nice to him. Why? He did not deserve any tenderness or mercy. He was a major asshole and he knew it. Damn!

Her hand rubbed his leg and she scooted closer in doing so. "I trust you." She paused. "If you believe this is bad, then I'm with you."

How could she be so trusting? He wouldn't even believe him. He finally looked up into her face.. When he did, his neck popped and sent a shiver of pain through his body and the two nights of cold, hard, aches came flooding back to him. "Thank you," he said in a low voice.

"What do we need to do next?"

He looked into her green eyes. He saw compassion for the hell he had already been through. "An unrested mind and body never plans well. What I need right now is a good sleep."

"We'll go to my place." She moved her hand up and reached around his chest, hugged him, then scooted back over to the driver's spot.

Melvin glanced over at her and said, "Thank you. That sounds great." He then fixed his position in the passenger side and waited for the car to start.

Chapter 38

It was near midday when Mike and Roger reached the FBI field headquarters near the capitol building. Side by side they entered the tan brick building through the double doorway, walked to the front desk where the receptionist was, and flashed their I.D.'s to her. She nodded and then they walked down the left hall. Roger carried a black cardboard box in front of him with his left hand. They stopped to look into the third room on the right where an older black-haired woman was sitting behind a desk.

Mike looked at her and said, "We have all the data and the local police have agreed to drop their investigation."

She looked up at him. Her blue eyes and small pupils resonated with glee when she smiled. "Good," she said in a husky voice. Her makeup was a mixture of bright reds for blush and lipstick and her eyes were heavily accented with a thick, black eyeliner. Her black hair fluttered a little as she rose from her chair and said, "Excellent!" When she was standing, she added, "Let's go back here and discuss it."

The three walked into the rear conference room. There was a mixture of screens, one very large, a collection of electronic devices, and a large table in the room. The lady turned to Mike and asked, "Do you have a flash drive?"

Mike was already reaching into his left coat pocket and pulled out a black flash drive about half an inch long. He handed it to her while Roger sat the box on the table. "Everything is supposed to be on here including a video feed from the convenience store."

She took it with her right hand and plugged it into a vacant port on the side of the table. The large screen in the front of the room lit up and showed a list of names on the left: Files, Documents, and Video. Mike, who was standing in back of her and to the left, looked at her and said, "Teresa, why don't we first look at the video."

Teresa looked down at the touchscreen built into the table that was showing the same thing as the big view screen and, with her index finger extended, tapped Video. A single file appeared on the right side and when she tapped it, they saw the video feed from the convenience store. They all looked up at the big wall screen.

After it played through, Teresa said, "We can't tell anything from this. This is like most other surveillance video: extremely poor quality."

When she looked back at Roger, he said, "Maybe not, but do facial recognition because we get a real good shot of him as he enters the store."

Teresa tapped one of the icons on the right side of the video and the view screen split into two horizontal sections. The right side had his image, the left, was blue on white and had the word 'Searching' above a thin, animated, horizontal line going from left to right. After a few moments, the left side of the screen changed to show a close up headshot photo of him and specific details.

Roger looked at the screen and cocked his head. "His name is Robert George Milgrew. The identification comes from sealed military records, but according to this, he's dead. Died 10 years ago in a plane crash."

Teresa's eyes scoured the faces that were onscreen trying to find an error in the match, but not succeeding. "Something extremely kooky is going on here. If this is correct, and it looks like an exact match, someone's tampered with the federal records database."

Mike looked at the other two and said, "This just got a lot deeper."

Chapter 39

Coming out of the command tent, Petry had a scowl on his face: full pouty cheeks, narrowed eyes, and a stiff, brisk walk. Nobody had seen or heard anything since they caught Tom and although Tom was on a slab at their facility, the only thing that was keeping him alive were machines. The EEG that was done as soon as he had arrived showed no signs of activity. The man was brain dead.

The medics at the lab were saying that he had either had a stroke or a ruptured embolism. Petry had discussed with others to use a CR gun to bring Tom back to life, but without a working temporal wall, who knows what they could affect. They could wipe out the technology for the temporal wall altogether, not to mention, affecting everyone's life in the process. No, the danger was just too great.

As he walked along, he could feel himself sneering at everyone. He did not want anyone around him right now. First, Rob sets out to investigate, second, the main man they were looking for dies right in front of Rob, third, they find out that his right-hand person is a traitor. To top that all off, they can't find hide nor hair of this other guy or even who he is. Such a mess...

When Petry walked into his tent, after sealing the entrance, he plowed face first onto his cot. His two hands were open on both sides of the lump where his pillow was and he started to knead the covers, finally balling the cloth up in his fists. Turning loose, Petry rolled over. Putting his arms behind him, he balled up his hands and lifted his torso then twisted and put his feet on the floor. The flimsy mattress made a noise as it shifted and the springs underneath creaked, echoing his mood. Petry lowered his head and put the fists in front of him. He groaned, then asked himself, "Why?"

He lowered his fists and stared at them, then opened his hands and rotated them as if looking for the answers he wanted, but nothing was written on them. He leaned forward and rose to his feet still staring at his hands and began walking toward the tent opening. He lowered the big hands and looked up. He walked slowly, kicking at the ground as he moved. When he got to entranceway, he parted the netting, unzipped the seam, and walked out. The icy wind blew into his face with a strong gust that pushed him backward. As he rocked back, Petry closed his eyes. When the gust died away, he opened his eyes, turned around and resealed his tent.

A young blonde woman was walking toward command center, noticed him, and stopped. "Mr. Petry, can I do something for you?"

Petry grabbed at both sides of his jacket, looked up and over at her brown eyes. He paused a moment, then said, "No thank you, Cindy."

"Okay," the young woman said as she resumed her walk.

Petry slowly circled around behind his tent and saw his black four-door sedan. He walked around to the passenger side, grabbed the door handle, and pulled it open with a click. The wind blew into the vehicle and Nancy's hogtied body lurched. Through the white cloth that wrapped through the creases of her mouth and around the back of her head, she grunted.

Petry stared a moment, then stooped and sat down on the cushy black sofa seat by her head. He reached over and grabbed the hand cord on the door, pulled, and, with a thud, they were closed in. He looked down at her dirty blonde hair which draped down her cheeks and partially over her eyes, finally covering part of the seat. As he sighed heavily, he looked up, down, and then back to her prone body.

He sat there a moment, then reached over and put a hand

on her back. He swirled his hand on her forest green jacket a moment, then brought the hand to his lap. "Old friend, I have no one else to talk so it might as well be you. After all, you won't hurt us anymore. I feel lost. You are the person who has listened to me all these years. This is the first time in at least twenty years that you haven't been at my side. Max and I get along great professionally, but I can't talk to him like I can you. I'm a hot head and I know it, but I never dreamed that you would betray me," pause, "us. I'm having to do everything alone now. It is very unnerving that after all these years, I am having to take direct charge of everything without anyone that I can really count on, like you. Forgive me for doing this, but it really upset me that you, of all people, would betray me and betray the project that we've worked so hard for. I have a horrible temper, as you know. Forgive me, my old friend. We could have had anything that we wanted: you, me, and the others. We were going to have it all. Masters of our own futures... I really hope that I can make sense of everything without you. Tom Soren is dead, no brain activity. The general and I agree that using a CR gun on him might have disastrous consequences so that option is off table. We were unable to get a single good fingerprint for the guy that was with Tom, not even DNA. Then, there's your reports. It would really help if I knew who it were you talking to and why you did this to the research. I really thought we had a good thing going."

He reached over and rubbed her back once more, patted her back, then retracted his hand. "I gotta go, my friend." Petry grabbed the silver door handle and pulled up. With a violent shove, he pushed the door open. The door opened wide and bounced at its extremity. With a duck of his head and a turn of his body, Petry lifted himself up and out of the car.

The cold wind began ruffling his jacketing and the noise in his ears was like the distant rumble of a freight train. He grabbed the metal edge of the door just beneath the glass and swung the door shut, turned his head toward command center, the side of which could be seen from his position and started walking toward it by first rounding the back of the car.

Nearing the center junction of tents, he saw Kelley, a larger size red head, walking away from command center. He whistled and motioned his extended arm toward her in a come hither style. She turned her head and her brown eyes saw him and she began walking toward him.

"Yes, sir."

"Where is Max at, Kelley?"

"Oh, I just left him in command center, sir."

"Thanks." Petry pivoted on his feet and began walking toward command center once more. Once inside the tent, he turned his head from side to side until he saw Max. "Max," he called out. Max jerked his head up from the tablet that he was looking at. He handed it to the woman at his side and started walking toward Petry.

"Yes, sir," Max said as he neared Petry.

"Let's go outside a minute, too many people in here." Once removed from the tent, Petry looked at Max. His brown eyes narrowed. "Max, she's about ready. Wait twenty minutes and then move Nancy to the supply tent. You stay with her. Keep her cuffed and gagged."

Chapter 40

Melvin had ridden in the back seat, lying down, as Margie drove them to her trailer house. It had been foolish of him to ride in the passenger chair to go out of town, but he dismissed the chance for people to spot him during that twenty-minute trip, at least, he hoped. He knew that people were looking for him and he wanted to avoid them like a bat avoids daylight. He knew that one tiny misstep could topple them both into a bottomless and deadly pit. The people that sought him would stop at no one and nothing to get the things back that Tom had rightfully took.

Rightfully, now there was a term that had meaning. Was it right for these people to plan world conquest at the expense of everyone else? No, of course not. Was it right for Tom to have stolen the one thing that allowed all of this cockamamie stuff to work? No. Ethically Tom was both right and wrong. Did that make him right? The answer to that was obviously no, but to protect everyone, Tom was willing to do wrong for the right reason.

Margie had told him that her trailer was on two acres on the westerly side of town. Good. It would give them time to plan. The search had obviously been Southeast. It would take time for whoever they were to regroup and refocus their efforts. Time was exactly what he needed right now because he had to find a way to deal with a major problem, the loss of his SANE book. Without it he was stuck. What on Earth was there to do? The book had the map and everything else they needed.

"We are getting pretty close, dear," Margie said as she turned the steering wheel.

"When we get there, is it possible for you to park alongside the front door?" Melvin asked looking at the light shining through the rear window.

Margie looked back at him saying, "Yeah, that's how I usually park anyway. It will be nearest to the passenger side door. I am turning in the driveway now."

Coming from beneath the tires, there was the crunchy, shifting sound of loose gravel being shuffled around. Melvin felt the car turn several times, shifting his body to and fro with each movement. Finally, with a bump, the car stopped and he could feel his body lurch forward and shift on the back seat. He hated the stops. There was an insecurity about feeling your body jolted forward nearer to the edge of the seat, even if it was only his flesh being jiggled around.

"We're here." Pause. "Let me go get the door unlocked and open before you try to get out."

He could hear her pull the door handle, bump, and with a click it unlatched. There was an extended metal whine of metal on metal when she pushed the car door open and then with a thud, it closed.

Footsteps around the front of the car were followed by the hollow wooden sound of, presumably her turquoise rubber slides on the steps. One, two, three, followed by three steady steps to the door. Pause. The dangle of keys, then ka-chunk and then the whine of a door...

Melvin's arm was dangling off the back seat when he pulled it to his chest. His hand was balled up and he decided to open it and place it over his heart. Ka-thump, ka-thump, ka-thump... Yep, still beating. His head was a foot away from the passenger door. He reached up with his right hand and clutched the door handle. He pulled. With a click it unlatched and he began to scoot toward the door. He heard hollow footsteps on the porch and the steps once more. The car door opened.

Margie peered down at him and whispered, "It's okay.

131

No one is around."

With outstretched arms, Melvin flexed his back muscles, sat up, and pivoted to a sitting position. Looking around, he saw that her property had a perimeter of assorted trees with various bushes mixed in. Most of trees the were small pines, but there were three big oaks, one in the front and two in the back on opposing sides of the yard. The only way a person could have seen into the yard, besides from an elevated position or through bushes, was the front driveway.

"Let's go, Margie." Melvin swiveled his feet and put them, one at a time, outside of the car. Margie grabbed his right hand with hers and pulled. Stiffening his back as he stood, he saw the wood porch, complete with handrails, in front of him. The steps were to his right side. The wood looked well cared for. There were no signs of rot or chips. The wood had a slight shine to it as if it had been water sealed recently.

He wriggled loose from her hand and began walking around the porch toward the steps when he felt Margie's hand on his back. He began to sprint around the corner and took the steps, one, and then grabbed both of the cold, but smooth, rails in his hands and swung himself all the way up. The door was still open and he got there in two giant steps, then felt the warm air brush against his skin. It was the first warm thing he had experienced, other than people, in several days, and he hesitated for a moment then smiled. "Ahhhh," Melvin said as he took a deep breath and walked in. It was a great change, at least for the moment.

He paused a moment more, felt Margie's hand on his back, and then stepped forward on the black and red shag carpet. When he was five feet in, he heard the door close behind him and the click of a lock followed by the clank and slide of a security chain. To his right was a step elevated kitchen with a wood grain island in the center. The kitchen was mostly mahogany with white and silver trim and beyond the entranceway there was a bar that stretched to the outside wall. To his left was the rest of the living room: a dark brown microfiber sofa, and a CRT television. There was a dark coffee table several feet in front of the sofa, but the room was absent of a recliner or any other place to sit. Beyond the living room to the left, was an open door in the center of the wall that led to the master bedroom. The bed was made up and had a white bedspread with rose flowers complete with stems.

Melvin stepped forward, turned around, and asked, "Where is your breaker box?"

Margie paused a moment and stared at his face, then pointed her index finger in the direction of the kitchen. Melvin turned toward the opening at the end of the bar and began walking. When he stepped up on the white linoleum, his brown sneakers squeaked a tiny bit as if the shiny flooring had recently been waxed. He could not let the slippery surface bother him though. He had to flip the breaker as soon as he could.

He walked past the dining table on his right to the closet door beyond and opened it. He saw a brown wicker basket and assorted cleaners on the shelves. A washing machine and dryer were against the rear wall. There was nothing even similar to a breaker panel in the room, so he closed the wood grained door and walked toward the next door. It was on his left and had been painted yellow. The door was mirroring the light from the decorative chandelier that was over the dining table behind him, but only partly, as his body was casting a shadow on part of it. Melvin stared at it a moment, but shook his head. "Can't do this yet," he mumbled.

Twisting his torso, Melvin grabbed the knob with his right hand and swung the door inward. He saw a filled walk-in pantry and a gray metal panel on the back wall. Ahhh, the breakers. He grabbed the broom and mop handles, one in each hand, and placed them alongside the shelves. As soon as he let go of them, they fell to the tile floor with a sharp tapping sound. He looked down at them. They just laid there, sprawled out on the white linoleum, much like his life: dead and motionless like he would probably be in a short time.

The tapping sound seemed to echo in the room and he heard Margie's footsteps come up behind him. "Need any help?"

He was already cussing silently, but managed to groan, "No! Fuck! This is how my life has been lately." He looked up toward the breaker panel and saw a metal ring and looped an index around it. When he pulled, he saw all of the black colored breakers were switched on, including the main one up at the top which extended over the rest about four inches. He put fingers of both hands on the top of the black plastic and pulled down. His fingers turned white, but the breaker did not budge. "Dang!" His hands and fingers lifted up and he rubbed thumbs against the tips. He removed the thumbs and put the fingertips on the switch again, pulled, then bent his knees. SNAP! "Damn, that's stiff."

The hum of electric motors around the house could be heard winding down and, after a few quick moments, they could not be heard. The house was silent.

With the hum of power vanquished from the house, along with it went Melvin's power. His already bent knees weakened and they fell to the floor. When they hit, there was a thud.

All of his energy had been spent in getting here and settled, and now, his body was saying, no more. It was time to surrender to stress. He lowered his head and stayed there, unmoving. He knew Margie was behind him. He had heard her walk to the door behind him and he could hear her breathing, but she was silent. He closed his eyes and inhaled deeply, held the air in his expanded lungs a moment, and then swallowed. When he exhaled, he heard brushing footsteps enter the room behind him. When the sound stopped, a moment passed, and then he felt open hands being placed in the center of his back. Even through his jacket, he could feel the warmth. The warmth of another human being... The very thing that he had fought his whole life against... Now, the warmth was somehow reassuring.

As the hands began massaging him, he heard Margie's very soft voice say, "It's going to be okay. You're all right. I'm here for you, Bean."

He paused a few moments, feeling her hands massage

him, then said, "I hope so. I truly do." He was silent a while more. Slowly opening his eyes, he found that his vision was blurry. He blinked his eyelids rapidly a few times and the shelving and cans before him came into focus. "Let's go in the living room and talk."

Chapter 41

Melvin seated himself on the right side of the mahogany sofa while Margie circled around to the left. As he looked around the darkened trailer, he sighed, but felt somewhat refreshed after his meltdown.

As a private investigator, there wasn't much pressure. He would do research into people's records sitting in front of a computer or follow some deadbeat husband, or something similar, but as far as real pressure on him, there was none. Was it performance anxiety? Maybe a form of it, but he figured it was more of a case of 'Save Ass.' It was a game that he was well familiar with because he had played it all too often. Not caring about people had a lot of advantages. Your actions or non-actions could not be manipulated for reasons of friendship, hatred, or the dreaded "love" factor. The more he thought about his advantages, the more in shocked disbelief that 'he' was to save the human race that he became.

When he looked at Margie, who was sitting over there silently, but patiently, he smiled in admiration of her silent consideration. She saw it and smiled back.

She always did give him his thinking space. It was appreciated because he had enough trouble dealing with himself and his own nightmarish brain, much less fill anybody else in on his mental status. This ordeal would quite probably kill him and her too. Him, for what he knew; her, by association, most likely...

Finding Tom after all those many years had been good

for him. He was pissed off, sure, who wouldn't have been to wake up to an idiot banging on your door at 4 A.M., but after he found who the idget was, sure he was happy to see him. Tom had been the only friend in his life, period. He had never been like other kids; they had friends running out of their ears. Sure, he had associated with lots of folks; associated, not a friendship. He preferred to live in his own world. He was never into sports or group activities. He just did his own thing and hoped that everyone else would leave him alone.

But, when Tom and he were working together in that old, rundown house, it had been fun somehow. A piece of him had finally been found with them working toward a mutual goal. Although he found the world full of idiots, scoundrels, and rats, there was Tom, a good guy. If there was one good guy on planet Earth, there might be another and what nobler project could one be involved in than to save the good people? He didn't know if Tom was really dead, but his heart was hurting. Was it intuition? He had no idea what the hell 'intuition' really meant, but he was fairly certain that what his quivering innards were telling him was the truth. That truth scared him even more than the forces that he was running from. To have lost Tom for all those years, then find him then lose him again would be cruel. He felt like that's the news that awaited him at some time or other.

How was he to cope? How would he carry out the plan that he and Tom had devised without his book? The book that had the details that he needed...

He stared at Margie's green eyes a moment, then at her medium long brown hair, straight, well kept, with a slight curl at the ends. Looking into her eyes, he saw the many questions just waiting for answers. "I suppose you are wondering why I shut off the power?"

"Yes."

"Well, Tom told me that the government can track nearly anything through electrical items: TV, radio, traffic lights, etc. By throwing the breaker, I've cut off all the spying gizmos."

Margie nodded. "Okay, Bean, but what happens when the refrigerator and freezer thaw?

"We have at least 12 hours before we have to worry about that. Besides, this is much more important. One disaster at time, girl."

Margie looked at him, flicked her curls back, and said, "What's our plan?"

Melvin raised both eyebrows and with wide eyes opened his mouth, but hesitated. "Our plan? Margie I called you to help me get safe, not to get you involved in this mess. The further I can leave you out, the safer you'll be."

"Too late! Like it or not, I am involved and I am going to help you through this mess."

"After the way I treated you?"

"Yes."

"Do you not understand that this could be the end of me and everyone around me?"

"'Til death do us part."

Melvin pushed his right hand at her. "You don't have to say that; we are divorced."

"That was your doing, not mine. I still love you even through all the crap that's happened."

Lowering his hand, Melvin leaned toward her a tiny bit. "You were staying out all those late nights..."

She looked at him a moment, then looked down at her twiddling fingers, then looked back up at him. "Yes, I was." Pause. "I knew you were drawn in and pretty quiet before we got married, but it was only a short time afterward, that you started coming home without even saying more than four words to me in the evenings: weekends too. I tried to draw you out," she glanced downward, "but I guess that I wasn't good enough."

Melvin saw her face turn splotchy red and tears well up in her eyes.

"I tried. I tried. I guess that I just wasn't enough for you at the moment, but I've always had faith in you and knew that someday you would turn yourself around." Margie hung her head as she moved her right hand forward.

Her hand jumped backward after having moved two inches. Melvin leaned forward more and reached his hand toward hers. When he grabbed her right hand, he knew that something in him had changed. All of this time, he had felt harsh at her, when in reality, he was being harsh with himself. Watching her shed tears over him was an uncommon experience. He had been assuming that the sum total of humanity was an uncaring, treacherous, and greedy lot, when there was one, yes one, human being on the whole accursed planet that cared about him.

He could only manage to sit there and watch her cry. He lifted his body up from the sofa and put himself nearer to her. He managed to slide loose from her hand in order to put his hand around to her backside. When he did, she tumbled over and put her head in his lap. His shoulders shuddered and she raised up immediately.

"Sorry."

He waived his hand at her, saying, "Just startled me is all."

"I was going out and doing different things just to keep active." She reached toward the end table and pulled a white tissue from the upright, pink square box, gathered some up between her fingers, and put it to her nose. Along with her side-to-side motions, she blew the mucus from her nose. The watery sound permeated the dark, still room. "I guess that may have been the wrong thing to do." Pause. "I don't know." Sniff, sniff... "Anyway, love is forever. I can't help myself, so I've been waiting. Perhaps you and I will both be ready for love one day."

Melvin rubbed her back with his open hand. "I didn't know any of this. You could have told me?"

She looked in his eyes. "I tried, but I knew that you had your mind made up. Besides, I did talk, but since you didn't talk back much, it was hard for me to tell if you even cared about anything." She raised the tissue to her nose once more, cradled her nostrils, and blew.

Melvin raised his left hand, palm toward him, and looked at it. It was his flesh alright, complete with the lines of his life. Within those lines was some sort of thing that would help him deal with this. He couldn't have been the cause of all her tears, could he? While he looked, she sobbed. He removed both hands and put hem to his side. Arching his back, he pushed himself up from his seated position, took a step, then leaned over her. He put his lips to the soft blonde strands of her hair and kissed her warm, soft head.

Margie looked up: her eyes, bloodshot, her cheeks, splotchy red like the rest of her face, especially her nose. "I love you. I always have."

"I love you too and I'm sorry. I'm guess I'm just not a good person."

"Yes you are."

"No, I'm not. I hurt everyone, do things to people like you: I'm hurtful."

"You may do that stuff to people, but because you have to. I see a good, honest, man that has the drive to accomplish things."

"That might be true."

"No 'might be' to it. You are! And when you want to be nice and sweet, you can be. You just need to find it inside you to latch on to the good things."

Melvin looked at her bloodshot eyes. Maybe they were telling him some hard truth. "Well, it would be extremely hard for me to pick out any good things in my life right now except for you."

Margie sniffed and turned her head toward the tan curtained double window behind her. Although it was made of thick material, she could still see that night had fallen. She turned her arm and looked at the cubic zirconia encrusted, small, oval watch on her right arm. "9:20! I had no idea that we had talked so long."

He bent over her body and put his arms around her and, with his head alongside hers, squeezed her tight. When he did, she put her arms underneath his and hugged him. He pulled his head back to where his mouth was next her ear and whispered, "I thank you for loving me through such terrible times." He felt her arms loosen so he backed away and straightened his back and legs. " I just thought..." He paused. "Well, forget about what I thought. Let's just go to sleep and worry about what to do next in the morning."

Chapter 42

Rob was in his own tent sitting on the far side of the bed. Having any time to himself was a luxury that he didn't often get, but he had told Matt that he just needed some down time. The truth was that he wanted some time to read in the book that he had picked up. From the tiny portion that he had read before, he knew something was amiss.

The line about 'bringing a dead roach back to life' had been weighing on his mind ever since he had read it. He reached both arms around to his back and grabbed his shirt tail, pulled the cloth up, and grabbed the black book with his right hand. He moved the book up from underneath his pants line, then brought it forward. Setting it on his legs with one hand, he re-tucked his shirt with the other.

'Book 325' was written on the top left corner next to the spiral binding. The lettering was in blue ink over an area that looked like someone had taken a knife or another sharp thing and scraped the lamination and black coloring off of the cover. He brought his arms forward and, held it for a moment, then opened the stiff paper front cover with his right hand and saw the name, 'Melvin John Travis', followed by, 'SANE Book 325'. Halfway down the white cover was written, 'Melvin here, Melvin there, Melvin everywhere, no friends, just job, and no chance of changing.' Rob smiled. The first page had Sept. 20th at the top, scrawled in scraggly lines of black ink.

He turned to the last page of the book. On the back cover

scrawled in black ink was the same message, 'Melvin here, Melvin there, Melvin everywhere, no friends, just job, and no chance of changing.' On the back page of the notebook was a floor plan of the base loosely scrawled in black ink. He had been inside the building many times for briefings and such. In different locations within the map, there were notes as to the security procedures and protocols. "What the hell?!?"

Rob shook his head and began turning backwards in the book. The next page had diagrams of bottles, drawers, and rooms with security details for each drawing. As he flipped backwards, there were a lot of empty pages before he arrived at pages of black inked handwriting. The last two pages were the only ones that referred to Tom's arrival, but these pages referenced time guns, conspiracies, and world altering events. "Whew! If this is true, no wonder they don't want anyone to know the truth," Rob said in a whisper.

Rob squeezed his hands together and closed the notebook. He shook it up and down for a moment, pinched his lips together, then hummed for a brief moment. His eyes narrowed, pushed along by his thinning eyebrows, then reached around to his backside, lifted his shirt, and reinserted the book into his pants in the center of his back. After his right hand pushed down at the top of the book, he used both hands to re-tuck his shirt neatly into his green camo's.

Chapter 43

When Rob stepped outside his tent, he blinked his eyes a few times, then raised a hand to shield his eyes from the bright sun on a cloud free day. Squinting his eyes, he slowly lowered his hand, but only slightly, and through slits he saw the image of a dark headed man walking by and called to him, waving his right arm. "Is that Rick?"

The man paused, turned toward him, and said, "Yes, what do you need, Rob?"

Rob lowered his hand and blinked several times to clear his vision as he asked, "Do you know where Matt is?"

"He should be coming up right behind me." After answering, Rick walked off down the corridor of tents.

"Thanks," Rob said as he removed his hand to his side. He turned his head to the right and looked and saw Matt walking in his direction. "Matt?" he shouted. When he saw that Matt had looked his way and recognized him, he raised a crooked arm in front of him, extended his index finger, and bent it repeatedly.

His second in command changed directions and walked toward Rob. When Matt was within a few feet, Rob said, "Matt, I want you to take charge here for a little while. I have an errand, but I want you to keep me fully posted by text messages, not by voice, not unless it is critical."

Matt nodded slightly. "Okay, boss. It's not like any of us know who in the hell we're looking for right now anyway."

"Yeah, this guy dropping on us sort of left a big hole, but

text me with any news anyway."

"Alright. What are you researching anyway?"

"It's nothing, really, an important personal matter."

"Well, the best of luck to you."

"Thanks," Rob said, then walked past Matt and through the center of their encampment. He looked at the green tents and shook his head. He was hearing his dad's words over and over, 'Just follow those orders, son.' In a whisper, he said, "Sorry dad, I just can't do it this time."

He reached a hand out toward his Escort and the silver door handle. When he pulled, the deep click reverberated in his mind. It seemed so hollow and meaningless, yet he knew it was a purposeful act that he was doing. While he searched his pocket for keys, a lump was building in his throat and he gathered a wad of saliva with his tongue and swallowed. He sat down, brought forth the key ring and inserted the appropriate one. 'Just follow those orders, son.'

He closed the door and said a loud, "No." When he turned the key, the car's engine started to hum with his purpose. He pulled on the gearshift, put it in Drive and mashed down on the accelerator.

He drove to Goodwood Blvd. and turned in at the East Baton Rouge Parish Library, found a convenient spot in front, and parked. The parking lot itself had various grasses and weeds busting through the asphalt, especially along the tire bumper areas. The red brick building had divots of missing mortar in numerous places. Here and there were chunks of bricks that had been carved out either by nature or deviants. "A dying breed," he whispered.

He clutched his hand around the door handle and pulled. There was that hollow click again. 'Just follow those orders, son.' "No, dad," he whispered as he got out. When he closed the door, it sounded a ka-chunk, this time without the echo of dad's voice.

As he looked around, he saw a nearly empty parking lot. There was a sliver of a smile on his face as he walked across the asphalt driveway to the elevated cement slab beyond. There were double glass-paned doors at the entrance with crusty gold-plated trimming. He pulled the handle of the right door and stepped into the lobby. As he walked forward, he could see a few people sitting at desks and a few walking around the large area. Rows and rows of books in an area bigger than the New Orleans Superdome and about fifty people roaming around.

The reference counter was ahead with two ladies behind it: both dark headed. He walked toward the first, who was the shorter of the two, and when he neared the counter, he stopped.

"May I help you sir?"

Rob nodded. "Yes, ma'am. I am looking for any and all personal records for a particular individual who is still living. It can be anything; even newspaper clippings would help."

The older lady behind the counter stepped toward Rob, and said, "Records on living people used to be difficult, but we have recently scanned all documents as text documents and now even the newspapers send us a digital copy of their issues."

Rob looked at her and asked, "So, then, where do we go?"

"Right over here, sir," she said. She raised her arm with a straightened index finger. At the middle of the counter was a double-door spring gate and the lady began walking toward it. With her legs, she pushed through the gate and walked toward the side room which she had pointed to, then lowered her arm. The room had a large, tan, wood door, and was glassed in, but on the inside of the glass, someone had put white paper ninety percent of the way up. The librarian put her hand on the silver knob, turned it, and walked in.

Rob walked in behind her. He saw several brown wood-grained tables in the room. All of them had a black border on their edge and all had folding, metal legs that extended to the floor. On the tables were rows of computers and microfiche readers.

"We rarely use the microfiche anymore unless it's before 1800, but we are getting ready to migrate 1700 to 1800 to digital files due to a grant that we recently received." She pulled two chairs out from under the table and sat down in the first, then motioned with a palm up hand to the other.

With a shake of his head, Rob sat down.

"I am going to help you search because, for right now at least, this search system is not easy to operate." She paused. "Okay, what name are we looking for?

"Melvin John Travis."

Chapter 44

"Petry! Petry!" Max was running through the encampment yelling. "Petry! Petry!" He quickly ran up the corridor, putting his head into each tent along the way. People around him, tablets in hand, followed Max with their eyes until a woman saw Petry entering the corridor and pointed towards him.

"Max, there he is," she yelled.

Max looked at where her finger was pointing, saw Petry, and ran toward him. "Petry, we have a major problem." He lowered his voice to a near whisper. "Nancy... "

Petry lunged at Max and grabbed both of his shoulders tightly. His face became instantly pale. He shook Max as he talked. "What do you mean??? What about Nancy???"

"She's gone!"

"Quiet down," Petry said in a hushed voice. "Do you want the whole friggin' camp to hear?" Petry loosened his left hand and then grabbed Max's left arm with his right with a tight grip. "Let's walk behind the tents." Petry turned loose of the shoulder and began pulling his captive into a brisk walk leading him behind his tent. His sedan was still there and Petry opened the near back seat door and catapulted Max into it, then shut the door. He walked around the back of the car and got in the other side. As he shuffled in the seat, he asked, "Now, explain to me, how in the hell a hogtied woman escapes?!?"

"Well, I sent two men..."

"You WHAT?!? You What?!?"

Max's face paled. "I sent two men instead of going myself because I was requested to be in command center."

Petry's face instantly became as red as the blood coursing through his veins and beads of sweat were appearing on his forehead. "Didn't I say that you, specifically, were charged with Nancy?"

"Yes, but that was during the investigation and then you made me second in command."

Petry blew air through his wide red nostrils. "Did I tell you that the investigation was over?"

Max paused, then quietly answered. "No, sir."

"Do you not realize the need for utmost secrecy?"

"Yes, sir."

Petry leaned forward and removed his butt from the seat, but remained crouched. He raised a hand and pointed an index finger in Max's direction. "Then how in the hell did this happen?"

Max slumped and then, with a raised arm, recovered. "You mean her escaping?"

"I mean all of it?" Petry screeched.

Max clasped his hands in front of him before answering. "I thought I answered that; maybe it wasn't satisfactory..."

"You're damn right it wasn't!" He shook his head. "Aw, hell, I guess it's an answer, nonetheless," Petry scoffed as he kicked at the black, carpeted floorboard. He lowered himself and re-took a sitting position, but still leaned toward Max. "Well, that is certainly bad news, my friend, bad, bad, bad." He put his right hand to his chin and sounded a low, but definite, hum. "We need to keep her treachery a secret. If news of this got out it might undermine the trust and resolve we need to keep going. We cannot let this get out. You know, everyone that knows the true reason for this research will be richly rewarded."

"I suspected as much, sir."

"Nancy was to join me; now you are. I trust you, Max. Power, money, control, it's all ours for the taking." Lowering his hand to his lap, Petry said, "Max, our priority right now is to get that witch back into our custody." He paused.

"If you want absolute secrecy, that's going to be difficult."

"Well, since you let her escape, absolute secrecy is a moot point, but we can contain who knows." He paused. "Round up two or three people that you trust. Make sure these people are going to be absolutely silent about this." He raised his right hand and pointed an index finger at Max. "There is a lot stake with this! If she gets government attention, the game is over."

Without hesitation, Max quickly said, "Yes, sir, we'll catch her." With wide eyes, he snapped a saluted in Petry's direction.

"Max, even in light of the screw up, I am doubling your pay. You have served well and your unquestionable loyalty is very important to me."

Max shuddered. "Why thank you, sir. I'm not sure that I deserve the raise, but, be assured, I won't disappoint you."

Petry looked at him with softer eyes and lowered his head slightly in a faint nod. "You do deserve it, friend. You are an up-and-coming young man. You will do amazingly well with the organization."

"Thank you, sir."

"Good. Now, go find Nancy."

"Yes, sir." Max turned and clutched the silver door handle and pulled. Klunk. The door opened with a whine and Max pushed on it and then extended his torso outside the car followed by his legs. Once outside, he grabbed the sedan door, swung it closed and then began walking.

When he looked up, he saw more dark clouds moving in from the west. "Damn, more rain," he said as he looked back down towards the corridor of tents.

He rotated his head from right to left and saw few people milling around within the corridor at the moment. "Good, everybody's busy," he said. Command center was twenty feet in front of the left so he did a one foot pivot towards it and sprinted to the doorway. Once inside the tent, he jerked the phone off the cluttered desk. Tina, who was sitting with her back to the desk watching the monitors, snapped her head around to look at Max. "What's wrong?"

"Nothing," he said sharply as he began to dial. "Team 6, this is Max. Contact code: Kappa-Pi 110."

"Code verified, Max. This is Tina, go ahead."

Max hung his head. When he spoke again, his voice was very hushed. "Tina, is Rob around?"

"No, Rob is out for the moment, but Matt is here."

"Lemme talk to him, please."

Max heard several shuffling noises through the phone, then finally heard, "This is Matt."

"Matt, this is Max over at command center. I need you, Ryan, and Brent, to meet with me."

"Where?"

"Command station. There is a small tent in the rear right as you come in. I'll be waiting for you."

"Be there in a few minutes."

Chapter 45

Roger was following Mike around the inside of the tan brick building they had commandeered. They had exhausted the background of 'Robert George Milgrew' and came up with a handful of nothing to show for it. Ten years ago the man had vanished from the face of the planet and there were no pictures, video's, nothing, from that point on. Teresa had even put a mole virus in the federal and state computers trying to get even a minor hit. All efforts came up with zero.

Why, or maybe how, in the world can anyone stay hidden for ten years? Maybe a better question is why would someone want to be dead and stay that way?

They would have no family, no 'real' friends, and no fun. Having to be always aware, always on-guard, and never really relaxing must be a frightening thing.

Every country has spies that live like this all the time, but at least they could always come home to a place they knew and obviously loved. They figment they were chasing didn't have any place of comfort that they could conceive of.

What kind of man was it that would forego a traditional life with a wife and kids? It was every young persons dream to have a life such as that. What propelled this guy? If they only knew that, then would at least have something to develop a theory.

That was the trouble; they had too many questions and zero answers.

Roger made several fast skips and caught up with Mike

in the hall. His fair-skinned cheek slightly glistened under the bright fluorescent lighing overhead when he turned toward Mike. "You realize since we have exhausted all of our avenues that we are going to have to depend on the police and their eyes on the streets."

Mike cocked his head down toward Roger and said, "Of course I do. I just issued the All-Points-Bulletin. They are to locate and follow only."

"And, I suppose, they are to notify us as soon as possible?"

Mike stopped walking, turned, and put a open, but tilted, hand in front of him. "Yes, why, do you have a problem with that?"

"Perhaps. Think about this. We have an unknown man, with a military background, who has evidently chosen to remain discreetly hidden for a long time, which means that he's smart enough to easily spot a tail."

"Hmmm, I see your point, Roger. I'll tell them to advise caution."

"Better yet, they can use GPS trackers."

"Possibly, if they can spot his vehicle in time to get a fix on him."

Roger squinted his left eye. "If only... We'll just have to hope that we get lucky."

Chapter 46

What a revolting development it had been... Caught off-guard and stepping on what he thought was a land mine... "Shit!" Rob sat in his sedan, hands on the steering wheel, contemplating his mistake. Unable to find anything much at the library other than ex-wives, now, here he was, parked at the courthouse about to go into a place that he knew he had to stay away from. There were cameras, guards, and a hundred pairs of eyes that would see him, but what else could he do? He needed to find this man.

"I have to know; I have to," he said, as he moved his hands and opened the Escort door. "Shit!" One mistake had totally disrupted his orderly life. Now, he had serious doubts about everything in his life. The chain of command and the orders he used to obey without question were being called into serious doubt. 'Just follow those orders, son,' was reverberating in his brain and had been ever since he found that blasted diary.

There was a strong, icy wind that blew through the cracked door as it opened by the push of an arm and clutched hand. Rob shivered. The thin jacket that he was wearing was no match for the permeating cold. Its plastic coating was supposed to block the wind from the body, but if it was working, Rob didn't know it. His flesh was stinging and telling him 'don't move any farther. Get under cover. Get warm.' Every moment that he persisted brought him further removed from his vehicle that had its inside warmed by a heater and wrought shooting pains of cold through more of his body.

When his body was fully outside and standing on the pavement beside his parallel-parked Escort, he grabbed the cold metal exterior of the door and slammed it shut. Rob looked around him and saw that there were several squad cars in the area. There were a couple of people walking in the lot, but not many. He had parked in the center of three aisles directly in front and, even through the cold, his nose could smell the mucky moisture of the Mississippi River three blocks away.

The building itself was a gorgeous limestone color with red brick walkways and gray concrete steps with intermittent black iron hand rails. Stretching his neck, he looked up at the building. It appeared to be seven stories tall with oodles of tinted windows for decorations. "Bureaucrats." Rob shook his head, looked down at the concrete beneath him, and stamped his foot against the pavement. "They just love overkill."

He stepped over the curb and onto the red brick, then went on up to the doorway. In the top center of the inner doorway was a silvery video camera that made Rob's gut ache. "No choice, no choice," he mumbled, shaking his head, then lowering it. Once beyond the doors he looked to his right and he saw engraved, overhead lettering, 'Clerk of Court.' It looked to be overlaid in gold. "Geez..." He walked through the eight-foot wide entranceway and straight up to the chest-high counter. In the back corners of the room, Rob saw two more cameras mounted near the ceiling. "Crap," he mumbled. Although the large room was filled with a dozen or more people being assisted already, he raised his hand to the nearby blonde woman and in his best southernmost dialect, said, "'Scuse me, Ma'am."

The woman turned ever so slightly toward him with unflinching blue eyes, and said, "Over there, sir." She pointed a finger toward a red spooler on the wall to his right that had a bit of paper hanging from its insides.

"Ma'am, I am from the governor's office..." Rob stopped talking because the lady was ignoring him and already talking with another person. Not wanting to cause undue attention to himself, he walked over to the device and tore off the ticket that was hanging out: 137. His eyes widened and he wadded up the reddish paper in his hand. "I don't have time to play friggin' politics." He turned around and went to the counter again.

Back into his southern drawl, although a bit angry, he hollered, "Miss!" He raised his right arm and waved at her. The mature blonde eyed him once again and pointed toward the ticket spooler.

"99?" another lady called out from across the room.

"Miss?" rob shouted. He walked toward the blonde, grabbed an ID from his pocket, and laid it on the counter. He slid the up-facing silvery-gold badge in her direction, bumping into the woman that she had been helping. ""Scuse me, Ma'am?" he said as he walked into the spot where the helped lady had been standing. The woman huffed and ran a hand over the top of her black hair, but took a few steps back nonetheless, stomping the floor as moved.

"Sir, you'll have to wait your turn," the blonde said as she sneered.

"I am a special investor from the governor's office." Rob glanced at hic mock badge then back up at the lady. It was a decent imitation of a generic investigator's badge and had been useful on numerous occasions over the past 20 years. "I am on a mission for the governor herself."

The blonde shook her head slightly with narrowed eyes. "Well," she paused briefly, "I suppose I can make a 'special' exception in your case." Her eyes flared and she shifted her stance. "What can I help you with?"

"Ma'am, I am looking for any kind of public records for a Melvin John Travis living in Baton Rouge."

The woman pressed her lips together and tightened her jaw before asking, "Do you even have an address?"

Rob bent down over the counter and shook his head. Resuming an upright position, he said, "No, Ma'am. Unfortunately, this boy did not give an address. We don't even have a license number on him."

The lady huffed. "Then you understand that this may be difficult." She extended her index finger in a come hither motion. "Come over here." She walked to end of the counter, next to the wall, and started typing on a keyboard there. In a moment, she said, "Other than address and phone, is there anything else you need?"

"Yes Ma'am, marital records, past places of residence, and anything else you can give me." He paused. "We need this information purty quick, Ma'am. We really appreciate ya helpin' like 'is."

The woman looked up slightly, rolled her eyes, and spoke in a low screech. "You're welcome." She filled her lungs and sighed heavily and hummed while she did. "This is going to take a while," she said as the clickety-clack of her typing began.

Rob looked at her scowling face and darting eyes that were reading information on the screen in front of her. "This here info is critical so I can wait for everything."

Chapter 47

Melvin stood in the living room and pulled back the burnt-orange curtain. As he looked out, he could not believe that an entire day had passed and that he was still without a plan. He had little time. The darkness inside and out only served to remind him that his escape from the pursuers, that he still had no clue about, was marginal and the future of everyone depended on him. His death was an almost certainty. He was trying to out maneuver people that nobody ever questions.

Was he trying to save himself or humanity in general? It was his crazy ass that in the nutcracker. As far as 99.9% of the world... SCREW'EM! Margie had shown him another side of people in the fact that she cared about him. He, who cares about no one, but himself....

In her revelation of warmth and caring for him, the world had changed. There was a glimmer of light in his life. Being in the same bed with her last night had given him something that he had selectively eliminated from his life, intimacy.

It felt good though. Warm, smooth, soft, sensitive... It had been a long time since he allowed himself to think such things as he was feeling now. Was he getting soft? The answer to that seemed to be, no, but now he felt as vulnerable as a flower in the wind. Should he give in to the warm feelings for Margie? Could he give up his singular philosophy of life?

To do so would make him good, like every other poor slob. Last night they were in the same bed and hugged each other for warmth. The closeness and warmth of another human body had made the fondness for Margie rekindle. Recent events sent his mind back to a simpler time, the way it was like when they were still dating. They were both about 15 years younger and, in his opinion, more daring and, he chuckled, more foolish. Everyone goes through being young and stupid. It was age and the hurts that one experiences that taught wisdom. Wisdom did not come from books, but actually living life and the hurts that went along with the process.

He supposed that there had been too many hurts in his life. Then again, his heart had always been cold.

There was Margie in the kitchen searching for them both some food. He had told her to go ahead and get stuff out of the refrigerator and freezer as he did not know how much longer they would be trapped. The stove was gas so they could at least cook. Strange? After being totally self-reliant for so many years, it seemed odd for anyone to be doing anything for him. He had always refused help from others because he didn't want to be beholding to any of the low-life's in this world and he didn't want to have to deal with their crap. That's what they were too, was crap, just simply crap.

Crap here, crap there, crap everywhere.... crap, crap, crap... Men crap, women crap, only Margie was different. She has waited 15 long years for him to deal with himself. That deserved recognition.

Melvin felt flush hands press to his back and start rubbing all around. It felt good. He could feel her warmth of her hands through his shirt and jacket.

"Whatcha thinking about?"

He closed the curtain, turned around, and put his hands on her shoulders and her hands went to his waist and began rubbing. "Same thing. What is my next step?"

"You mean "Our" next step?"

He looked down slightly and into her soft brown eyes.

159

"Yes, 'Our' next step."

"Come up with anything?"

"Nope. Frankly, I'm stuck. I can't even attempt to go in without the diagram. I just have to hope that something comes up or that something comes to me. Until then, we can hide out here, hopefully."

"Well, I trust you." Pause. "Come on, dinner's ready." She grabbed his hand and pulled him toward the kitchen.

As Margie stepped up into the kitchen, she said, "Although I went ahead and cooked all the frozen stuff, tonight's menu is rib eye steak, baked potato, and green beans."

Melvin saw the plates already fixed on the table to the right. Besides the plates were silverware, water glasses, and red-white napkins, and a tablecloth underneath that had intermixed red and white squares. There were two chairs pulled out in front of plates on opposite sides of the table and the two other chairs were pushed under. Even in the dimly lit room, Melvin could see the flame reflections of the two lit candles off of the high gloss chairs. To his left was ample counter space, including the island, nearly overflowing with cooked meats and vegetables.

"Excellent! In the January cold, this ought to be good for a few days." He grabbed the back of the closest chair and sat down. Meanwhile, Margie circled around the table and sat in the opposite chair. Melvin picked up a knife and fork.

"I'll say the blessing," Margie said.

Melvin's face turned red and mumbled, "Okay."

With heads down, Margie said, "Dear Father, thank you for the food and thank you for the opportunity to help Melvin thwart such disastrous plans. Amen."

As heads raised, Margie could see two tears on their way down Melvin's cheeks.

Chapter 48

Melvin and Margie finished their meal and talked by the glow of the candlelights. New topics were slim and very depressing. Without a formalized plan, they were stuck. A deer would have a better chance of infiltrating that base than they would so there they sat until some idea with a reasonable chance of succeeding came to them.

Past topics were mostly about them. Reminiscing about how they met, fun times, etc. Melvin was startled to realize that she remembered going to the Kinnilworth Park. They had had a picnic there three weeks before their wedding. They laughed at the kids playing there. Him laughing? Did that really happen? He couldn't believe that he was ever the man that she was describing.

As she talked, Melvin began thinking about the box that Tom had given him. He had hidden it in Margie's house while she was elsewhere in the house. They could not let that box fall into the wrong hands. He knew that he could withstand torture, but what about her? Could he let it happen to her? That would be difficult to do given his new found affinity for her. The situation sucked.

As he looked across the table at Margie, he could not help but to be amazed at her self sufficiency. Here is the image of a woman that had cared for all of her own needs for all these years in addition to buying this land and trailer. She had a job as a secretary for a law firm. What a wonderful and difficult achievement. As he looked at her blonde hair swaying as she talked, he remembered how much he liked it. Being blonde was one of the attractions that started his interest in her, that, her face, and near-perfect figure.

She had taken good care of herself these many years which showed her resilient mind. She would need every bit of that strength if they were caught by their unknown enemy. As he stared at her beautiful face, he could not help but break the conversation to inject some reality. "You know, if we are caught, there could be dire consequences."

She looked at him, set her hands on the table, and leaned forward. "Of course, do you not think I know that?"

Melvin slumped. "Yes, but I wanted to say it outright." He swallowed. "It needed to be said. As we talked, that just kept running through my mind. I don't want anything to happen to you."

Leaning back, she said, "I can appreciate that and I don't want anything to happen to you either. Here," she said as she slowly got up from her chair and walked around the table and stood behind him, "let me try to relax you." She placed her hands on his shoulders and started kneading his shoulders through the jacket.

Melvin hung his head as she rubbed and swung from side to side in small motions. Uncontrollably, he started moaning ever so slightly. His achy body was still recuperating from his nights with Tom. The pains were almost healed, but not quite, and the question of how long he would need to fully recover was uncertain. All he knew was that her hands felt good. Emotionally, he knew that it might take forever to get over this, if they managed to live past this ordeal that is.

The more she rubbed his shoulders and neck area, the warmer he got. He could feel the warmth in his shoulders first. Her boobs were near his back. The swaying motions made them gently caress him. The warmth felt so good. Then he felt the bottoms of his feet tingle. It was the first time in days that he could even feel them. The tingling slowly trailed up from his feet to his legs, they were actually warming. Her hands were stimulating the circulation of warm blood.

Her kneading hands felt so good. The warmth in them was being delivered to his entire body. His eyes popped open when he felt the warmth reach his crotch. Willie was heating up for action.

No, this can't be happening! All of the sudden, his gut began to tremble and his heart began to pump hard and more rapidy. His face became warmer. Willie was awake!

Did he really want this? He couldn't deny that his body obviously wanted a rekindling of the fire that was once between them. The driving desire that he felt was stronger and more powerful, more passionate, than he had ever experienced before. The lust he felt was infiltrating every cell of his body. He could not control the flame that had been lit within him. His heart burned at the very center, wanting, needing to satisfy her. The flame ignited his mind and was forcing him to act. He needed her; he wanted her. He wanted her body, mind, and most of all her heart. He had to act. He had to.

He lifted his right hand from his lap, grabbed her left hand, then brought her around in front of him, ducking his head in the process. He backed away from the table and pulled her torso into his lap, cradling her shoulders in his right arm.

Before he could do anything else, she said softly, "Are you sure?"

He cradled her knees with his left arm, stood with her in his arms, then looked deeply into her eyes. Putting his face near hers, he said, "I have never wanted anything more." He pursed his lips and kissed her.

Chapter 49

Matt, Ryan, and Brent arrived at command center from Team 6 headquarters soon after Max called for them. He had given them very generic instructions because he did not want any talking going on before he had a chance to talk to them privately. He led them to an isolated rear tent and told them the pertinent details. The meeting was short, but they all agreed to search the other team sites first. Max would search her tent in hopes of finding some kind of clue as to her whereabouts.

As the four exited the tent, Max looked over his shoulder toward the rear of Nancy's tent. "Dang!" Her car was still there. He had hoped that she was dumb enough to take it because all the cars had trackers. What a shame. It would've made things so much simpler.

When he walked to the front of her tent, he grabbed the zipper, and pulled it up. Max spread the netting with his hands and stepped inside. The white sheet and gray wool blanket was laying over the foot of the bed and various clothing was scattered on the ground, on her rumpled white pillow case, and laying on her purse. He walked over to the purse lying on the near side of the bed and grabbed it with both hands. Picking it up, he searched through it with his left hand holding one edge steady and taking everything out with his right. Inside was miscellaneous stuff such as a hair brush, lipstick, tissues, pens, wallet, and some loose change.

"Women," he muttered as he dropped the purse back

onto the bed. Using both hands, he took everything out of the wallet, but did not find anything worthwhile, so he turned to the night stand. He opened the top drawer and tried to remove it from the stand, but found that its rollers stopped abruptly. Ka-thunk! He looked inside the drawer and saw that it was latched at the rear and would not come out. Max did not want to take the time to figure the latch out and began sifting through the drawer with his hand. He did not see much, pens, string, more tissue. Underneath the drawer was a cabinet, but when Max opened it, there was nothing in it. The drawer was still out, so he looked behind it, nothing. He leaned up and over to look behind the cabinet, nothing.

He bent to his knees and looked underneath the bed and saw a polyester black bag. With his right hand, he reached underneath and grabbed its two black strap handles. Quickly he pulled it toward him and then set it up on the bed. Max pulled the zipper and the compartment within he found panties, socks, more tissue, power cords, a capped blade razor, and several other things, which he threw onto the bed. With the bag nearly empty, he turned it upside down over the bed and several small items spilled out, a few items bounced to the ground. "Too heavy." Turning the bag inside out, he noticed a velcro seal that was made into the bottom along the edges so he gripped it with his right hand while holding the edge with his left and ripped the flap loose.

"Aha!" There was the object of his search, a phone. It was black and had a security keypad built on top. He reached into the compartment and grabbed the phone and threw the bag on the bed. "Petry will want to see this." He quickly exited the tent then turned around and pulled the zipper down.

Max walked around the encampment for over an hour looking for Petry. His black sedan was gone and the people that he talked had not seen him for hours. He had all but given up when he saw a black sedan drive up beside him at the edge of the corridor.

The passenger window rolled down and Petry called out to Max from the driver's seat. "Why the long face?"

Max walked up to the driver door and peered into the open window. "I've been looking everywhere for you."

"Well, now you've found me or, rather, I found you. Step in and let's talk."

Max walked around to the passenger's door, opened it, stepped in, and seated himself.

Petry leaned toward Max taking his right hand from the steering wheel and placing it flush against the seat. "Okay, what's happened while I was away?"

"Well, in the process of trying to find Nancy, I thought about it, and she must have been communicating with them through an unknown phone, correct?"

"Correct, because all other phones are monitored."

"Well, I searched her quarters and found this," Max said as he held up the phone in his hands. He began twirling it to show all sides. "There is a security code panel on top, but no dialing pad so it must be have a preset dialing number."

Petry reached out to take the phone, saying, "Good work, Max. We'll have figure out the unlock code." As he gripped the hard shell and turned it, he looked at the top and said, "This is a 20-button keypad, 8-digit display. We'll have to find Nancy; it's unlikely that we'll be able to figure this out on our own."

"You're right." Pause. "By the way, where did you go?

Petry paused. "I just tapped some resources that I know trying to find Nancy."

"Any luck?"

"Not a bit."

Chapter 50

Eric was walking out of his headquarters when he thought he heard whispering coming from his left. He turned and walked behind his tent and had his arm jerked by a soft feminine hand.

"Come on?" said Nancy as she pulled him into an open car door. She scooted herself to the far side while pulling him.

"Okay, okay, you don't have to pull so hard." Eric crawled in the car and sat down. He grabbed the handle on the door and pulled it shut. He looked at her eyes and saw pinpoints. "What's up?"

She paused while she swallowed. "Eric, I need your help. I need to monitor this investigation, but my association with the organization has been ended and not by my choice either."

Eric raised his hands and shook them, saying, "What in the hell are you talking about, Nancy?"

She took his left hand into her right. "My friend, I am trying to save my family's lives and others too"

"How? Why? What's going on?"

She rubbed his hand in hers. "I can't tell you anything more."

Eric shook his head. "Then I'm afraid I can't help."

Nancy's hand trembled while she rubbed. "Eric, I am undercover and was assigned to Earth Incorporated to investigate what they were up to. I've been undercover for a long time." Her eyes looked down at their clasped hands. "Now, my cover's been blown." She looked up into his eyes again. "We've been friends ever since you I got you into the Army and I have to depend on you."

"This's all very weird. What in the heck were you investigating?"

"The legitimacy of the organization and the ethical and security aspects of the research. I found problems in all three areas. I've been waiting to seize the stuff that Tom Soren took off with to stall their efforts. It was only then that I was to file my full report."

"What is the research anyway?"

"It deals with time reversion. It gets complicated, but they have a way, for example, to make you a younger man without taking you back in time."

"Wow. A fountain of youth."

"Sort of, yes, but they could even wipe out your existence altogether. There are just too many problems associated with the process though. For instance, what happens to the uncounted actions that you've done in your lifetime? I need to get the equipment that Tom stole and get it to my superiors. I need to stop them."

Eric looked at her from feet to head. His eyes narrowed, then went back to normal as he moved his hand free from hers and rubbed his chin. "Why should I stick my neck out along with you?"

"That's easy. Because your life, your family, along with everyone else you know and love are at stake."

"How?"

"Think about it, Eric." She put one perpendicular hand on top of the other. "How many things would change in the world if something wiped twenty or thirty years out of your life? You might not even have kids or be married."

After a long pause, he said, "Alright. I'll help." He paused once more to swallow. "But... if this is some trick..."

She grabbed his hand again. "It's not. Remember when I asked about if you could change the world for the better?"

Eric pulled his hand loose and nodded. "We still are in

limbo because we are not sure who the second man was."

"That's too bad."

"Yeah." Eric's eyebrow's raised suddenly and his eyes grew wide. "Hey! Why don't you hide out in my tent?"

Nancy leaned back a bit and raised flush hands. "I don't think so."

"Sure, it'd be great. Nobody ever comes to my tent except me and I can bring you the details as soon as they happen."

"She shrugged. I'd be in the middle of the very people that I am trying to avoid."

Eric raised both hands in front of him and his torso bobbed. "That's the ticket. They'll never think to look for you in the most obvious of places."

"That's true."

"Better still, I can give you some sheets to hide yourself."

Nancy put down her hands and closed her eyes a moment. With an open mouth she exhaled, her eyes half opened. "Okay, I will stay in your tent." After a pause, she stressed, "Temporarily."

"Good," Eric said. "I think you'll be very comfortable in there." He clutched the car door handle and with a click, unsealed the lock. "When I open this door and make sure no one is around, climb out and quickly crawl through the back tent panel."

Sliding toward him, she said, "Okay."

Eric turned to face the door, opened it halfway, then all the way. He looked back at Nancy while lifting himself up and out of the door, saying, "Okay. Quick!"

Eric moved to the opposite side of the car door and waited on Nancy. She scooted over quickly and got out of the car and did a quick sprint to the backside of the forest-green tent where there was an oval zipper seam. There was a kaplunk sound as Eric closed the car door as she pulled at both zippers that were at the top center of the entranceway. The zipper pulls had the high pitch sound of a mosquito. Several beads of sweat appeared above Nancy's brow and she lifted her right hand and wiped her forehead as she ducked and entered the tent.

Nancy went inside about three feet and then kneeled down while Eric turned around and re-zipped the opening. He turned and grabbed at the thin, black, metal stand to his left on which some gray blankets hung, saying, "Now, let's get you comfortable."

Chapter 51

The fan and fixture in the middle of the ceiling was still and dark, but the morning sun was beginning to illuminate the green-curtained window on the East side of the trailer. Melvin and Margie were not bothered by the near darkness or morning chill of a house without electricity because they were basking in the heat of each others arms. They were closely layered in each other's arms with the cover of a sheet, blanket, and a comforter sealing them in.

After the pleasure of their love being aroused and, once again, cemented into their relationship, they had both spent the rest of the night bathing in one another's skin. She nestled her head close to his chest while his chin was atop her head holding her near. She moved her head back, then up, so that her arms around each side of his neck tightened a bit. "We may be dead tomorrow, but for now, I'm happy," she said in the midst of a sigh.

Melvin looked at Margie's prone body alongside his and remembered how much he missed closeness. Intimate closeness is a thing that he had not allowed himself, but, now, life was different. He needed her help. He needed someone to help him. Tom had come and gone like the flash of a camera. While he was there, Melvin felt better, purposeful, and, now, Margie was here to help him.

How can life get so twisted around? He had it all figured out. He was happy to be himself. He was happy with himself, only himself, and, at the time, he was all that mattered in this whole universe. That was all moot now. Kaput! Finito! In his desperate attempt to find answers and a way of resolving this mess, he had dragged Margie into this. It was an act of desperation.

For the first time since he was a youngster, he didn't know what to do. Her being here, being in the room, comforted him. Desperation could drive a person to so many acts, both good and bad, some downright despicable. Which side was he on? As he pondered the question, he reveled in the feel of her body. Was he just feeling the security of being beside an independent, stable woman?

"I'm happy too," he said as he looked into her eyes. Thank God she didn't use the 'L' word. He didn't think he could say that, at least not yet. For him, it was sufficient that she was filling a need and a void in his life. Yet, he could not deny that there was a stirring in his heart. Those heart tugs were why he bedded her.

He, many times had he heard that matters of the heart were the most complex of all. Complex? What did that really mean? He was just a stone-cold bastard, nothing more. Was he just using her? Did he 'really' feel something for her? Bedding her felt good, but was that just sex? Was he feeling desire for her or desire to fulfill his need for help.

It was the first time he had had sex with anything other than his fist since the time that they were married. Females... Humph! They were like all other human beings - flawed, imperfect, and hard to deal with. Women might be worse than men because they were typically more emotional than men. Yuck! If they, and others, would just use their logical brains for something other than door stops then the world would be better off.

He looked into her brown eyes and studied them. He wondered if he was looking for flaws in her character, but the only vision he saw was soft eyes and a pleasant smile that signified enjoyment and affection.

"What are you looking at?" asked Margie softly.

Melvin shook his head against the pillow, making a light brushing noise. "I dunno, something pretty, that's for sure."

172

His one upright ear distinctly heard her verbalize an 'Awww,' in appreciation. His gut tightened as her arms tightened around him.

"Whatever we need to do, we'll do it together."

There it was. Reality! "I have no idea what we're going to have to do. I've thought about it a lot recently. The only thing I do know is that the longer we stay here, the more likely we are that someone will find us."

She squeezed her arms. "That's likely to be true, but if we go out, we have a greater risk of being seen."

Melvin could feel his chest tightening. His muscles were waking up to the notion that they were still in big trouble. "That's true, but somebody, somewhere, is going to figure out who I am and where I went."

Her arms loosened far enough for her to pull back and look into his eyes. "Yes, but do we have to rush out just yet?"

"No, I think we're safe here for today."

Her eyes looked down. "Good," she said with fervor. Her arms tightened again and her head moved in to lay on his neck.

Chapter 52

Melvin and Margie laid in each others arms and under the warm covers of the bed until the brightest spot behind the curtain was far above the top of the opening. Melvin had guessed the time to be Eleven O'clock, but when he rolled over and looked at his trusty Timex, it was closer to noon. After they were up and dressed, he asked Margie if she had a gun in the house. He knew better though. Margie had always hated guns. Oh well, it was worth a shot. She hated guns, but eventually they were probably going to have to use them if they had any chance of straightening out this mess.

"I need to check on things," he told her.

She slowly pulled her arms away from his body and said, "Okay, Bean. I'll be waiting right here."

He scooted backwards and rounded the corner of the mattress with his feet and legs. The cold in the room stung his bare flesh, but he continued by pulling the covers back and sitting up on the side of the bed. He saw his rumpled clothing that was tossed on the floor from the night before and put them back on. They were cool, but he knew his body heat would warm them up in a jiffy. He turned, leaned, and patted the covers back down around Margie.

"Don't shoot. I'm unarmed," came a shout from outside the front door.

Melvin, who was walking from the bedroom to the living room abruptly stopped. He looked back at Margie and whispered, "Don't make a sound."

"Please! I'm alone." Pause. "I only want to talk to you." Longer pause. "Please! I need to talk to Melvin John Travis." Pause. "I am not here to catch you or take you in. I only want to talk."

Margie had quietly walked up behind Melvin. He looked back at her and whispered, "Don't make a sound." Her face was pale and he knew that the risk was great. He had spent the last few days of his life running from the unknown and, now, here it was at the door, begging to come in. 'Just talk,' maybe, but more likely, 'eradicate.'

If they were here to kill them, then they would have the house surrounded with no way of escaping. If it was,'just talk,' where was the harm? The two options weighed in his mind on an invisible scale. If the masculine voice was or wasn't telling the truth and he didn't answer, what then? Would they watch the house or even come back with other people to help.

His stomach was queasy and his guts wreaked of the sloshy, groaning, pains of diarrhea. As he was walking softly toward the front door, the voice worked upon his mind. 'Please, I need to talk, only to talk.' The silence after every statement grated on Melvin's nerves. 'Let me help you,' was the famous campaign slogan of Governor Jimmie Davis of Louisiana. Actually it was, 'Won't you he'p me,' but it was ringing in Melvin's ears nevertheless and help was what they needed right now. Was it a coincidence? Could be, but he was lost in the doldrums right now.

He reached out and put his hand on the cold silver doorknob. "Let this turn good," he whispered as he turned the knob slowly. The sound of the latch being set free was loud in the quiet house, but no one put force on the door to Melvin's surprise. He slowly opened the door and stepped into the crease, peered out, and saw a man that stood about six feet tall with mildly graying hair, receding hairline, wrapped in army green clothing. His Escort was parked beside the Plymouth Neon, but there was nothing and no one else that Melvin could see as he leaned out the door and looked around.

Melvin opened the door wide while he backed up. "Come in."

"Thank you," said the man.

Once he was inside, Melvin quickly gave the door a big shove and once he heard the click, he put his fingers to the lock and twisted. As he turned around, he braced himself against the door, but, for the moment, he had no choice but to follow through with whatever the heck this guy wanted, up to a point. For all he knew the place could be surrounded any moment. "What do you want?"

"My name is Rob Milgrew. I found your diary and I am here to tell you that I'm on your side. They're lying to everyone about who you are. I read in your book and after checking some things out, I believe that what you wrote is the truth. This technology needs to be destroyed." There was a long pause. "Did you hear me? I am on your side."

Melvin could feel the air brushing his eyeballs. He had expected many things, but never this. "Of course it's the truth!!! Would I lie to myself?!?"

Rob held up flush hands. "I didn't mean to offend, but as crazy as what you wrote sounds... I had to check some things out, you know."

Melvin stood in silence.

Rob clasped his hands together. "No tricks! I just want to help you! This has got to be stopped!"

Melvin looked at the man's face studying every line and wrinkle. He was youthful looking despite the gray hairs. The only thing in his face that showed his increased years were the wrinkles around his eyes. His skin, loose, but defined, had a spongy look. On a kid, they would call it baby fat, but on an adult, it was just called flab. The green eyes had intensity, but whether the motives behind them were for good or bad, Melvin had no idea. He started to say something, but Nancy came up and whispered in his ear.

"Melvin, I think we should trust him."

He inhaled deeply and sighed. Looking at Rob, he said, "Well, thank you. First, you can call my book anything you want, but it is not a friggin' diary! It's a journal! And if you've read it, you know the whole story."

"Don't be alarmed." Rob reached around behind him, lifted his shirt, grabbed the book, and brought it forward, re-tucking his shirt in the process. He extended the book toward Melvin, saying, "Here's your book back, although, I don't think the security diagrams on the back will do you much good."

"Why not?"

"Well, after Tom Soren escaped, they changed every security procedure. For instance, the elevators have key cards now."

"How do you know?"

Rob put his hands on his hips. "Because, as one of their top security people, I am in and out of that place often for briefings, etc."

"You might be useful at that. And just what the hell are they saying about me?"

"Everyone is being told that you are a terrorist and want to detonate a nuclear bomb. One thing I don't get though. Who was Tom Soren anyway?"

Melvin sighed and lowered his head for a moment. "Tom Soren is a good man that never really got to live life. He was recruited before graduating from high school by some organization, I don't know who."

"Earth Incorporated."

"Okay, he was recruited by them and was kept as a veritable prisoner all his life." Pause. Melvin raised his head high. "Wait a minute! You said 'was'."

"Yes. Tom is dead."

Melvin dropped to his knees and hung his head.

Chapter 53

With tears running down his cheeks, Melvin said, "Dead! Damn it! I was so very much hoping that he was okay." Pause. "Deep inside I knew though."

Rob stepped forward and started to reach out his right hand, but withdrew his arm quickly to his side. "I'm sorry. I didn't mean to bring bad news."

Melvin saw Rob try to extend a hand, but ignored the action. He wiped his face with the tops of both hands. After sniffing several times, he said, "It's okay." He had already resigned himself to never seeing Tom again. He supposed that a death announcement was always a shock, no matter how prepared you were. Poor Tom never really lived.

Losing a friend to death was heartbreaking. Losing your ONLY friend to death was disastrous. As he knelt there in front of Rob and Margie, Melvin felt naked, bare. Humanity had been stripped away. He felt like an empty shell. Everyone looks to a friend, a God, or someone else to look up to, measure themselves by, or get help from. He had always looked up to Tom. Even though Tom hadn't been around since high school, he had always talked to him. The people that Tom worked for were responsible for his death. They were the ones who enlisted him. They were the ones who took him away. His death was on their hands. If they had not been delving into this crap, none of this would ever have to happen. Grrrr!

Those bastards were trying to play gods at everyone

else's expense. Everyone's life is a mess, that's a fact of life, but at least it was their mess and a result of their own choices. They didn't need some wacked out nut jobs revamping 'their' world at 'their' will. How dare they?! To hell with their sorry asses! It was time that they got screwed instead of screwing with everyone else.

Tom was killed by them. First, they killed his future, then they killed his dreams, and finally they killed him with pressure. He was a good man. He was living life his way until they whisked him away.

The bastards that ruined his life must pay! They must!

Melvin raised his knee, put his foot to the floor, and stood up quickly. With his right hand curled into a tight fist, he threw an uppercut into the air. "Fuck'em all!"

Rob backed up and raised a flush hand. "What?!?"

"To hell with everyone that's leading this crazy scheme. They are screwing with everyone's lives: me, you," Melvin turned to point at Margie behind him, "her, everyone. I just want to kill'em all right now." He swung a fist into the air. "We're going to make them pay for Tom and everyone else!" He motioned toward Margie with pulling fingers of one hand. She walked forward to his side and wrapped an arm around his waist. "By the way, this is Margie."

"Yes. I know. She is the only person that my research had you connected to. She's how I found you. When I arrived and saw that her car was here, but the lights were off, I knew you were here."

Melvin thought a moment and cocked his head. Snapping his fingers, he said, "You read where I wrote about Tom telling me about the electronics, didn't you?"

"Yeah."

"I'm glad it's you, not the others."

Rob nodded. "Me too." Pause. "When I began searching, they had no idea who it was that was with Tom, but that ain't gonna last too much longer."

Melvin looked down momentarily and then stared into Rob's eyes. "Yeah, we know. We figured on leaving here tomorrow."

"Well, since I found you, trust me, they won't be long after me. We'd better make plans quick."

"And just what is your experience with these things? How do you know what they'll do?"

Rob lifted his hands in front of him and opened them both. When he spoke again, the hands bounced in front of him. "Well, my background is military, but more than that, I am one of the leaders in the search to find you. I have about 20 years of experience in these types of searches and they seldom go well for the searchee's." He paused. "Of course, I had an advantage in finding you. I had your di... Err, journal."

Melvin considered the statement for a moment while nodding. Rob, if that was really his name, could be leading them into a trap, just telling them what they wanted to hear. Sure, he and Margie needed answers and this guy seemed to have them. It was a perfect fit, too perfect. That was the trouble.

If they followed this guy's lead, they could walk right into a trap. For all they knew, this guy had a homer on him, in which case, they were done for anyway. He didn't want to die. Save thyself, sayeth the wise man. He couldn't let this guy lead them, regardless.

Melvin raised his right hand in front of him. With a bent elbow and an open hand at shoulder height, he said, "Okay, Rob, we'll listen to your advice, but remember, what I say is what we do."

Rob lowered his hands to his sides. "Okay, Melvin, you run the show. I'm just here to help."

Chapter 54

Max walked into command center and saw Petry sitting behind the desk holding the encrypted phone with both hands. There were two people, both female, watching the monitors over on the right. On the left, there were three people, two males and one female, with headphones on. A few people were holding tablets in their hands. Most of the noise in the room came from the walls of the tent being beaten by the January wind outside. There was the salty, moist, nauseating odor of heavy perspiration in the room that made Max move a hand up to his nose and rub. Petry's eyes were darting over the keypad of the phone and his hands were turning the phone. Once in a while, Petry would tilt his head at different angles.

Max walked up to the desk holding a tablet in his right hand by his side. When he was at the edge, he said, "Petry, sir."

Petry hesitated, then looked up from the keypad on the phone. "Yes, Max."

"We finally have a lead, Petry," Max said as he raised the tablet and laid it atop the desk. It was more facing Petry, but Max could see it legibly as well and extended his index finger to the screen. "Watch this?" The tablet screen pictured a doorway with signs. The upper part of the door was made of clear glass, but decals and paint were stuck on the outside. Beyond, an arm could be seen reaching toward the door. After a moment the door opened and a man walked in the door. In the background another man could be seen jumping into a small car. Max touched the screen again and the image of the car froze. He slid his finger to the left slightly to the point where the man was getting into the car and pointed to the man in the background. "This is from a video camera inside Robert's Grocery. The time index on these is the exact day and time that our guy escaped."

Petry raised his head along with one eyebrow. "Have you done facial recognition?"

"Not yet. The guys at the base are working on it. The CCD cameras that most of these little shops use are not the best."

"Good work, Max." Petry took one hand off the phone and pointed it around the room, pausing as he did. "It's a pity we couldn't do all of this video and audio monitoring back at the base."

Max shook his head. "Yeah, it would've been nice, but, unfortunately, all this wireless tapping equipment has a limited range."

"Well, with any luck we'll have a positive I.D. on this guy soon."

"Let's hope so."

Petry put his hand back on the phone, scooted his chair backward with a nudge of his butt, and raised up from the chair. "Max, follow me."

"Aye, aye, sir."

Petry began walking toward the tent opening. When he passed Max, Max grabbed the tablet from the desk and started walking behind him. When he was outside the tent, the wind started fluttering the sleeves of his jacket. He shivered, then quickly interlaced his arms.

They walked the short distance to Petry's tent and went inside. Petry sat down in the rear chair at the desk and braced his forearms on the sides while holding the phone.

Max stared him a moment before he said, "You seem fascinated by that phone."

Petry looked up. His eyes were wider than normal and bright. During a brief pause he blinked several times, then finally answered. "Not fascinated, intrigued." He took his right hand away from the phone and pointed his index finger toward it. "Max, aren't there ways of detecting which of these keys have been pressed repeatedly?"

"Why yes, human skin secretes a light acid. That would breakdown the surface of buttons and the molding around them after repeated use. Also, the buttons that are pushed more are the ones more likely to be scratched. A couple of other things... but that's an 8-digit display! Even if we could figure out which buttons, getting them in the right order before tripping the fail safe would be a miracle."

"Fail safe? You mean like security..."

"Exactly. It can be set for any number of tries and once you go past that, it becomes a paperweight. It sends a destroy code to everything, chips, circuits, you name it."

"No way of getting around it?"

"If there is, I don't know it."

"Hmm...," Petry put his right hand to his chin and rubbed with his thumb and index finger. After a long pause, he said, "I think it's enough that I just know the correct keys." He took his hand away from his chin and picked up the phone and extended his arm toward Max. "How long?"

"Including travel time to and from the lab... maybe 12 hours," said Max as he took the phone.

"Set a speed record."

Max snapped his free hand up to his forehead and saluted. "Yes, sir."

Chapter 55

Although there were very few sprinkles that had come with the wind, Eric could still smell moisture in the air as he drove up to the encampment in his white jeep. There were numerous people circulating about at the far end where command center was, but very few on his end.

The Jeep slowly came to halt as Eric mashed gently on the brake petal. Afterward, he maneuver of the gearshift knob into Park. Pulling the door handle, he pushed the door open, and stepped out. Splash! His left foot came down in the top edge of a mud hole.

"Crap!" He looked down and saw his foot in water and quickly picked it up and moved it over to the dirt, gravel mixture several inches farther out. Seeing how wide the water was, he pulled his wet shoe back to doorway's edge, then spun around, and catapulted himself over the waterhole.

With a stretch of his arm, he grabbed the door, gave it a shove, and started walking down the corridor. There were eleven tents in all: five on each side and the command center tent at the end. The corridor itself was ten feet wide made up of grass and dirt with mud holes scattered about so that if he were not careful about where he stepped, he would end up getting his Dockers wet again.

An average looking blonde man was coming toward him. "Excuse me. Do you know where Petry is?" asked Eric with a raised hand.

The blonde paused and put a hand to his head. "I think

the last time I saw him, he was in his tent talking to Max." He pointed a finger. "Last tent on your left."

"Thanks," Eric said, putting his hand back at his side. The guy walked away after saluting. Eric walked forward until he reached Petry's green tent. It was unzipped, but not open and Eric could hear voices within. "Knock, knock. Petry, sir, are you in there?"

"Come on in," a voice said.

Eric parted the opening and pushed through the netting. Inside, Petry and Max were both sitting in chairs. There was a tablet on the desk that was lit up. Both men were still.

"How are you two?" Eric asked.

A chorus of, "Okay," came from both men.

Petry waved an arm. "It's nice to see you, Eric, but what are you doing in this area?"

Eric looked down and cleared his throat.

Petry turned toward Max and said, "Max, would you give us a minute."

Max grabbed the tablet off of the desk with his right hand and stood up. The chair behind him tipped back a little and he grabbed it with his other hand and set it upright. "Certainly, I need to check in with command center anyway.'

When he exited, Petry motioned his hand to the vacated chair and Eric walked to it and lowered himself into a rigid sitting position.

"What's up, my friend?"

Eric lowered his head for a moment, but remained silent.

"Take your time. I'm here for you?"

He raised his head and looked Petry in the eye. "I... I don't know quite where to start."

"Anywhere? Usually the beginning works best."

Eric nodded, but paused. Slowly, he asked, "Well, first let me ask you if there's any information about this operation that I don't know about?"

With a turn and tilt of his head, Petry said, "Certainly not! We are assisting other government agencies in an attempt to stop a nuclear threat. Earth Inc., as you know, is a covert military operation and since the bastards we are pursuing stole the nuclear know-how from our end, we are helping in the search." He laid his hand on the table. "The bastard was one of our own! I trusted him! Now it's my fault."

Eric slumped. He inhaled deeply through his nose, then exhaled through his mouth. "Well, sir, I was recently told a crazy story that Earth Inc. was being investigated by the FBI for dabbling into reverse time technology"

"WHAT?!? That's totally ludicrous! Where did you hear this?!?"

Eric's eyes blinked several times. "From Nancy."

Petry hesitated a brief moment. "That traitor! We knew that Tom had an accomplice, but I would've never suspected my second in command. Damn! Damn! Damn!" Pause. With a jerk of his head, he asked, "How long ago did you talk to her? Do you know where she went?"

"DAMN IT! I knew it sounded too wild!" He hung his head and shook it vigorously several times. When he looked up, he said, "Geez! She almost had me convinced too. I was hoping and praying...

Petry leaned forward. "About what, old friend?"

"Well, part of me wanted to help her, the other part was praying that she was wrong."

Petry leaned back again and threw his hand softly to the desk where it made a shallow, boomp. "Do you know where she went, Eric?"

Eric's eyes narrowed. "I want nothing to do with a traitor." He paused. "I talked to her no more than an hour ago and I know exactly where she went."

"WHERE?"

"My tent!"

Chapter 56

Rob was there 'to help', or so he said. Melvin considered the statement as he stared at Rob's green eyes. Over the years, he had become a connoisseur of people and how to make judgments about them. People could generally act how they wanted to be believed and they generally succeeded, but the eyes were the windows to the soul. He had tried to put it down in words what makes soft eyes or hard eyes, but had never quite been able to describe it.

The best that he had ever done was to show the positions of eyebrows, eye socket shape, and pupil size, but actually writing down hard eyes or soft eyes still seemed the best way of describing them. Over the years, he had become pretty adept at judging people by their eyes. Green eyes, however, had always given him trouble. He could read all other colors with amazing accuracy, sometimes even being able to predict the how, when, where, of their actions.

With green eyes though, he was often wrong. Now, he was being put to a life test. As he stared at Rob's green eyes, he saw purpose, caring, and focus. His eyes were not soft or hard, but simply resolute. The pupils were not large or small and there were significant facial positions. Those green eyes showed nothing to make a determination so he would have to listen to his gut.

What a revolting development that was. Empirical evidence was always best, the provable, factual stuff. Hunches could be disastrous. Ordinarily, he would call his police buddies, but that would be highly ill advised. They were looking for him and would alert others as well. It seemed as though it was a hunch or nothing so he put his right forearm where his guts would be and looked down at the shag carpet.

The red and black fibers indicated danger and trouble. He already knew that, no help there. He wanted to believe in Rob. They needed for there to be help somewhere, someone to trust, something to provide direction. He rubbed around his gut, which was slightly upset. C'mon, man! Tell me something...!

Melvin took his arm off his stomach and looked up at Rob. "I guess we're a go then. Tom and I had decided to go into the base and steal the rest of the research and destroy everything."

"That's what I figured from what you wrote and, I agree, we must destroy every bit of this technology. It is far too dangerous."

Melvin opened his stance, and let out a gush of breath. Immediately after doing so, all three heads in the room abruptly turned toward the front door. Knock, knock, knock.

"Robert Milgrew," a male voice called out, "This is the FBI. We know you're in there. We want to talk to you."

Melvin's head spun toward Rob with glaring eyes. "You were followed," he whispered sharply.

Rob lifted his hands in front of him and shrugged with eyes so wide that they looked nearly white. "I had no idea."

Melvin's face was red from anger at himself. He had led Margie into doom. If they were watching Rob as he entered, they knew that he had opened the door. Damn it! He couldn't hide. He looked down at Margie at his side. With wide eyes pulled by lifted eyebrows and an open mouth, she looked at him. He was supposed to be the one with answers. The only thing that he knew was that he could at least protect her.

He waved his hand toward the open bedroom door. "You go in there and hide. Keep quiet," he whispered.

She closed her mouth, then started scooting backwards toward the bedroom door. Melvin waited until she was behind the threshold, then waved his arm and whispered, "Close the door."

He saw Rob take a few careful and slow footsteps toward the door. Melvin felt like a sinister thief that was about to get caught and be thrown in jail. Perhaps jail wouldn't be such a bad idea right now. At least they would be protected to some degree. Then again, if this was the FBI, what did they want with Rob? Was it Robert or Rob as he introduced himself as?

With the magnitude of what he knew, even a federal prison would not be a comfort for long. Or, as his dad had told him, you can hope for the best, but you have to plan for the worst. They would find him wherever he was and hook him on drugs, torture, or whatever they had to do to get the missing piece of a controlling empire. Powerful people wanted more power. It was an addictive drug and they would stomp on anyone to get it. Human nature was so very predictable.

Regardless, dying today was definitely not in his plans, but if it happened that way, he could at least say that he lived life on his own terms.

When Rob reached the door, he looked back at Melvin, who nodded, then put his hand to the lock and turned. He grabbed the doorknob, turned, and pulled the door open three inches.

Putting part of his head into the sunlight that shone through the crack, Rob saw two men. One was tall and dark headed with a meat grinder face, the other, shorter, with a graying fringe of hair. "I'm Rob Milgrew, can I help you gentleman?"

The taller man said, "I'm Mike Curry and this is Roger Christian. We're here in connection with an ongoing investigation. We would just like to come in and ask you a few questions."

"In what regard?"

"May we discuss it inside?"

Rob backed up pulling the door as he did. "Come on in."

Frightfully, Melvin watched as the door opened and the

two men stepped in. His insides were quivering again. Letting the FBI, or anyone else in here, was the last thing he had wanted, but, if they were denied entry, that could add complications to an already difficult situation, not the least of which was arrest for obstruction of justice.

Mike and Roger both opened their coats and took out the leather I.D. wallets and opened them. "We should have shown these outside the door, but this is an unusual situation all the way around," Mike said.

"That's okay," Rob said eyeing the badges as he put his back to the door and closed it with a stretch of the arm.

Roger motioned his arm toward Melvin and said, "That's the man we're supposed to be on the lookout for, Mike."

Mike took his eyes away from Rob and saw Melvin to his left. "Yes, it is."

Oh crap! Here we go. Melvin stepped forward from the far corner. "Probably so, but, I'm telling ya, it's all a big mistake."

Roger pulled the Glock pistol from his waist looked at Melvin and said, "Sir, we have nothing against you, but don't move."

Mike put his hand on top of Roger's gun and pushed it down. "Roger, let's not rush things along. The bulletin on him that we got didn't say much of anything."

"Thank you," Melvin said.

"What 'is' going on here?" Mike asked, still looking at Melvin. He turned to look at Rob. "Robert, according to military files, you died in a plane crash almost 20 years ago and, then, within two days, you've been caught on video in two separate places... and then we catch you with someone that the military is trying to catch..." Mike lifted his left hand, palm up, shrugged, and said, "I don't understand. Explain."

Rob looked at Melvin, shrugged, and asked, "Do we dare?"

Chapter 57

Dares are mostly meant for school-age kids, but adults have to learn when to be daring and when not to be. There are lots of dares that you deal with as you grow up: steal, lie, skinny dip, run through the graveyard, and much more. The lessons you learn from these things were about calculating risks. Any dare had a risk associated to it.

"Dare?" Melvin asked as he looked at Rob. "They wouldn't believe it. Hell! I wouldn't believe it!" He pointed a hand at his chest.

Mike looked at Melvin, tilted his head, and threw his hands up in front of him. "Believe what?!?"

Rob looked at Mike, over at Roger, then back at Melvin. "It's entirely your show, pal. What do we do?"

Melvin looked down and shook his head. "You just wouldn't believe it." You just wouldn't." He slowly picked his head up and looked at Mike.

"I don't know about that. Try me?" Mike said.

"If you weren't in on the research or saw what I saw from Tom," Melvin paused, "then you'll think I'm crazy."

"Well, we'll see won't we," said Mike as he looked between Melvin and Roger."

Melvin looked at Rob again, then back at Mike, and frowned. "Look..." he said, then paused and pointed. "Wasn't your name, Mike?"

"Yes," Mike said, nodding.

"Mike, we are on the good side and are trying to prevent

some very bad people from doing some horrible stuff. ... Can you let it go at that?"

"I'm afraid I can't, Melvin," Mike said. He shook a perpendicular hand in front of him. "We've got to hear a lot more or we'll be forced to arrest you both and my suspicion is that there is a lot more to this story than what we've heard so far." He paused, taking his hand down. "If we were any other agents, you'd be handcuffed right now."

Melvin put both hands to the front of his face and covered his eyes with multiple fingertips. "There is a lot more to our story, but I'm afraid you're going to think we're both crazy."

"If we do, then we'll have to take you in, but we'll just have to see about that," Mike said. "Who is this Tom Soren anyway?"

"Tom Soren was my best and only friend in life. He disappeared right after high school."

"Hold on a second," Roger said as he pulled a device off of his belt with his right hand. He switched hands and with an extended index finger of his right hand, he began fingering the screen. A few moments passed. "Aha! I was right! We have an open case from a police report filed by the parents of a Tom Soren dating back some 20 years ago. It says here that the boy had a high I.Q. and disappeared right after high school."

Melvin pointed at Roger and with a wide-eyed nod exclaimed, "That's him!"

"Okay," Mike said as he turned his head from Roger and began staring into Melvin's eyes. "We have a genius that disappeared 20 years ago, a man that's supposedly been dead for 20 years, and you, who we're supposed to be looking for with no idea why. Would you care to tell us why we're all here, Melvin?"

Melvin paused while he looked at Mike's unflinching eyes staring at him. Mike and Roger could have just arrested him and Rob immediately, but didn't. They were also well within their rights to have shot them, but haven't. They were also seemingly unaware of the CR guns and the time research and Earth Inc. Was this all a ruse to gain trust? Could be. If it was, it was an elaborate setup. He was not even sure that he could trust Rob yet, much less, the FBI.

An old cartoon expression came to mind: 'Heavens to Murgatroyd!', which roughly means, 'Help! My table is hanging from the roof!'

Everything was just totally getting messed up all at once. Melvin felt like he was sitting right in the middle of Niagra Falls. He was being pressed against a wall by turbulent forces which he had no control of. They were all foreign to him and they were about as trustworthy as the California fault line. In the true spirit of humanity, they were all going to shake but nobody knew where, when, or how much.

He was dead sure of one thing though. He couldn't play word games any longer because Mike and Robert would arrest them if he stalled any longer.

After breathing a heavy sigh, Melvin said, "Okay, but you are going to think we're crazy!"

Chapter 58

Petry's face turned blood red. "How did Nancy come to be hiding in YOUR tent?"

Eric looked up as if searching for answers on the roof of the tent, then down into Petry's flaring eyes. "Like I said, her whole story sounded fishy to me, so I wanted to keep her nearby, or at least where I knew where she would be."

Petry glanced down regaining his composure. "That was great thinking on your part. You get a gold star for that one. Now let's go get this hussy." Petry put both hands on the arms of the chair, gripped, and pitched forward. Extending his legs and back, he stood. He pointed toward the entranceway with a lone finger and said, "Let's go, Eric."

Petry exited the tent, followed closely by Eric, and began briskly walking toward command center. He took five steps then stopped. Eric plowed into his back and Petry dropped to one knee and caught himself with his hands. SPLASH!

Water covered Petry's right hand, the other was mud soaked and he roared. "I HATE COLD, WET WEATHER!" Picking his hands up, he slung them again and again, then put his left hand on the upright knee. With a grunt, he managed to stand and slung his hands some more.

Eric quickly apologized for the incident to a red-faced Petry who simply said, "S'ok." Petry then pulled the phone from the attachment at his waistline, pressed on it a few times, and then put the phone to his ear. After a brief moment, he said, "Hello, Max. Do you still have Brent, Ryan, and Matt?" Pause. "Good. Get them together and meet me outside of Eric's encampment. Don't enter the camp and keep quiet until I get there." Pause. "Thanks. We'll be there very shortly. Petry out."

Petry took the phone away from his ear and pressed a button to hang up, then looked at Eric. "Follow me."

Petry turned toward the back of his tent and strutted a few paces to his car. "Get in the passenger seat." He clutched the door handle, popped it open, and lowered himself into the driver's seat. As soon as he reached for his door, Eric opened the passenger door. Two butts plopped down inside. KAPLOOMP!

When the car engine started, Petry put the gearshift into Drive and they were off.

*

The drive only took a few minutes and they parked near the edge of Eric's camp. There had been no conversation during the trip. As soon as the car stopped, Petry looked around and quickly saw Max's Jeep parked near the corridor entrance with him and the others inside. They appeared to be talking amongst themselves.

"Damn it!"

Eric looked at Petry with wide eyes. "What's the matter?"

"Nothing you need concern yourself with," responded Petry as he gazed at the men in the Jeep. He grabbed the door handled and yanked at the latch. There was a popping noise as the door was freed and he gave the door a big shove. The icy wind entered the car, making Petry shiver. He started to get out, but the wind blew the door back toward him and he stiffened his arm to keep it open. He grimaced and moaned.

Eric exited the car and walked around to meet Petry who was waiting on him and rubbing his elbow. The two walked toward the Jeep and when they neared the vehicle, the four men saw them and hopped out. The six men came to a standstill not far from the Jeep and still outside of the camp.

"Alright, men," Petry said quietly. "We're after Nancy Birch. She's holed up in Eric's tent which is off the main tent to the left." He pointed at the tent. "That tent!" Brief pause. "What we want to do is go into that tent from all sides and all at once. Don't fire at her; we need her alive, but take any action necessary to capture her. We'll surround the tent and the four of us will go in. The other two will remain outside as a second line of defense. I fought wars alongside this woman and she is as dangerous as they come. Brent, Matt, you be on the sides to relay the 'Go' signal, while it'll be Max and I on the front side, Ryan and Eric on the back. Now, let's move out quietly."

Few people were in the encampment as the six men went to their designated locations for the assault. The sky was clear, for the moment, but the wind blew strong and made their jackets ruffle. All got into their positions quickly. Petry, stood at the front, right side, and motioned his hand to Matt.

They could not go in quickly as there were zippers to undo on each end, but as soon as they started, a gunshot was heard by all. As Max entered the tent, he pulled the Glock from his side and shouted, "Put the gun down, Nancy."

Nancy stood up and dropped the pistol as she did. The gun made a soft bumping noise when it dropped and, subsequently, Nancy's hands shot into the air. Ryan entered the tent, after a moment, shouting, "Eric needs help! This bitch shot his hand!"

"Max," Petry said, "Have you still got your cuffs?"

"Yes, sir."

Petry pointed to Nancy. "Then use'em."

Max unhooked the silvery cuffs from his beltline and unhinged both sides, walked over to Nancy, his eyes narrowed and his face was red, grabbed her wrists and sealed the cuffs around her wrists. He grabbed the connected chain between the cuffs and jerked downward. Nancy grunted with the thrust. "Hush! Anyone that would shoot my teammates deserves whatever they get. Be thankful! If it were up to me, you'd be dead!"

Chapter 59

Nancy rode in the back seat of Petry's car back to command center with Brent and Matt on each side of her. Eric was in the front passenger seat with a towel wrapped around his bleeding hand. Ryan and Max were following closely behind them in the Jeep on Petry's orders.

Petry looked over at Eric and asked, "Is it hurt bad?"

Eric shook his head, but winced. "Nah, it went right through the center. It just hurts like an erupting volcano." He gripped the small red and white towel and grimaced, followed by a grunt.

"Well, hold on. I'm pulling into command center. There is a first-aid kit in the back right tent." Petry stepped on the brake and threw the gearshift into Park. Eric got out first, while Petry turned and leaned between the seats.

"You two take Miss Traitor here to the rear left tent and, for your sake, she better not escape."

"Aye, aye, sir," they both said in unison. Brent opened his door with a click and they all three scooted in the direction of the driver's side. Each man cupped his arm underneath hers and dragged and pushed her along.

Petry clutched his door handled, pulled until he heard the click, and pushed his door open. Ryan and Max rushed over to help contain Nancy from the Jeep.

"Where do we take her?" asked Max.

"Back left tent, the supply tent" replied Brent.

Max's eyes opened wider. "I was wondering if we would

ever use that area for anything other than to look at. I thought we were going to use the back right tent for interrogations?"

Brent and Matt were completely out of the sedan now and, with his free hand, Brent pointed to Nancy. "Petry said no. Since the bitch shot Eric, he is in there using the first-aid kit. I tell ya... You think you know someone... Geez!"

"I see."

While Brent and Matt walked with their arms cuffed around Nancy's, Ryan and Max walked behind them with their hands on their guns. Brent and Max walked with small strides and careful footsteps toward the tent while Nancy looked to be waddling as she thrashed her arms and body against their leadership. While she didn't say words, she grunted occasionally.

Although the pace was slow, Petry followed behind them toward the tent. There were others in the corridor that started to look on and Petry grimaced, then waved a downward arm toward them. "It's okay. Go on about your business. Seeing that the tent was sealed, Petry trotted around the five of them and got to the tent before them, grabbed the bottom zipper and pulled it up. The two sides flapped a bit in the wind making a popping noise. Nancy and her captures were nearing the tent and rather than letting go of her arms, walked in sideways, followed by Max, Ryan, and then finally Petry who, upon entering, pulled the zipper back down.

There were two metal fold-out chairs on the left-side wall. The entire back wall was lined with cardboard boxes with words written on them: paper, T.P., pens & pencils, tablets, supplies, and assorted others. All of the boxes had drawers that could be pulled out to reveal the contents.

Petry motioned a loose right hand toward Max and said, "Max, why don't you go check on Eric." Max clasped his hands together and blew on them as he started walking toward the entranceway. He nodded his head along with a verbal acknowledgement and promptly undid, stepped out, and redid the mosquito zipper.

Nancy stood silently, her arms still entwined with Brent and Matt's. The room was silent except for the wind beating the tent and it stayed that way for a few minutes, that is until Petry started shaking his head. "Nancy, Nancy..." Pause. He tilted his head. "Would you gentleman excuse us for a bit? Just wait outside."

A chorus of yes sir's came from the three and they promptly exited the tent.

Petry walked toward Nancy and circled around to her back. He lowered his head toward hers and, when it was pressed against her hair, put his mouth up against her ear. His right hand began stroking the length of her blonde hair from her neck down to the tips. "I know you well," he whispered. "I know you enjoy this." Pause. "We shouldn't be against each other. We should be fighting whoever or whatever's making you act this way as a team. I know that you're not the power-hungry type." Pause. "'My friend, let me help you." Pause. "You know, I found your encrypted phone." He licked his lips. "I can get you out of whatever trouble you're in. You know I can. Let me help."

Nancy stood there quietly. After a few moments, she whispered, "I'm in too deep. You can't get me out of the trouble I'm in. I've screwed my life up, don't let me mess you up too..."

Petry turned his head slightly more toward her ear. "Even you don't know how powerful my connections are. I can even talk to the president if I need to."

"My family is at stake. My family! Do you know what that means to me???"

"Yes, I do. We've known each other all these years. I know what your life means to you, but I swear that I can help you. I can get you out of any trouble you're in. You know I can!"

After a few moments of silence, Nancy finally said, "What do you need from me?"

Petry smiled slightly. "Good girl," he whispered. "I need the encryption code for your phone and I need to know who it is on the other end."

Pause. "Do you swear that you can get me out?"

"I swear. After I do my thing, then you'll never be

bothered with them ever again."

"Okay, Petry, I am going to trust you. The unlock call code is A3D15C971. The phone is a direct line to Senator Lucy Gold."

Petry paused a moment. "Good girl! I'll get you out of this." He backed away from her and walked to where the tent opening was. "Wait here," he said, then turned and pulled the zipper on the tent. He turned back toward Nancy, looked into her brown eyes and paused. "Brent, Matt, Ryan... Get back in here."

The three men parted the zipper seam and re-entered the tent.

Petry waited for all three to turn around, then said, "Brent, Matt, grab Nancy under the arms again, just in case. I don't think she'll try anything, but, you can't be too careful." He exited the tent and pulled the zipper behind him, then walked across the corridor and called out to Max, who stuck his head outside the tent. "Max, stay with Eric in here. I'll be back in a few minutes."

Chapter 60

Margie's trailer was mostly dark. The sunlight that was shining through the curtained windows provided the only light on a dim situation. Melvin had only just finished his final words on the hows and whys of why they were all standing in the center of Margie's living room. Rob had long since finished telling that he had been 'killed off' by Earth Inc. to become their 'do all, be all' militant leader of whatever situation they wanted him to do or handle at any particular time.

Having said all that information, Mike and Rob had that dumbfounded look that you get from your dog the first time you pretend to throw a ball for him. Melvin had to make them understand that this was no joke and that they were not insane.

"Melvin," Mike said, "do you know how crazy this sounds?"

"Yes, I do, 'we' do. My future, your future," Melvin pointed to Roger, "his future, and all of your families' futures depend on you believing me, right here, right now. A future of their making, not someone else's." There was a pause of silence. "If I'm crazy, you'll know it right away. ... Look I, we, don't want anyone to get harmed, we just want to put a stop to something that could easily destroy everything we know or ever have known or have ever existed."

Mike looked at Roger who lowered his head slightly and rubbed his chin. "Roger, what do you think?"

Roger paused, then said, "It's your call."

"Hmmm....," Mike said. He looked at Melvin and Rob for a while, then at Rob's pseudo-army uniform and each of their faces. Finally, he said, "Okay, for the moment, we're on the same team, but I have to call this in."

Melvin's eyes flared, but before he could say anything, Rob shouted, "No! You can't do that!"

Mike leaned back. "And why not?"

Melvin said, "Because they're monitoring all electronics."

"That's impossible!' Mike leaned forward again. "Our communications are encrypted."

"Impossible for you and not for them," Rob said. "All electrical devices can act as transceivers, encrypted ones too. Even TV's and traffic lights... So, no, it's us here or nothing."

"Well, what's your plan?" Roger asked.

Melvin looked at Rob. "Shall we go in?"

Rob hesitated, hung his head briefly, then looked up, "Yeah, I guess it's up to me."

Melvin stared at Rob. "Yes, it is." There were bad days and worse days in life, but this day was all messed up. Topsy-turvy didn't even come close to describing this mess. Not only didn't he trust Rob, now the F'ed up bureau of rotten buttholes was involved. A huge question was nagging at him too. If the military was looking for him, shouldn't the FBI know about it?

The fact that they didn't know about him or Tom could only be answered one way; Earth, Inc. was a rogue operation. Had they gone off the reservation? Was it some super-secret research operation? "'Wait, wait...'"

"Yes," Mike said.

Melvin looked down and fell back into a seated position on the sofa. "Ahhhhrrrggg!" Long pause. "I don't trust anyone except Margie... I need her friggin' opinion."

All eyes were on Melvin when he raised his head. Hands still to his head, he shouted, "Margie! ... Come out here, please."

The door to the bedroom clicked as the doorknob turned

and slowly opened. Mike and Roger reached for their sidearms.

"It's okay, fellas," Melvin said taking both hands away from his head and stretching them out in front of him, palms down, with downward motions of each.

Margie opened the door fully and walked to Melvin's side. She put her right arm over both of his arms and gently pressed downward. When his arms were in his lap, she moved her arm up in front of his chest and wrapped her other arm behind him. She positioned herself on his left side and sat on the arm of the sofa. She looked down at him and straight into his eyes. "I heard everything that was said, Dear, and I think you should work with these gentlemen." She leaned over and kissed him on the forehead, then lifted her head just enough to turn her head sideways and lower it back down to the top of his head.

He sat there contemplating what the only woman that he had ever any measure of trust in had said. With her adorning his head like a mother goose rubbing on her hatchlings, he felt a warmth begin to grow deep within him. Here were three people, other than Margie, that he did not know or trust that were willing and able to help and, yet, he felt alone and at war with the world.

It was freakishly perfect. His insides were as tight as a vise holding a two-ton pipe. Could he ever stop worrying that people were against him? His past experience would say no, but recent events would seem to indicate that not all people were notoriously bad. Something had to change if he really wanted to keep the world free. His life had always been crap, but he had to trust in something if he really wanted this problem solved for this world and the worlds beyond this one.

He lifted his right hand up to Margie's arm, looked up into her eyes, and softly asked, "Do you really think so?"

Margie rubbed his right arm while she answered, "Yes, Bean, I really think so."

Melvin turned his head toward Mike and said, "Okay, I guess we're all working together." He paused. "What Rob said was true. You can't talk to anyone else, I'd say, within a hundred feet of any electronic device, even street lights.'

"Don't worry," Mike said.

"We must infiltrate the Earth, Inc. site," Melvin said. "To do that, Rob has to go with us. He knows the layout and the security.'

Roger stepped forward. "We'll have a lot of people behind you to keep you safe."

"No, you won't," Melvin said. "From what Rob said, this facility is underground. A small contingent will have a better chance of success."

Mike looked over at Rob. "I tend to agree."

Melvin looked up at Margie. "And, Honey, you're staying here and away from any gunfire."

She leaned back, looked down at him with narrowed eyes and firm cheeks. Her right arm withdrew into an arm with a pointed finger at the end and poked his shoulder. "Listen, mister, I hate guns, but wherever you go, I go. We're in this together and don't you forget it."

Chapter 61

Petry walked into his tent and grabbed the encrypted phone off his bed with a jerk of his right hand. The lab had determined that the most used keys on the unlock pad were the ones that Nancy had told him about. Unless she was more clever than anyone knew, the decrypt code she had given was the correct one.

As Petry held the phone, he gripped it with both hands and started spinning it. "Hmmm..." He laid the phone back on the bed a moment and mumbled, "I suppose indecision is the root of all failures." He jerked the phone back up and strutted through his tent opening.

When he emerged outside the tent, the strong icy wind pushed on his front causing him to stumble, and finally kneel so that his right knee fell into the water hole underneath. Splash! The cold water quickly soaked through the thick jean cloth and drenched his knee within. "Damn!" Pressing his hands to the ground, he steadied himself and then got to a standing position again.

He walked around to the back of his tent and looked at his black sedan. Walking to the back door, Petry clutched the door handle of the rear driver's side. When he pulled, it clicked, and he opened the door just enough for him to push his body through and lower himself onto the seat. He grabbed the leather handle on the door, pushed out a tiny bit, and then slammed the door closed.

Petry looked down at the phone's keypad. "Here goes,"

he said. Holding the phone in his right hand, he pushed the buttons on the keypad, 'A3D15C971,' which Nancy had told him.

The phone began ringing, one, two, three, four rings went by before a female voice said, "Nancy! Where the fuck have you been?!?"

"I'm not Nancy, Ma'am. Nancy is out of the game."

"Then who the hell are you?!?"

"My name is Petry, Ms. Gold. I'm an interested party.

The voice became sharper and louder. "Don't ever use my name again, you imbecile! How do you know the fuck who I am?!?"

"Nancy told me under duress."

The high-pitched voice became even sharper. "Well, that's one death certificate signed!!! How about you?!?"

"I'm not about to die. I actually think we can help each other."

Ms. Gold's softened a bit. "How?

"I have the military and science research contacts that you don't have. You have the power and the political contacts that I need."

"You could be right."

"There's some things you need to know about our search though. Tom Soren is dead and there are quite a few more people here that know the truth than I am comfortable with."

"Deal with the situation as you see fit. Get the research from the lab and contact me when you have it."

"Partners then?"

"Yes, partners. Be warned though, I can be your worst fucking nightmare if you try to burn me!"

"Then I will take care of things. And,

don't worry, I want exactly the same things as you."

"Good! You will be very richly rewarded for your works."

"I know. Thank you, Ma'am."

#

Chapter 62

After he hung up the phone with the senator, Petry smiled and took several deep breaths. With a quick nod of his head he grabbed the handle of the car door latch beside him. Still holding the phone with his right hand, he pulled the latch with his left. Ka-chunk! The sound permeated the stillness of the car and Petry shook his head as he pushed the car door open.

He scooted his legs around to the opening and shoved them outside. With his feet now solidly on the ground, he leaned forward and rose up from the seat, walked a few steps, then, with a good swing of his arm grab, he closed the door. Ka-ploomp!

Walking around to his tent, he, once again, placed a right hand on the phone and ran his left hand across the back and felt of the belt clip. Using both hands, he maneuvered the clip to where it was facing his body and with an up-down motion fastened the phone to the waist of his pants. He took his right hand and shoved it into his pocket. With tumbling fingers, he jangled the keys to the sedan.

He was now at the entrance of his tent and with a duck of his head and forward steps, he entered. He walked around his bed, then kneeled on his right knee. Reaching under the bed, he removed a twelve-inch-long tan box. Petry took the black top off, grabbed the Glock pistol with his right hand and the matching black, silencer with his left. He screwed the silencer on the tip of the barrel, then unclipped and removed the cartridge, turned it over, looked at it, then reinserted it into the gun.

Putting his left hand on the bed, he stood up, then lifted up the front edge of his jacket, and jammed the tip of the silencer into his pants. He pulled his jacket forward and pulled it down over the Glock, then exited the tent.

A young blonde woman came rushing up to him from the far side of the corridor and yelling his name. "Petry!" Petry turned his head toward her. She rushed up to within a feet of him, splashing her right foot in a mud hole along the way.

He looked down at the wet foot. "You ought to be more careful."

"Avoiding mud holes around here would be a miracle. They're everywhere." She quickly continued. "Petry, you are wanted in command center immediately."

"What is it?"

"I don't know. I was just told to find you. Your phone doesn't seem to be working."

"Thank you, Kim. I'll find out."

Petry pivoted on his right foot and started walking. It was only a few steps before he reached the tent. The entranceway was open and he walked on in. Looking around, he saw the usual monitoring going on, nearly everyone's eyes and ears were glued to their assigned task. Tina, from Team 6 was sitting behind the desk looking at a tablet.

When Petry propped his hands on the desk, Tina looked up. "Oh! They found you."

"Yeah, Kim told me. What's up and why are you over here?"

"We have a positive identification from the video at Robert's Grocery and no one seemed to be able to locate Max or Rob," she said as she leaned forward in the chair.

"Max has been with me on a special project. Rob, I don't know about. Never mind that, what's the I.D. of this guy?"

She stood up. "Melvin John Travis."

Petry swung his arm like he was a tennis pro. "Well, what the hell are you waiting for? Let's get this bastard!

ALIVE!" Petry backed away from the desk, spun around on his right foot and walked out.

Outside, Petry looked up and saw dark clouds in the western sky. "More rain... Perfect." He walked all the way to end of the corridor and towards the left tent. The tent entrance was open and when he entered, Eric and Max turned around long enough to say 'Hello,' then turned back toward the table along the back wall where they were pecking through a large, yellow, metal case.

"How are ya'll doin'," Petry asked as he lifted the front edge of his jacket with his left hand.

Max, staring at Eric's lifted hand, said, "Oh, I think he's going to be alright."

Petry pulled the Glock from his waist, aimed, and there were two whispers from the gun. The bodies of Max and Eric fell to the floor. Petry shook his head, saying, "No. I don't think so." Pause. "See you later, guys."

He exited the tent with a smile and turned around and closed the zipper. As he turned around to face the opposite side tent, with a full rotation of his head, he saw no one even close to his position, then strutted across the corridor. When he arrived at the tent, he grabbed the bottom zipper and pulled it up. Before stepping inside, he called out, "It's just me, guys."

When he stepped in, Brent and Ryan still had their arms interlaced with Nancy's and Matt was standing off to the left side and behind the others slightly.

"Has she said anything more," Petry asked, looking at Brent.

"Not a word," Brent said.

"I didn't figure she would," Petry said as he began to spin around. He faced the tent door and said, "Excuse me, fellas, but I thought I heard something." When he turned back around, the Glock was firmly in his hand again.

"Oh God," whispered Nancy with a shaky voice.

Petry pointed the pistol at Matt first, fired with a whisper. A splotch of red appeared on Matt's forehead and as Matt dropped to the ground, Petry quickly aimed at Brent.

Brent and Ryan were already scrambling for their guns, but were hindered by the arm that they secured Nancy with. The Glock whispered again and Brent's forehead became blood soaked. He began falling to the ground. Ryan had gripped his left hand on a right-side hip-holstered gun when another whisper from the Glock impeded his progress.

The interlaced arms fell out from Nancy's body and the bodies fell to the floor. Immediately following the last shot, Petry pointed the Glock in Nancy's direction.

Now free from being held, with a scraggly voice, she asked, "Why?"

He looked deeply into her eyes. "Because I'm a son of a bitch." He pulled the trigger.

She threw up an open hand. "Waaaiii...."

"Sorry, dear," Petry said as he fired. He stared as her body fell to the ground. "You were a pretty dame. It's a pity that you had to marry that bastard husband of yours. What a dick!" He shook his head and took a last look at her bloody forehead as it hit the ground. "I always keep my word, dear friend. I got you out." He turned around, exited the tent, and resealed the tent..

He spun his head in both directions and saw few people milling around. Smiling, Petry turned toward command center. He carefully avoided the mud holes, stepping over some, then circled around to the rear of his tent. Fishing into his pockets with his right hand, he grabbed the door handle of the black sedan, and pulled. Click. The door swung open as he pulled the key out, and stepped down into the car. Smiling, Petry shifted his butt in the seat and stuck the key in the ignition. He pulled the door closed as he turned the key. The familiar song of the engine made the car vibrate under him.

"Now to the next step," he said as he grabbed the gearshift.

Chapter 63

Melvin and everyone concerned agreed that Margie's trailer was not safe for them any longer; so here they were, under the roof of a black limousine, being transferred to a safe house while the feds did some stuff on their end. He was sitting next to Margie, holding hands, which he had not done in years wondering what was the matter with him? He was turning soft, which was the most hideous thing that he could think of. Soft? Him? He shook his head in sheer disbelief.

He wriggled his hand loose from hers, set it over into his lap, and began rubbing it like it was diseased. How could he? When he looked down, red streaks began to appear on the hand, yet he felt no pain. What was happening to him?

When he looked up, he saw Rob sitting in front of him eyeing his hands. "What's the matter," he asked.

He grimaced. "Nothing, just nervous, I suppose."

"Well, don't let it bother you. I've had reason to be nervous all my life, from wars to everything else you can think of and I've come out on top every time. Be prepared is my motto."

"Thanks," Melvin said as he looked back down. While his eyes were trailing downward, the dark interior of the door caught his attention and he turned his head toward it and looked. "Do you guys realize that there is no door handle?!?"

Rob and Margie both swiftly looked at the doors, but it was Rob that was the first to speak up. "Son of a ... We've been sold out!"

"That or they thought my story was too crazy to be believed."

Margie turned to Melvin who was already digging at the side panel of the door. Her clawing made noise, but she was getting nowhere because of the seamlessness of the door 's interior. "So much for trust, huh?" She turned toward Melvin and asked, "I wonder where they're actually taking us?"

Melvin threw his left hand up and brushed her shoulder in doing so. "We're not waiting to find out."

"What's the plan," she asked.

"I don't know."

Rob patted his waistline with his right hand and found his phone, then took a firm hold. He raised it up in front of him.

Melvin bobbed his head and said, " I don't think calling anybody will do us any good. We..."

"No, no... You don't understand. I'm not calling anyone. I have a frequency generator on my phone."

"A what?!?"

Still with his head down, Rob said, "A frequency generator..." He looked up. Both Melvin and Margie were staring at him. "Look, most of these door mechanisms have wireless remotes..."

Melvin interrupted, saying, "...so if you hit the right frequency, bingo, they'll open up."

"Exactly!"

Margie looked at him and tilted her head. "How do you know these things, Rob?"

"When you live life on the edge like I do, you play 'save ass' too many times. You learn to be prepared for anything. 'Save ass' is what I'm best at." With a nod of his head, he said, "Unfortunately, we don't have the luxury of waiting for the right time, so I'm just going to have to set it and hope we're on a slow turn. Also, we're to going to have to move like mad dogs because, the second the door pops, the driver will hear it."

Melvin leaned forward as he stared at Rob. "Do you have any more good news?"

"I think that's it, but we do have the element of surprise on our side. It'll take a few minutes, but both doors will open and we'll just have to see,which one faces better."

"Okay," said Melvin, followed by an, 'Alright,' from Margie.

"Here goes," said Rob as he touched the screen.

The compartment became totally silent and Melvin could see that Margie was holding her breath. She was facing him and looking toward the door on his side of the limo. Melvin looked at her face, then her hands. Her face was pale and both hands were balled up and as white as a freshly washed sheet. He turned to face his door and nudged her as he did.

"Any second now," Rob said.

There was chorus of Ka-thunk's and both doors cracked open. Melvin gave the door in front of him a shove and saw a wooded area filled with pine trees and a barbed-wire fence in front of them. The area was about fifty feet away.

This was a fine mess. The chances of them making it to and over the fence before being shot were slim and the car was already slowing. Margie said, "Let's go you guys! We don't have all day!"

Dang it! "Well, come with me," Melvin said as he hopped out of the car. Have you ever played football? Not the tame 'touch' version, but genuine 'tackle' football? Feature all 11 guys on the defense tackling you all at once, they have protective gear, you don't, and throw in a dozen twirls and summersaults for fun. If you add a few scoops of gravel to that scenario and go at it at thirty miles per hour, you might have it. Never had Melvin been so jolted.

After the tumble from the built-up highway, Melvin tried to put his scraped hands to the ground and stand. He knew that he had to make it into the trees. He simply fell back to the ground on his first attempt, toppled over by the world spinning around at about a hundred miles per hour.

Barely able to focus, he managed to look to his right and saw Rob, then, beyond him, Margie. Both of them were trying to regain balance with legs of rubber and extended hands. "Run," Melvin shouted as he tried to crawl. He managed to crawl two inches before putting his hands to his knees and standing up. He stammered toward the tree line. His dizziness slowly dissipating, his stammer became a stumble and the stumble became a run.

When he looked over his shoulder, he saw Rob and Margie recovering into a run also. Far down the road, the limousine had pulled over to the shoulder and was backing up. A few people on the interstate were pulling over to the shoulder as well. Two men got out of the limo and looked over their shoulder at the stopping cars.

Melvin turned his head toward the tree line, grabbed the top wire, then looked back at Margie and Rob who were near the tree line, and back at the limo. The two men had gotten back in and were driving away.

A few people had gotten out of their vehicles and were running to meet them. A man with a scraggly, overgrown beard called out with crackly voice, "Ya'll need any help there, sonny?"

His truck had a few dingy brown rust spots and the thing had bedding rails made of brown wood held up by rusted struts. Melvin could see straws of hay in the back. Well, one thing was for sure; if they refused one offer, then they would look like idiots. You don't jump out of a fast-moving vehicle and not need help. Another thing was, if they refused help from one person, all the rest would drive off too.

Melvin waved his arm, "Yes, we need any help anyone can give." He and his companions staggered their way up toward the people coming from the small incline that the highway was built on. He didn't get very far when a dark-headed man grabbed his hand. Looking up into his face, it was absent of age lines, and his eyes were rounded.

"Let me help you, sir," the young man said as he stretched his other hand out.

Melvin reached toward the hand, grabbed, and used it to steady himself. His legs were still a bit wobbly, but working at least. As they walked up toward the interstate, he couldn't help but think that here he was again, getting help from people. In this case, he didn't even know the guy. He could feel the blood rush to his face. This was infuriating and shameful. He ought not have to take help, but at the moment, he was in no position to argue.

"Thank you," he said begrudgingly. As they reached the cusp of the highway, it was one last heave ho, and Melvin had had enough. Bending over, he wriggled his hands free and put them to his knees. "I gotta take a breather."

The young man took a step back. "I completely understand. ... If you don't mind my asking, what happened?"

Not about to bring anyone else in on a situation that was totally upside down anyway, not to mention completely out of control, Melvin simply said, "It would take far too long to explain, but we're the good guys."

The young man motioned his arm in the direction that the limo drove off. "Who were those guys then?"

Melvin looked down the highway too, but he was looking at Margie and Rob propped on the old truck. "Look, man," he looked back at the youngster, "it's a totally backwards situation. Leave it alone. You'll be a lot happier." He straightened up, stretched backwards, and walked on the shoulders of the interstate toward his partners. "Ya'll okay?"

Melvin could see Rob's mouth say something, but the noise of a passing 18-wheeler drowned out the sound. As soon as he was next to them both, he re-asked the question.

"I think so," Rob said as Melvin looked at Margie, mussed hair and a few scrapes on her left cheek, echoing Rob's statement with a simple hand gesture and nod.

Other than a dirty face and rumpled clothes, Rob seemed to take the jump the best of the three. It was Melvin's guess that it was because that he had jumped last and that the limo had probably reduced speed, but it seemed too ironic that the one person that was most suspicious had the smallest amount of damage. Yet, there Rob was, trapped with he and Margie. Whether on purpose or accidental, it was compelling evidence that Rob was really on their side, but not convincing enough.

The old geezer leaned over and rolled the passenger

window down. "Ya'll need a ride somewhere's?"

"Rob," Melvin said, "what road is that base near?"

"Off of Highway 61. There's a turnoff north of Baker and just south of Zachary. It's a dirt road that leads to several wooden shacks in the middle of a big field."

"I's knowed where dat be. Pass by dere e'ery od'der day. My maw live in Sa'nt Francisville."

Melvin chuckled and then smiled. "Well, mister, can you take us there?"

Rob stepped toward Melvin and held a hand out. "Melvin, you realize, of course, that everybody knows we'd be headed there?"

"No choice, Rob."

"I was afraid of that."

Margie stretched her arm out between the two men. "If we're going to do this, we're gonna need a distraction."

The young man who was listening behind them spoke up. "I can help ya'll."

Melvin turned around, as did the others, and said, "Sonny, did you see what we just went through? Why would you want to get involved?"

The young man looked Melvin straight in the eye and put his hands on his black leather jacket. "Didn't you see the sign on my truck and trailer I'm pulling?" Pause.

"No."

"I'm Darrel The Daredevil." He took a bow, saying, "Darrel P. Roberts, at your service."

Margie pointed at him with wide eyes. "Darrel The Daredevil! Didn't you just finish a gig in New Orleans?"

"Yup! I was shot out of a cannon over the mouth of the Mississippi and parachuted down on the other side."

"Well, Mel, that answers your question right enough, doncha think," asked Margie.

Melvin turned toward her. "Geez! A woman with an attitude."

"You asked. Now, what do you think about him helping?"

'Another person,' Melvin questioned himself in his mind.

Will this never stop? So, okay, he trusted Margie. He sort of trusted Rob, but needed his knowledge. So they couldn't solve things on their own. Did they really need these two others? Well, 'couldn't' was a strong word, a better thing would be, 'couldn't in a timely manner.'

"I don't really care what you're up to," Darrel said.

"That's good because you really wouldn't believe it anyway," said Melvin as he eyed the average size guy. He stood about 5'5" with a slim, wiry frame and it reminded Melvin of a telephone pole with its featureless appearance. His chest seemed bigger around though. His shirt sleeves were stretched tight on his arms and ripples were apparent.

Darrel went toward the blue truck, with its plethora of rust spots, walked up to the open window, which the geezer was looking out, and said, "Old man..."

"Names's Bob Brown."

"Mr. Brown, if you could bring these people up there, I'll go with you and start setting my stuff up. Anybody there will be focused on me."

"Will do, young'un."

Melvin hung his head for a moment. When he looked up, he turned to Darrel and Mr. Brown and said, "Thanks!" He paused while he looked at Bob, "Mr. Brown, is there enough room in the back for us?"

"P'urt near."

Melvin looked at Rob who was already walking towards the bed of the pickup. After he peered into the back, he shouted over the whisk of a passing truck, "There's enough room."

Melvin looked back at Bob, "I think we'll ride back there."

Bob looked at him and winked his right eye. "I'll open this here back winder so we can talk too."

"Alright," Melvin said as he started walking away.

Chapter 64

Melvin stared at Margie through a lot of the ride. The hay was getting strung throughout her hair. She was smiling and having fun with it, but the only thing it did for him was make his nose run. As he sat there rubbing the mucus away from his nose, he wondered if it was even possible to get things more messed up. Oh well, these people were a means to an end.

The cold wasn't making the ride any more or less pleasant. He didn't think that he even remembered what warmth felt like, at least not for more than a few moments. He reached over and wrapped his arms around Margie. She giggled. She had no idea that he was hugging her for warmth, rather than being affectionate, yet some part of him enjoyed her breath on his skin. Or was that just warmth?

Rob stayed near the center of the pickup bed for unknown reasons. There was plenty of room where they were. The only talking had been between he and Margie, except for when Rob told the driver to stop at where Highway 61 meets the Bennett Road cutoff.

Darrel's truck had been right behind them the entire trip. Occasionally, on a turn, Melvin would get a glimpse of Darrel's trailer. The only thing he could ever see was that it was long and that underneath one side was red with something blue on top.

"We're here," the old man said through the six-inch cab window.

The truck turned slightly and the sound of crunching gravel could be heard underneath the tires. Melvin's arms loosened their grip around Margie and found their way to his sides. His body bounced around a bit and his body was pressed against the cab by the force of the brakes as they were applied.

Darrel's truck pulled over behind them. He opened the door and did a one hop getting out.

When Darrel came to the back of the pickup, Rob got to his knees and went to the back corner. "Darrel, there are two main entrances to this place. One, on Highway 61 about a mile further, the other, on Bennett Rd about two miles further, which is the one we want. How much time do you need, after you get there, to set up for the diversion?"

"About ten minutes," Darrel said.

"Okay," Rob said, then paused putting a lone finger to his cheek. "I'll give you a ten minute head start, then we'll go. The roads are unchained, but be sure that you park next to a shack."

"What's in those shacks?"

"Don't worry about that," Rob said motioning downward. "Just be sure that you're parked next to one.... Wait! How will we know that you're set?"

"World War III, man, World Was III." Darrel grabbed the tailgate with both hands and shook his head. "What in the name of Chicken Pox is going on here?"

Melvin chuckled. "I thought you were a daredevil?"

"I am, but, crap, I don't want to get arrested or nothing."

Melvin looked at Bob. "How about you, Mr. Brown?"

The old man looked backwards through the window and smiled. "Sonny, I seen plenty in my day and one thing I learned good is if it looks bad, it's usually because it's right. Hell yeah, I'm in."

Melvin looked back at Darrel. "Man, I could tell ya what's going on, but, I promise, you don't want to know."

Darrel pulled his eyebrows down and in and shook the tailgate with intensity making it rattle. "Let's do it!" He turned loose of the tailgate with a jolt and swiftly turned back toward his truck. He did a step getting in, grabbed the door, and slammed it shut.

The engine cranked with the low rattle of a diesel. Melvin heard the gears change into drive and the familiar rumbling sound of the thing as it started moving along. He sat up and looked out between the wooden slats of the pickup. The trailer was at least eight-feet long. On top of it was a blue tube, with a vertical black ring at the far end. At near end was a dingy-orange hand crank. Melvin recognized rust when he saw it and crossed his fingers in the hope that it still worked. The middle of the thing was a red, white, blue, yellow logo with the lettering: 'Darrel The Daredevil.' Patriotic at least...

Melvin hit his head with the fleshy part of his right hand. "That's the canon!"

Chapter 65

Margie had been hugging Melvin ever since Darrel had left. Melvin didn't mind, it was keeping him warm at least. If he could do it to her, then this was fair. The sky was filled with dark clouds, looking like they might try to rain. It was later in the evening, but he wasn't exactly sure of the time. He had long since stopped wearing a watch and his phone was in a million busted parts somewhere on Airline Highway. The sun wasn't visible. There were not going to be any Indian tricks, telling time by the sun, or any of that sort of junk.

Late evening would be a good time to try to infiltrate anyway. The question was no longer what to do, nor how to do it, but rather do or do not. Melvin still didn't trust Rob completely, but now it was trust or trust not. He had proven himself worthy of a good deal of trust and Melvin didn't see any need to back down now.

As they turned down the dirt road to Earth, Inc., there were noises that sounded like the Fourth of July coming from where Darrel should have been. The dark sky lit up with brilliant flashes. KABOOM! KABOOM! When the old geezer stopped the truck to turn down the road, Melvin told everyone to 'look sharp.' Margie and Rob gave the OK sign and Melvin told the old man to pull up next to the shack.

It was about fifty yards away and the truck stopped within five foot of the front door to the shack. The three of them jumped out of the back of the pickup.

The shack was about ten-feet square made of darkened

wood that was bowed outward at the top and bottom in places. Where the wood bowed there were creases, but only darkness could be seen within them. The threesome rushed towards the door at the front and Rob reached up to the top left of the door and lifted the brown rust-covered metal latch midways up on the right side.

When the door opened, the three quickly walked inside with Rob being the last. Melvin heard the door creak shut and the latch click itself back into place. He heard the noise from the truck's engine fade as it drove away.

Inside the shed, Melvin saw only more wooden walls and he put his right hand to his stomach. Had they been sold out? His gut said, yes, but to have come all the way out here for nothing was a little hard to believe. So, as he stood waiting for either a trap to be sprung, or anything else, he watched Rob walk past him toward an inner wall of the room.

Rob reached up the inside of the right wall in the center of the room with his right hand and Melvin heard a click. The wall in the center of the room began moving. It separated beginning at the center and disappeared. Beyond was a well-lit tan room with metal walls, complete with mid-height silver runners.

Melvin removed his hand from his stomach. "An elevator!"

As Rob motioned them all inside, he said, "Yes. Like I said, the whole thing is underground."

Once they were all inside, Melvin looked at the panel. Six black and round buttons were there: S1 through S6. The panel itself was silver with a black digital display at the top that had the words, 'Locked - Ground,' in green lettering. There was a slot above the display that was credit card size. Melvin opened his mouth to ask which floor, but Rob held a lone finger to his lips, so he closed his mouth.

Rob turned toward the panel, then put a hand in his right, front pocket, and pulled an I.D. card. Putting it into the slot, he said, "Robert Milgrew." The display changed to, 'Ground,' after a buzz.

"Okay," Rob said. "You can talk now. When the elevators are at ground floor now, they are locked and sound sensitive."

"Gee, thanks for telling us," said Margie glaring at Rob.

Rob raised a hand and said, "Sorry, my goof. It's okay as long as it doesn't hear anything else while I say my name. This is some of what I mean by saying that there are security things have changed."

Melvin wondered if forgetting to warn them was really an accident or not. Did Rob just try to sabotage them by not saying something? He looked over at Margie, who hated guns. Why did he allow her to come in with he and Rob? It was a big enough gamble for him. He should've just tied her to a chair and left.

Wait a minute... He was actually sounding like he cared about her. Well, of course he cared. It didn't take much to care if another human being died or got hurt. Caring for her as a living being meant nothing. Nothing at all... Zip. Nada. Nothing. Besides, it was her tough luck if she was in love with the proverbial asshole that he was.

Melvin turned toward Rob. "Well, just remember pal, we could all lose our lives over just one simple mistake."

Rob pushed 'S5.' "I'll be more alert for all of us. ... The only floor that I can't access from the elevator is, '6,' so I'm assuming that what we want is down there. Maybe there are stairs or we might have to lift a key from someone."

"Let's hope," Margie said.

Chapter 66

"By the way," Rob said, "the elevator will stop at 'S1' for a security check. If I show'em my I.D., we should have no trouble. Just stay in the elevator."

The elevator stopped and the doors opened up into a hallway that extended a good ways in front of them. There was a small desk facing the elevator and a white helmeted young man sitting in the left chair. His green togs ruffled when he stood.

"Please show your I.D. badge, sir?"

Rob walked to the table, showed his badge, and waited.

"Who's with you, sir?"

"Just a few of my team members."

The young guard stared at Melvin a moment and then began reaching his finger toward the wall where large red and blue buttons were. The red button was on the outside and the reaching hand was veering toward it. Quickly, Rob reached across the table and pulled the man's body toward him and bent him over the desk.

"Help!" Rob pulled at the young man, his arm still outstretched. "DON'T LET HIM TOUCH THAT RED BUTTON!" Melvin and Margie rushed out and Melvin grabbed the man's arm, bodily forcing it down to the table. Margie grabbed the man's torso and tried to hold it. Rob grabbed the neck and twisted. There was a yelp, a pop, and then a motionless body sagged onto both sides of the table.

"Press that Blue button, Melvin," Rob said turning loose

of the neck. It dropped like a pile of lead and a low harsh buzzer sounded. "Back to the elevator."

They rushed into the elevator and when Melvin turned around, he saw the limp body across the desk.

Seconds passed. The display showed 'S5', finally, and the three rushed to exit the elevator. Rob unbuckled the strap on the brown holster that held his Glock and stretched the arm across the opening. Melvin could still see some clumped brown dirt stuck to the barrel site from their death-defying leap from the freeway.

Rob cupped his hand around his mouth and whispered, "Be very, very, careful in here. Most things in here don't react well to anything out of the ordinary."

Rob removed his outstretched arm. He put his hand to beyond the corner of the door, leaned over slowly beyond the eclipse of the wall, and looked both ways. There were two men far down on the left and a floor cleaner down a bit on the right.

Rob, still holding the door, leaned back toward Melvin, and said. "Our best hope is the maintenance guy on the right. Just be casual and walk like you own the place." Looking forward again, Rob walked out onto the white-tiled hallway floor and faced the white jump-suited maintenance man closely followed by Melvin and Margie. The man was stooped over a floor cleaner facing away from them.

As a private investigator, Melvin seldom was afraid of bodily injury, his own or someone else's, but, here he was, in a place that he didn't even know existed until Tom broke in on a cold winter night fixing to kick some poor slob's teeth in. All of this was aimed at stealing and destroying technology to try and save the friggin' planet, which he didn't like anyway. If it wasn't so real, he would say it was the plot from, 'The Three Stooges Save The World.' He smiled at the thought; that's a movie he would actually like to see.

Rob walked up to the janitor and said, "Hey, buddy." The man went on vacuuming so Rob tapped him on the shoulder. The guy looked up and then down, turned the vacuum off, then looked back up. "Hey, buddy, I forgot my keys. Can you let me in the office," he asked pointing to the large wooden door on his right.

"Sure thing," the thin man said as he reached down for the keys fastened on the right side of his belt line.

The wad of keys jangled a bit as he pulled at them one by one and found the correct key. The gold plaque beside the doorknob had recessed black lettering that read, 'Conference Room.' The keys jingled as the man fingered through the them until he found the right one and inserted it.

Turning the key and knob, he gave the door a gentle push and said, "There you go."

Rob grabbed the back of his collar with his right hand, put his left arm over the man's arm and around his chest, and shoved the guy forward into the room. He resisted and called out, but then Melvin shoved his way in on the right side of the guy. Once inside the room, Margie closed the door with a thud and then the three men fell to the floor, narrowly missing the brown conference table that nearly covered the length of the rectangular room.

Rob pushed his arms against the medium-tan carpet and, with a grunt, was the first to get up, grabbing the keys along the way. Melvin was to the right side of the janitor and started kicking his legs a bit to untangle them, but not succeeding until Rob moved the limp janitor's legs a bit. Melvin was then able to push his hands to the floor, curl his back, and stand.

"Ack!" Margie rushed toward Melvin.

"What is it!?"

"You have a bloody cut on your forehead about an inch long."

"He'll live," Rob assured her. "Just tear off a piece of your shirt to dab the blood. There's blood on his hands too, but I don't think it's from him."

Melvin looked down at the limp janitor while Margie did as instructed. "Him?"

"Yeah, but we can't worry about it now."

'Can't worry about it,' Melvin thought. There was a man who could be dead or dying on the floor in front of him. Did life really mean so little? He was doing this to save life, not kill it. The thought occurred to him to quit all this, but he had already crossed over. This was the point of no return. The only choice now was to continue. "How do you do it," he asked, still looking down at the body.

Rob looked at him. "Do what? Kill or press on."

"Both," Melvin said looking up at Rob.

"You do it by focusing on what needs to be done, what has to be done." He then began sifting through the wad of keys in his hand. "There's no key to 6th floor stairwell, if there is one. Grab the badge from off of his shirt." He motioned down toward the body.

Margie was still doctoring the cut on Melvin's forehead. Rob walked over to the body and stooped down. With both hands, he rolled it over, and unclipped the I.D. from his jacket.

"We'll just have to hope this does the trick," Rob said as he brought the keys up as he straightened himself.

As he was walking toward the door, Margie asked, "What if these keys don't do the job?"

"Then we're sunk," Melvin said.

Rob looked into Melvin eyes and said, "Oh, I think it will. Don't forget, I know this base pretty well."

Chapter 67

Melvin thought he knew what he was getting into when he agreed to help Tom, but he didn't. In the office with them was a dead body, a person, and as they were getting the vacuum cleaner into the conference room to hide it, he couldn't help but think about 'what if' he hadn't been so anxious to destroy the technology. Would this man still be alive? Or the guard? Would these people really have succeeded? Probably, but would it have been so awful bad? He would never know now.

NO, NO, NO. Self, he thought, no matter what the possibilities may have been, you can't screw around with this stuff. People had a right to screw up their lives however in the hell they want. They shouldn't be dicked around by rich assholes who were power hungry, money hungry, imbecilic, fools, and idiots.

He reached around the door and twisted the lock, pulled his hand out, and then pulled the door closed.

As they walked back down the hallway, Melvin noticed that it was empty now and that the area was very quiet. He pulled his hands together and it dawned on him that the air was warm. He looked up at the ceiling and admired the marvelous air vents. Since he was warm, he put his hands back by his side, but started rubbing the thumb and index fingers of both hands.

They all stepped back onto the elevator and Melvin ushered Margie toward the rear. When the doors closed, he inserted the janitor's card into the slot and pressed, 'S6'. There was a pause. Melvin's heart skipped a bit, but then the elevator started descending. When it stopped, the doors opened again.

Rob held his hand to the door and slowly put his head out. There was a large room, as big as a football field, beyond with glass shields at several of the desks and tables. The room was bi-level with a giant 200-inch screen that was wall mounted at the bottom level. There were two cubby holes, wall-mounted bins on each side of the large room and one doubled sided on a floor stand in the center of the room. Computer screens were all around, mostly off. At the bottom, underneath and the to right of the screen, was a small cubicle about four feet square and on the left was a door with a glass pane in the middle that had the word 'Computer' on it. Rob looked left and right. There were two short hallways with offices on each side. No one was around, but several small boxes were stacked in the left hallway.

Before Rob stepped into the room, he re-inserted the janitor's I.D. card and then removed it again. "Now." He stepped onto the floor and motioned them to exit.

"Where do we start," asked Melvin as he stepped toward Rob.

Rob was slow to speak, but finally said in a lowered voice, "I'm not really sure. I've never been down here before. I knew the security procedures from people talking about the changes, but I have never been here."

It had seemed like such a simple plan to Melvin, break in and destroy all the technology, and make sure that this couldn't happen again. Simplicity is often over rated. It's all the little details that just get summed up in a few short words that would confuse anyone. Like English spelling class, i before e except after c, but wait, there are exceptions. Do this before that, but, hey wait, not this time. Details can seem so minor to the mind, but they made up the difference between success and failure every time.

Everything had to be destroyed, but where should they start. A fire would be hindered by the sprinkler system that he saw overhead and it would alert everyone that, 'hey, something is wrong.' Besides, they couldn't do that if they ever hoped to live past today. They had little hope of that anyway, but Melvin would rather not rush things along. Not that his life was good anyway, but it was HIS life and, up until a few days ago, it had been on HIS terms.

Nobody said anything. They all looked at each other's blank faces until Rob went toward one of the computers. He bent down and looked under the desk, followed by looking through the drawers, and finally going around the desk and looking at the back.

"Hey," Rob called out.

They both walked toward Rob and Melvin asked, "What is it?"

"These are terminals," Rob said pointing at the monitor.

Margie put a hand in front of her while shrugging her shoulders. "So what does that mean?"

Rob looked at her. "It means that they are plugged into some kind of mainframe or super computer. If we take that out, destroy its drives, and shred everything, that'll take care of it. We also need to shred all the papers here and I'll bet that main computer is down here on this level because I haven't seen it on any other level. I noticed that each desk has a paper shredder too."

Melvin quickly grinned and raised a hand. "What're we waiting for then? Turn around. There's a door back there that says, "Computer.""

Chapter 68

The three of them had been shredding papers for almost an hour when Rob asked Margie to go to go into the door marked 'Computer'. He had given her the I.D. and keys, but when she tried turning the silver knob, the door was unlocked.

When Melvin saw the door open with such ease, he dropped the papers in his hand onto the desk and ran toward her. The door was only cracked when he arrived. He wedged his body between her and the door, pushing her to his left and behind him.

He raised his right arm and put his flattened body to the door and pushed. His arm was closely followed by his head chicken necked into the room. When the door fully opened he saw a roundish block that had silver-gray panels around its surface and a mesh of blue at the top and bottom. The object was in the center of the room. The front of the device was flattened with a fifteen inch screen and folded-out keyboard in front. At the top center was red lettering with the word, 'Cray,' written on it.

"This must be the computer and, lucky for us, it has a direct terminal. The devices here on the right must be for the data and on the left are the backup tape drives."

Margie looked from right to left and stared at the metal racks of devices. There were green, yellow, and red lights blinking everywhere. "So how do we knock all this out?"

Melvin looked back at her. Her brown eyes were being

pulled open in all directions and looking at him. Unfortunately, he was an investigator that had about as much in common with computers as a sack of wet mice.

He looked at her half-opened mouth. The same mouth he was loving to kiss just a short time ago. Feeling himself drawn in, he took a few steps toward her, bundled her up in his arms, and put his lips to hers for a deep, passionate kiss.

"Alright, you two," Rob called out.

Melvin turned loose and started walking past Margie. She caught his arm in hers and moaned, "Later."

"Yes, later." Melvin freed his arm and walked toward Rob. "We need you in here, bud."

Rob finished inserting the page in his hand into the small black shredder he had moved from the floor to the desk and then turned toward Melvin. "Coming," Rob said as he turned around and walked into the computer room.

He walked toward the terminal on the front of the computer, stopped at the keyboard and began typing. A few minutes went by before Rob said, "I'm in."

Melvin could only see Rob's back, but Rob's arm seemed to move faster and fast. The keyboard clicks seemed to grow louder. Every now and then, Rob would pause a moment, then resume pecking at the keyboard. Rob lifted his right arm and put an opened hand on the top of his head. He stood there and paused, then with a low voice that rumbled like a motor boat shrieked, "Argh! We're in hot water!" He slid the hand from his head down in front of his face.

Melvin wailed, "Damn it!"" He rushed toward Rob, putting a hand to his back. "What's the matter?!?"

Rob turned around. His face was almost colorless and his eyes were wide. "Someone has erased everything! There's not a single bit of data left!"

Chapter 69

Melvin could not believe his ears. He leaned forward and looked at the computer screen and pointed to it with his right hand asking, "Whaddya mean, 'no data,' there's gotta be something?!?"

Rob turned toward Melvin with fixated narrow eyes and said, "No, man, you don't understand, even the backups have been erased! This 'super' computer is just," Margie raised her right hand," like a newborn baby, it doesn't know anything."

"I'll go check down the halls," Margie said as she lowered her hand. "Maybe the information is simply stored somewhere else."

Rob looked at her and said, "That's not a bad idea. I don't know why they would have any computer with no data, but we'll look around."

"I'll take the left. You two take the right," Margie said. "That stuff has to be here somewhere." She turned and walked out of the computer room.

"Gotta be, otherwise we're sunk," Melvin said following her.

Melvin was followed by Rob's footsteps closely. As he weaved through the desks, a sense of foreboding came over him. What was the matter?

As he and Rob started walking down the right hallway, he looked behind him and saw Margie going into the first door on the left. His first thought was to go to her in case she needed help, but he snapped his head around to the door beside him. Melvin grabbed the knob, turned it, and shoved. Stepping inside the door, he raised an arm to the wall, found the light switch and, with a slight twitch of a finger, turned it on.

The office held a desk, a filing cabinet, and a terminal screen. Just to be on the safe side, he walked around the desk and looked underneath. There was nothing but a few pieces of trash on the floor. He saw a few family photos on top of the desk, nothing more. A scratch picture of a snowy mountaintop was on the wall above the desk. He leaned over and grabbed the bottom edge of the frame and lifted it. Nothing.

As he walked by the door on his way out, he grabbed the knob with his right hand and pulled. When he was beyond the edge of the door, he looked to his left to see how Margie was doing and his hand fell from the doorknob. Margie was standing in the middle of the hallway with a gun held to her head. There was a rather tall man standing with devices hooked to his belt behind her pinning her arms behind her in some way.

"Rob!"

When Rob exited the door on the other side of the hall, he looked at the direction which Melvin was facing and turned his head. "Petry! You bastard! What the hell is going on?"

Petry's hand tightened its grip on the pistol. "I could ask you the same thing, my friend, Rob Milgrew. What's your angle, Rob?"

"No angle, pal. This time reversion mess needs to be destroyed. You're a smart guy, Petry, surely you realize the harm it can do?"

"I'll bet this idiot has told you all of Tom Soren's fears about how it could destroy everyone's lives, huh?"

"Yes."

"Well that's the paranoid delusions of a super geek. Tom was brilliant, but too fearful. This stuff could also make everyone's lives better."

"By wiping away from existence a few people, huh? But

what if you change too much?"

"I prefer dealing with reality, buddy."

"But 'what if'?"

"The reality is that I'll be protected, regardless. Everything important about this project is in these two boxes. You three were shredding garbage. ... Look, Rob, just kill this guy and we'll find or re-develop the secret to the time chamber. It's been done once so I know it's possible. Once we have that, whatever changes in the timeline there will be, we'll both be protected. I have millions of dollars to start with already. Otherwise, you all die..." Petry jabbed the gun into Margie's head. "...starting with her. Think about it, buddy. Wealth, power, and we could control the fate of civilization. There's a lot wrong with the world and you know it. Why not wipe away a few bad eggs and get rich and powerful in the process. Otherwise, all three of you die. It's your choice."

Melvin looked into Margie's contorted face and saw tears welling up in her eyes. His heart hurt deep within. The pain was in his every limb, crevice, and nook of his entire body. As she was hurting emotionally as well as physically, it occurred to him that this is the way people describe love.

No, this could not happen to him. He was a certified bachelor and loner. He was supposed to be alone forever. They had their time and it didn't work out. How would he feel if she was killed? He knew his body was in agony. He wasn't sure what to do or say. If she died, what would he be like?

He put his arms up and said, "I'll do anything you want, Petry, just don't hurt her. Please? I beg of you." Melvin looked over at a wide-eyed Rob, turned facing Rob, and starting walking backwards down the hallway. Rob reached around the back of his clothing and pulled a pistol out. He aimed it at Melvin who was still backing down the hallway.

"Stop," Petry shouted. Melvin continued. "Stop, or I'll shoot." Melvin continued backwards. "Shoot him, Rob!" Melvin continued and was only a few feet away from Petry now.

Rob, gun still aimed at Melvin, did nothing.

"KILL HIM!" Petry took the gun from Margie's head and pointed it at Melvin.

When he did, a gunshot was fired. KA-PLOOMP! Melvin looked at Rob's gun aimed to the right of him and he looked back at where Petry had been standing. He saw Petry's body on the floor limp. There was blood coming from the center of his forehead mussing up the white semi-clean floor.

Melvin turned around quickly and rushed to Margie who was still frozen in position and wrapped both arms around her. He kissed her on the lips several times. "I love you!"

Margie blinked her eyes several times. "I love you, too!"

He spun her around and saw silver, metal handcuffs. "The keys must be in his pockets," he said as he bent down and searched in Petry's pockets. He felt keys in the left pants pocket and brought them up with clenched fingers. "Here we go." He sorted through the keys and found the one for the cuffs. The silver key sparkled a bit as he put it into the slot and turned. The cuff clicked and popped open. Margie sighed as he undid the other cuff, then quickly spun around and threw her arms around his neck.

"I love you," she said.

As he brought his arms underneath hers, he wrapped them around and whispered, "I love you, too!"

Rob looked at them both. "I don't want to interrupt your cooing and gooing, but we have a dead body on the floor."

Melvin turned and looked at Rob. "Well, I guess we do. Is there a rolling cart somewhere around here? Maybe we can take him out with us."

"That's no good, Bean. We need a way to make the body disappear."

"He'd make great fertilizer," Melvin told her.

"Be serious," Rob said.

Melvin looked at Rob and said, "I am. Murderers get caught primarily for hiding evidence, distancing themselves from the crime. This way, the body will be nearby and he'll make a great garden."

"I guess that's true," Rob said.

"Sure I am. We might as well put his sick, twisted body to good use. All we need is a cart to get him outside."

A wide-eyed Rob held up a finger. "I think I saw some kind of a cart with a big basket in a back room."

"Go get it."

Rob turned around, walked down the hallway, and went in one of the offices at the far end. Melvin grabbed Margie's hand and knelt down in front of the two boxes that were on the floor. Using one hand, he flipped the lid off both boxes. Inside both were a mixture of papers and several flash drives.

As Rob came back into the hallway, Melvin turned loose of Margie's hand and scooped the bigger box in his hands. Standing up, he said, "Margie, can you bring that other box?"

"Sure," she said as she bent down and grabbed the lone box from the floor. Melvin was already walking toward the nearest desk by the time she looked up.

Melvin had already set his box down and was shredding by the time Margie got back to the desk. Melvin looked at her and said, "Grab another shredder and start feeding it." She walked to her right, grabbed the shredder, and brought it back.

When she set it on the desk and started feeding the tooth monster paper, she looked back at Rob who was handling some kind of device. Petry's body was still on the floor. "What's up, Rob?"

Rob looked away from the device and back at her. "This is a preset, code-locked phone. Petry was obviously keeping in touch, or working for someone else."

Melvin cocked his head and then raised an arm in Rob's direction. While his other hand was still stuffing the shredder, he asked, "Any way to know who he was calling?

"Sure," Rob said as he clipped the phone to his belt. "All you have do is pull the chip. The encryption part of it is a wash though. Enter the wrong code three times and it's a paper weight, chip included."

"How do you know these things?" Margie asked as she put more paper in the shredder.

Rob grabbed Petry's body with both hands, grunted, and

lifted. The body's waist was on his shoulders and, as Rob began pitching the head forward and down into the white bag, he began grunting, "Like I said before," the body dropped into the bag and his voice evened out, "when you live life on the edge you learn how to play, 'save ass.' I guess I'm doing pretty well, I'm still alive."

Melvin took down his hand and went back to feeding the shredder. "I'd say so...Glad you're with us. So how do we destroy these flash drives properly?"

"Simple," Rob said as he poked the legs into the bag. "We get a hammer or something to whack'em with and just beat the heck of'em."

"Well, I don't think we'll find a hammer here," Margie said.

Rob started pushing the rolling bag toward the elevator. The silvery rim was bent some under the weight of Petry's body, but the platform above the rollers was bearing most of the weight. "Other than that, we could find a microwave, but some of the recent flash drives are shielded."

Melvin looked up saying, "Well, go find a club then."

Chapter 70

The task of shredding was complete in twenty minutes. Rob found two steel weights that were the size of bricks that he and Melvin used to smash all of the flash drives into piles of rubble. They put the piles in the sack with the body of Petry and straightened the office.

There was silence in the elevator as the three stood waiting for the doors to open at the ground floor. Melvin's arms remained at his side. They had accomplished everything that he and Tom initially set out to do. Now, could they escape with their lives? How long could they live?

The bell of the elevator dinged and the doors opened. The cold air smelled fresh and clean as it entered into the doorway. The three of them exited with the hamper. Rob pulled from the front, Margie on the side, and Melvin pushing. When the doors closed for the final time, Melvin heard the hollow metallic sound of sliding metal and thought about those two men dying for the cause. How senseless it had been. They killed in order to preserve humanity and freedom. A noble cause to be sure, but how do you win a war against something by becoming what you are fighting against? He shook his head, then looked at Margie and smiled.

Rob let go of the hamper and turned around. He walked forward and pulled the latch for the door. When it opened, the three walked out rolling Petry's body in the hamper. A bright search light illuminated their bodies from the small side road.

"Halt! Stay where you are! Put your hands in the air!"

Oh crap! Caught already. Melvin snarled. "Fuck! We're dead, guys! Do exactly as they say! Damn it!" Melvin's hands shot up as did Margie's and Rob's. He knew they would be killed, but he figured that they would at least have a few days. At least a few hours... Well, there's one thing he could truthfully say, he lived life his own way. Not many people can say that. It may have took some really big brain bashing, but in the process of everything, he found love. The last day of your life was not the best time to find love, but he was better for it.

Love is something he thought was the fictitious ramblings of men and women, both sexes. They were too weak to live life by themselves. ...Pathetic losers... The world was crammed too full of them. They needed to love! They needed to have someone in life to share with and do things with. They required a life partner to help be complete people.

His and Margie's relationship was totally different, it was a love based on strength. Strength of character and a total lack of dependency... He was independent and she was too. That jive about a man's strength is a woman's weakness sort of mess was hogwash. Margie was a complete, well-rounded person and he was too. Probably not the first time in history such a love existed, but pretty close, and now they were going to die with each other. He just hoped that it wasn't too painful. He could handle it, Rob too, but Margie would have a tough time.

"Stand still."

Two men began approaching them, one tall, one medium height. Both men were slim and cast long shadows on the ground. As they approached, their shadows grew longer and the details, which started as pitch-black blurbs, became more pronounced and detailed. When the shadows began to overlap his toes, he was able to distinguish dark hair on the tall one and a graying fringe on the other.

"Don't be alarmed," the dark-headed one said.

Melvin leaned slightly forward trying to distinguish the

figures. Squinting, he asked in a high pitch that trailed off, "Mike?!?"

"Yes, Melvin, it's me. Roger's with me."

"I had the impression that you thought we were all crazy?"

Mike and Roger were steps away from them when they stopped walking. Roger raised a hand and said, "We actually believed your story as fantastic as it was. There were too many concrete details for us to discount the possibility."

"After you escaped we had no choice except just help clear the way for you to accomplish what you needed to," Mike said.

Melvin shook his head and raised his right palm. "Then why the limo with the sealed doors?"

"Standard procedure. When we don't know exactly what we're up against, we safe guard everything," Roger said.

Melvin lowered his hand. "What about the old man and Darrel The Daredevil?"

Mike glanced behind him. "They were free to go, but they hung around to tell you goodbye." He looked down at the white hamper. "What's in there?"

"A man named Petry," Melvin said. "He was going to kill us all to keep this thing to himself. He was greedy and power hungry. He had a gun to Margie's head and..."

"We know all about it. We tapped into the video cameras and saw everything," Mike said with his hand in front of him.

"Good deal." Melvin grabbed the encrypted phone from the hamper and handed it to Mike. "Petry was either working for or with whoever this phone connects to".

Mike looked over his shoulder and shouted, "Todd." A young man rushed to his side. "Todd, I want to know who this phone connects to and where they are and I want it ten minutes ago. Before we leave here tonight..."

"Yes, sir," the young man ran back into the darkness.

Mike looked at Melvin, then to Rob and Margie. "I hate that you've gone through all of this, but what was done has preserved the fabric of freedom and the constitution."

Melvin squinted and then smiled, "Well, sir, it's an honor

to serve the world." He grabbed Margie's hand into his. "Along the way, I discovered what 'right' really means."

Melvin didn't really know how long everyone talked before Todd returned. He was simply relieved to know that the ordeal was finally over. He still felt anger at getting involved so unwittingly. Tom had sought him for help and had said that he was his last hope. He never elaborated much about that, but it was easy to assume that several others had been enlisted before him and had been killed. He could not help but frown at the thought. The evil-minded people had been willing to kill so that they could rule destiny itself. He balled up both hands at his sides into fists and trembled.

"Are you cold, Bean?"

"Yeah, that's it," he said. The night air was chilly so he wasn't exactly lying, just not telling the whole truth.

Todd ran back to the group waving his arm as he came closer. "Mike! Mike!" When he came near, Melvin could see a paper in his hand. "You'll never believe who that phone calls."

Mike turned, looked at the paper in his, and asked, "Who?"

"Senator Lucy Gold! It's a private line in her office."

Mike looked at Melvin, "You don't worry about this. We have everything we need to take her down. Other than that, you're free to go, but I, personally, want to thank you all for helping to protect our nation."

"Oh, by the way, you all are under direct orders not to reveal anything you know about this incident to anyone. It's for your own good as well as the country's."

Melvin tilted his head. "What about the Earth Inc.?"

Roger stiffened. "This actually is a military laboratory. We'll inform the NSA, military, and other agencies that you may or may not know about. This whole place will be shut down tonight and everyone involved with it will be rounded up and investigated."

Melvin smiled and nodded. "Good."

Chapter 71

It was 12 A.M. when Mike's car pulled into the driveway at Margie's. Melvin and Margie had spent little time talking to Darrel and the old man, who had been given the same 'forget' instructions, but when Mike had offered them a ride, they seized on the opportunity. Rob didn't ride with them, but stayed with Roger to help them prosecute the senator. Roger told them not to expect to hear anything about it in the news because it would be the FBI filing charges in a Department of Justice case. Due to the nature of the investigation, the matter would be held in the strictest of confidence.

When Mike's car stopped. Melvin opened the back seat passenger door with a click and he stepped out, closely followed by Margie.

When she was out, Melvin bent over and looked inside the car at Mike. "Thanks for everything, Mike. It sure has been exciting." He managed a laugh. "Of course, exciting's not always a good thing."

Mike's dark eyes widened as he leaned over the top of the front seat. He chuckled and smiled. "Well, I don't know about exciting, but it's been very different. I'm just glad it's over and everything is destroyed."

Melvin knew there was something left to do, but said, "Me too. Take care." He started closing the door.

"You too." His voice changed pitch. "Hey, one thing!"

Melvin caught the door as it was about to close and yanked on it. "Yes."

Mike leaned over and pulled something from underneath his seat and passed it to Melvin.

"A gun!"

"It's my backup piece and it's only for tonight. We've just dealt with some big baddee's. I just want you to feel safe while we round up these people tonight. Ordinarily, I'm not supposed to do this, but I know that you're an investigator and know how to handle a gun."

"How do you know that?"

"Hey! We do our research, too.

"Thanks," Melvin said as he stuck the gun barrel in his pants. He slammed the car door shut and they started walking toward the steps to the trailer.

Margie looked at his hands. "What did he give you?"

"He let me borrow a gun fo..."

"Are you crazy?!? You know how I feel about those things!"

"For tonight? Just for protection?"

Margie shook her head. "I suppose."

"You're going to have to overcome your 'gun thing' with me being a P.I. It's required for the job."

"I suppose."

He turned his head toward her and said, "Let's have a bonfire before we go to bed."

She snapped her head toward him. "Are you crazy?!?"

Not again! As they began stepping up on the porch, he said, "Fortunately, no. ... Do you have a barbecue pit?"

"On the other side of the porch."

He reached out with his right hand and grabbed the silver doorknob. Turning it, he said, "Go get it set up, but don't light it. Is it a gas pit?"

"Charcoal," she said going down the steps. "Matches are on the kitchen counter."

"Be back in a second." Melvin turned the knob and walked in. He walked to the counter, pulled the gun from his pants with his right hand, and laid it on the counter. Looking from far end of the counter he searched for the matches. Spotting them near the counter's end, he picked them up and stuck the small matchbook into his right pocket.

Melvin turned toward the bedroom and walked over to the red and black shag carpet into the bedroom and to the right wall. He knelt down and put both hands to the paneling. He felt and, after a moment, found a crease. Inserting fingers of both hands, he pulled the wood away and reached his right hand in. After his hands fished around for a moment, he found a hard case and grabbed it. "Aha!" He pulled the case out, looked at it a moment while turning it around, and then laid it on the carpet. Melvin pulled his fingers out, put his hand to the paneling, straightening it, and stood up. Picking the case up from the carpet, he said, "You are the last piece."

The black case felt cold in his hand. The cold reminded him of the death and misery that could have been associated with it and the men that died in the base. Their deaths preserved free will for everyone. There are many choices that we can make in life. Now, more than ever, he was determined to make the best of his choices.

So his life had been, cold and barren, so was the case now. He had found his mate and the warm feelings in his heart about her. Did it make him weak? No. He could appreciate the beauty of her inside and out without being weakened. Their two worlds could be as one without the ill-fated dependency that has doomed so many people to their miserable lives.

Melvin walked out of the front door with a smile on his face. Margie had pulled the grill around near the front of the steps and had poured charcoal into the pan. The can of starter was in her hand. After he walked down the steps, he put the case over the coals and opened it up. The gun, the tube, and all the other contents spilled onto the coals. He threw the case in there as well.

Melvin pointed to the grill. "Pour the lighter fluid all around these boys. Use the whole can!"

"Aye, aye, sir," Margie said. She popped the red lid up with her index finger, turned the can upside down, and pointed at the coals. A steady stream of the fluid came out dousing the coals in the fluid. The odor was an assault on

Melvin's nose. Using his thumb and index finger, he pinched both of his nostrils together. The squeezing of the blue and white can made a rude metallic popping noise, but finally, there were more pops than fluid. "That's it."

As Margie turned and walked to the porch, Melvin ran his right hand into his pocket, grabbed the matches, and pulled them out. Using both hands, he pulled a match out and positioned the striker and match. He turned his head toward Margie and told her, "Here ends a very bad chapter in science and humanity."

With a quick pull of his arm, the match sparked and lit a flame. Melvin threw the match onto the coals. The coals, objects, and case instantly were ablaze with red-orange flames leaping three feet high. Billows of streaky gray smoke began to rise above the flames and the smell of starter fluid cooking off permeated Melvin's nose. Never had the scent of a fire smelled so sweet.

He wrapped his right arm around her and they watched the fire for a while. Minute by minute they stared while the flickering flames reflected in their eyes. Several of the objects began to blaze, while others simply became deformed, gnarled by the fire. As they stood there watching the fire burn up the past days' troubles, Melvin could feel a flame burning in his heart for the human being beside him.

He now had two friends in his life, one living, one dead. How would his life be different? Changed? He could see that most of the pieces from the case were burned up now. The time gun was all that was left and it was melting instead of burning. It was misshapen so Melvin looked into Margie's eyes and asked, "Ready for bed?"

"Are you kidding? I'm exhausted."

"Well, then," Melvin said as he opened the vents on the pit and closed the lid. "I guess you better get your butt in bed."

"Roger." Margie slipped from his arm and turned toward the steps.

Melvin turned and followed her.

Chapter 73

BAM! BAM! BAM! "HEY, MELVIN," a sharp and scraggly voice shouted.

Melvin lay there in bed when he heard sounds that pierced his brain. His ears twitched in revolt. He turned onto his right side hoping his imagination was overactive and trying to re-live, in some weird way, the horrid events of the past several days.

BAM! BAM! BAM!

'Go away,' his mind said. He didn't want to deal with nightmares today. He didn't, he didn't, he didn't.

BAM! BAM! BAM! "Melvin, I need your help!"

The sharp tone of the voice grated on his nerves. It caused a stabbing pain that started in his low back and it traveled toward his skull. It was a searing pain that, with every advance, became more pronounced, more urgent.

BAM! BAM! BAM! "I know you're in there, Melvin."

When the pain reached his skull, Melvin's eyes popped open. He saw that Margie's eyes were open and staring at the ceiling.

"I wished he'd go away!"

Melvin rolled onto his back and pushed with both hands and legs. "DAMN IT!" His body bounced and flounced until he was on his feet. He ran into the living room naked. Growled and snarled as loud as he could and shouted, "Go away! Go away! Go away!" He looked around a moment, saw the pistol on the bar, grabbed it, and fired three rounds in the air.

White particles and chunks fell down upon his face.

Margie, who had followed him into the room, put her hands on the outside of his shoulders. In a low voice, she shook her head and said, "Bean, we really must do something about your temper."

***